"Conner, I don't want you throwing money at me," Lucy said. "I mean it. You don't owe me anything."

But she was wrong there, Conner knew. "I owe you everything," he corrected her. "Lucy, you got me through this whole holiday season."

"I wasn't doing it as a favor!"

"No, I know. And I'm not trying to make this into some kind of trade deal. It's just…I see you and Emma, and I want to—"

"You want to help us," she said, "but that's not your job. Is it?"

Maybe not technically, but he'd be damned if he was going to give up caring for her. "Lucy…"

"I'm asking you to promise me something. No more gifts. I mean it."

She was serious about this. He gripped her hand. "No more gifts," he pledged, knowing even as he spoke that there had to be something else he could give her—and yet aside from another two weeks of entertainment, what the hell did he have to offer?

If only he could love her.

Dear Reader,

Step into warm and wonderful July with six emotional stories from Silhouette Special Edition. This month is full of heart-thumping drama, healing love and plenty of babies!

I'm thrilled to feature our READERS' RING selection, *Balancing Act* (SE#1552), by veteran Mills & Boon and Silhouette Romance author Lilian Darcy. This talented Australian writer delights us with a complex tale of a couple marrying for the sake of their twin daughters, who were separated at birth. The twins and parents are newly reunited in this tender and thought-provoking read. Don't miss it!

Sherryl Woods hooks readers with this next romance from her miniseries, THE DEVANEYS. In *Patrick's Destiny* (SE#1549), an embittered hero falls in love with a gentle woman who helps him heal a rift with his family. Return to the latest branch of popular miniseries, MONTANA MAVERICKS: THE KINGSLEYS, with *Moon Over Montana* (SE#1550) by Jackie Merritt. Here, an art teacher can't help but *moon over* a rugged carpenter who renovates her apartment—and happens to be good with his hands!

We are happy to introduce a multiple-baby-focused series, MANHATTAN MULTIPLES, launched by Marie Ferrarella with *And Babies Make Four* (SE#1551), which relates how a hardheaded businessman and a sweet-natured assistant, who loved each other in high school, reunite many years later and dive into parenthood. *His Brother's Baby* (SE#1553) by Laurie Campbell is the dramatic tale of a woman determined to take care of herself and her baby girl, but what happens when her baby's handsome uncle falls onto her path? In *She's Expecting* (SE#1554) by Barbara McMahon, an ambitious hero is wildly attracted to his new secretary—his new *pregnant* secretary—but steels himself from mixing business with pleasure.

As you can see, we have a lively batch of stories, delivering the very best in page-turning romance. Happy reading!

Sincerely,

Karen Taylor Richman
Senior Editor

Please address questions and book requests to:
Silhouette Reader Service
U.S.: 3010 Walden Ave., P.O. Box 1325, Buffalo, NY 14269
Canadian: P.O. Box 609, Fort Erie, Ont. L2A 5X3

His Brother's Baby

LAURIE CAMPBELL

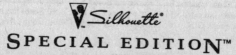

SPECIAL EDITION™

Published by Silhouette Books

America's Publisher of Contemporary Romance

For my writing friends who've kept on reading through the longest gaps—Daphne Atkeson, Connie Flynn, Kathy Marks and Betty Sheets— with thanks for still believing in me!

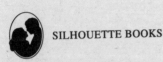 SILHOUETTE BOOKS

ISBN 0-373-24553-X

HIS BROTHER'S BABY

Copyright © 2003 by Laurie Schnebly Campbell

Visit Silhouette at www.eHarlequin.com

Printed in U.S.A.

Books by Laurie Campbell

Silhouette Special Edition

And Father Makes Three #990
Unexpected Family #1230
Good Morning, Stranger #1314
Home at Last #1386
His Brother's Baby #1553

LAURIE CAMPBELL

spends her weekdays writing brochures, videos and commercial scripts for an advertising agency. At five o'clock she turns off her computer, waits thirty seconds, turns it on again and starts writing romance. Her other favorite activities include playing with her husband and son, teaching catechism class, counseling at a Phoenix mental health clinic and working with other writers. "People ask me how I find the time to do all that," Laurie says, "and I tell them it's easy. I never clean my house!"

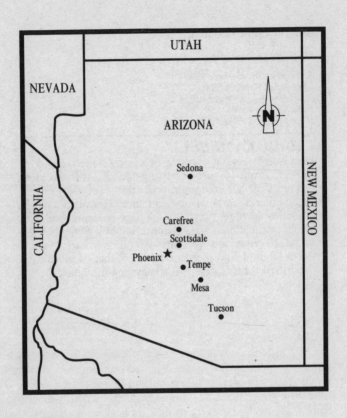

Prologue

Not even Kenny could be late to his own wedding.

Could he?

Lucy Velardi dropped her last two quarters into the courthouse pay phone and punched in the number they'd shared for the past five weeks. It was silly to be nervous when he'd probably just missed his flight back to Scottsdale. If she hadn't left the house early to pick up her dress—a dress that revealed no sign of the reason for this marriage—he would have called to let her know.

Wouldn't he?

Sure enough, the answering machine held a message in his familiar, lazy voice. "Hey, babe, it's me. Look, I'm really sorry, but I, uh, I won't be coming back. I got this chance to play on the Asian tour, and…well, I just don't think us getting married would be such a good idea after all."

What?! Lucy almost cried out before realizing the message wasn't finished yet.

"I mean, I'm really not ready for a baby, you know?" he explained. As if she *was* ready—but they had until October to prepare. "And once you think it over, I bet you'll feel the same way...because a baby just wouldn't work out right now."

She would never feel that way, no matter how badly this unexpected pregnancy had complicated her life. How could anyone dismiss a baby so casually, so—

"But don't worry," Kenny continued, "I'm putting a check in the mail you can use for, uh, taking care of things. Call it a house-sitting payment, okay? Because, listen, you're welcome to stay in the house until next January."

He sounded relieved, she realized numbly, as if that offer made everything right. As if all she cared about was his money and his house.

"Nobody ever uses it except for a few weeks after New Year's," came his blithe assurance, "so it's all yours until then. I know you gave up your apartment, but the family really *needs* a house-sitter, and I bet you'll do a great job."

At least she'd have a place to stay until after the baby was born, but what she'd wanted was a family for her baby. For little Matthew, or little Emma—names she'd already begun using in her imagination, because they sounded so good with Tarkington. But now neither she, nor the baby, would share Kenny's name.

"Anyway," he concluded, sounding as cheerful as if he'd suddenly finished a difficult task, "I'm really glad I got to know you—we had some great times, huh? Well, take care of yourself.... Bye."

And that was that.

Lucy held on to the phone receiver, staring blindly at the lobby beyond her. At the flat white wall, the fluorescent light, the cluster of people in line near the door...until a shrill beep in her ear made her realize the message had ended long ago, and her fingers were starting to cramp.

She couldn't quite draw a full breath, she discovered while hanging up the phone. Couldn't quite shake the chill from her hands, her lips, her face. Couldn't quite make herself think, or cry, or even move—although she would *have* to move, because she couldn't spend the rest of her life standing here in the courthouse lobby.

But she couldn't do anything right now except breathe. In short, unsteady gasps. She felt as if she might burst into tears at any moment—which would be a good thing, because tears could be spilled and then forgotten—but right now she was too stunned even to cry. She had never experienced anything too intense for tears before, Lucy realized, anything like this mixture of disbelief and anguish and desperation and—

And, in a way, relief.

Which didn't make sense, but she needed to hang on to any comfort she could get. Any comfort that would give her the strength to head back to the bus stop for the dismal trip home.

Alone.

No, not alone, she reminded herself as she made her way outside into what felt like blinding sunlight. She still had the baby inside her...a baby who would never hear a word about this day. Who would never know that its father hadn't wanted a child.

But his belief that she could even consider terminating her pregnancy proved she'd been right in thinking last week, the day before noticing her period was late, that she and Kenny didn't really belong together after all. Their first three or four weeks had been dizzying; a frenzy of love-at-first-sight exhilaration and passion and fun. But lately, she had begun suspecting that the relationship wouldn't last.

And that, no matter how much she might have enjoyed

the giddy whirlwind of life with a high-flying golfer, because she didn't really want it to last.

But the baby would never know that, Lucy resolved on a shaky breath as she made her way back to the bus stop bench. Emma or Matthew would hear only the good things about their father, would hear only about the first month when she *had* loved Kenny.

Because all she could give her child was the comfort of feeling wanted and loved. And no matter what happened, she was going to love this baby.

Her baby.

Hers alone.

Chapter One

November 28

There was a woman in his living room.

And she was tickling a baby.

Before Conner Tarkington could ask how she'd gotten in here and what she was doing on his sofa, the woman shot one startled glance in his direction, grabbed the baby and immediately angled her body to shield the pink-blanketed bundle from view.

''Who are you?'' she demanded, rising from the sofa with the baby almost hidden behind her, as if she were facing down an intruder. ''How did you get in here?''

Great defense, he had to give her that, Con thought with a mixture of admiration and annoyance. Put the blame on *him,* act like he was some kind of burglar or something, rather than a bone-weary attorney who'd just flown from Philadelphia to Scottsdale and found a stranger in his family's house.

"I used my key," he told her, holding up the platinum key fob his mother had given him last night, after a farewell dinner during which no one even attempted a toast. "Who are *you?*"

"The house-sitter," she answered defiantly, although her guarded stance softened a bit at the sight of his carry-on bag. As if she might be willing to consider the possibility that he wasn't some random invader. "And the Tarkingtons aren't coming until January. So if you were planning to visit them—"

"I was planning," Con interrupted, "to bring in my stuff, dump it on the floor and get some sleep." Nine hours of flying, counting the layover in Chicago, was a small price to pay for escaping the holiday season at home, but it was still nine hours of teeth-gritting torture. He would never admit it to anyone, but flying scared the life out of him, and while the past few weeks of twenty-hour workdays was his own choice, all he'd wanted for the last hour was to collapse into bed.

Alone.

Although, if he were in a mood for company, he couldn't ask for better than this woman. In spite of her ragged jeans and disheveled tumble of dark curls, she seemed to radiate more sensuality than any woman he'd noticed in a while. But considering the wary suspicion in her eyes, it seemed pretty certain this house-sitter wasn't a "welcome to Scottsdale" gift.

Not that his law partners would set up that kind of gift, anyway. Not that *anyone* he knew would—except maybe his brother, and he hadn't talked to Kenny in months.

"Nobody said the Tarkingtons were expecting a guest," the woman protested, drawing his attention back to the problem at hand. His family had believed the house was vacant, but she'd obviously appointed herself as some kind of gatekeeper. And when he glanced beyond her to the dining room, where a baby swing rested against the doorway, he realized why.

"Oh, hell," Con muttered. "You're living here."

She didn't even attempt to deny it, probably because the evidence of a baby in the house was impossible to hide. "Until January," she confirmed, moving the gurgling baby to her shoulder before repeating her original question. "Who *are* you?"

He extracted the driver's license from his calfskin wallet and flashed it at her. If all she wanted was a show of identification, rather than the self-analysis he'd endured when his partners insisted on a shrink, he could answer with no problem. "Conner Tarkington. And you—"

"Conner…" she repeated, and then her face went white. "Tarkington? You're Kenny's brother?"

If she knew Kenny, that might explain how she'd gotten in here. Kenny had always attracted the kind of gorgeous women who appreciated fast living and fun times, and this one was beyond gorgeous, with her vivid coloring and soft, full lips. But she wasn't dressed like the "show ponies" who used to follow Kenny home from golf tournaments. And it was hard to imagine his brother choosing a woman with a baby.

Much less inviting them to stay.

"Yeah," Con answered, dropping his coat on the chair by the door and watching the color return to her heart-shaped face. "He moved you in here, huh? Told you to make yourself at home?"

She straightened her posture and gave him a cold look. "He *told* me," she said, "that his family needed a house-sitter. I'm supposed to leave them the key in January, but…" He saw the moment his look of disbelief must have reached her, because she suddenly faltered and drew a shaky breath. Clutching the baby tighter against her, she whispered, "Oh, no. He was making that up?"

Oh, yeah. Kenny had outdone himself with this one. Instead of sending her off with a charming thanks-for-the-good-time gift, he'd installed her in the Tarkingtons' vacation home with an imaginary job.

"Look," Con began, before realizing he didn't even know this woman's name, "I'm sorry, uh…"

"Lucy. Lucy Velardi." Her voice was still very small, but when she shifted the blanket to present the baby—a baby he really didn't want to look at right now—there was an unmistakable pride in her bearing. "And this is Emma. My daughter."

Great, so now he had to play bad guy to a woman *and* a child. It had been almost a year since Kenny's last discarded girlfriend showed up at Con's office, but just because he'd been out of touch for a while didn't mean his brother had suddenly decided to take responsibility for his own messes. No, that was still—as always—Conner's job.

All right, then. Time to see if he'd retained his skill at smoothing things over during the past six months of rebuilding his life from the bottom up. Time to start the job, get it done…because he already knew there was no sense in delaying a blow.

"Lucy," he said swiftly, "I'm sorry for whatever my brother told you, but if my family wanted a house-sitter they'd call an agency." The stricken look in her eyes was all too familiar, but he'd delivered this kind of speech so many times that by now he knew better than to watch the woman receiving it. "I appreciate your looking after the place, but—"

"But it wasn't a real job," Lucy interrupted, "was it?"

That was different, Con realized with a flicker of surprise. One more intriguing contrast from the usual show ponies. Normally they protested that Kenny *had* to be telling the truth when he'd promised them a Porsche or invited them to Hawaii or talked about five-carat engagement rings, because no one had ever shared a love like theirs.

But this woman wasn't asking for money….

"Well," he answered, wondering what his brother had promised her, "it's a real job, in a way." After all, she had obviously kept the place clean, watered the plants, taken care of whatever the housekeeping service normally handled the day before anyone arrived. "But it's my job now." At least until his mother and Warren arrived in January. "So you and Emma can get back to—"

"Right," she interrupted again, standing up and adjusting the baby's blanket with a quick, decisive gesture. "Absolutely. We'll be out of here in no time."

"You've got somewhere else to go, right?" Of course she did, he realized as soon as he'd asked the question, because otherwise she wouldn't be so ready to leave. Still, any house-sitter deserved more notice than she'd gotten…no matter what she'd already collected from Kenny. "You need any money? I mean, if you've been doing this for a while, I owe you—"

"No, you don't," Lucy said fiercely, heading for the dining room where a tall stack of envelopes rested against a printer's box. "Kenny already paid me back in March, and I've been addressing envelopes for a temp service, besides. And last week I started the early shift at a diner downtown. They got a Code of Variance, so I can bring Emma. We just—"

"Lucy. Wait a minute." She was speaking too swiftly, moving too rapidly, and he had the feeling she was balanced on a very thin edge of panic. But when she turned to meet his gaze, he saw nothing but determination in her coffee-brown eyes. "You sure you're okay? If you need to make some calls, if you need any help—"

"I don't need any help!" she snapped, shifting the baby from her right arm to her left with a touch as gentle as her posture was rigid. "I take care of myself. And Emma."

And Emma, right. The baby he still wasn't letting himself contemplate looked surprisingly small against Lucy's trim yellow T-shirt, although he couldn't remember exactly how big a baby was supposed to be. Had Bryan ever been so—

Don't go there.

"All right, then," Con answered her as well as himself. He had to stay focused on action, not on his son. "I've got some stuff to bring in, but let me know if you need any help, uh, lifting a suitcase or anything," he concluded. "All right?"

Lucy fixed him with a steely glare. "Look, I don't know how much clearer I can make this," she said evenly, "but I am not taking *any*thing, *any* help, from any Tarkingtons."

From the fury with which she practically spit his name, Kenny must have really done a number on her. Which meant that, unlike the women who hinted about Porsches, she must have given her heart completely....

God, she must've loved him.

His brother had spent the past four years breaking hearts all over the PGA tour, but never the heart of a woman like this one. A woman who obviously wasn't in it for the money, who wasn't clamoring for some kind of reward. No, this naturally sensuous, vibrantly fascinating woman had loved Kenny Tarkington.

A fact which left Conner feeling curiously regretful.

"'Feelings are our friends,' remember?"

"I hear you," he acknowledged, mentally shoving his therapist's reminder aside. He didn't need—or want—any feelings right now, not while dealing with yet another woman his brother had abandoned. A woman who, unlike the usual two-month girlfriends, must have believed Kenny's glib promises of love...and who needed to know there was little chance of him returning anytime soon. "Last I heard, Kenny was playing the Asian tour."

"Well, he can *stay* in Asia," Lucy retorted, with a flush of color that seemed to light her entire body. "And you can stay, uh, here. In your house. Emma and I will be out in no time." She whirled toward the table, picked up a stack of envelopes and shoved it into the box, then turned back to him with a final plea. "Just do like you said. Get your stuff, dump it on the floor, and...and go to bed. Okay?"

She wasn't going to watch Conner Tarkington bring in whatever luggage he'd left in his million-dollar car. Or watch him unpack in the luxurious master bedroom she'd kept scrupulously untouched. No, Lucy vowed as she headed for the guest room, she was going to grab a change of clothes, Emma's freshly washed diapers and her milk from the kitchen, then get out of here before the last fragile shreds of her pride collapsed.

Her friend Shawna had offered to make room on the couch for overnight guests, and Shawna's husband Jeff could pick them up when he got off work at midnight. So all Lucy needed to do was pack whatever she could carry to the nearest all-night donut shop, and wrap the baby in enough sweaters to keep her warm during the walk...because she sure wasn't going to wait around here.

Not after vowing to raise her daughter with the hard-won knowledge that accepting men's favors was stupid.

But Conner Tarkington wasn't making it easy to concentrate on packing. Maybe he wasn't deliberately trying to distract her—he seemed intent on nothing but the trek indoors and out and back again, with a laptop computer and a series of airline-labeled file boxes—but in spite of his haggard face and crumpled executive shirt, the man looked incredibly good.

And she had no business thinking that way.

So the sooner she got out of here, the better. "We're going to be fine," Lucy told Emma, folding a dozen cloth diapers into her pink-plaid bag. She still hadn't saved enough for a move-in deposit, and asking for help from Kenny's brother was out of the question, but there was no sense in worrying her daughter. "Because Shawna—you remember her, she's got those blond corn-row braids—will let us spend the night at her place, and tomorrow Mommy's going to find another job.''

The diner had been perfect, because she could keep an eye on Emma while fixing sandwiches for businesspeople, but it didn't pay as well as the upscale restaurant she'd worked at until February. She had quit waitressing when Kenny wanted to spend more time together, although she'd returned to work the day after his farewell message. But by then it was already too late to qualify for health insurance, which made it all the more frightening when she was ordered to stay in bed or lose the baby.

Still, with the rent taken care of, she'd been able to devote every envelope-addressing paycheck to the medical, grocery and utility bills—and to start a meager savings account for moving out in January.

Which was still five weeks away.

''We're just moving a little early,'' she assured her daughter, tucking the flap of the bag into place and heading for the kitchen. ''Not into the trailer park with the nice trees, because that costs more, but tomorrow we'll look in the paper and find, uh, somebody who wants a roommate with a seven-week-old baby. A *wonderful* baby.''

Emma gurgled as Lucy kissed her forehead, and when she closed the refrigerator door she saw Conner depositing another armload of boxes on the dining-room table. ''We're almost out of here,'' she called, and he turned around.

It was bizarre, she thought with a guilty flicker of awareness, how much the man looked like Kenny. Dark hair instead of blond, but the essentials were unchanged. The same rugged build, the same cleft in his chin, the same vivid blue eyes…except Conner's gaze was harder. Darker.

More intriguing.

And it was a little unnerving to realize that some ancient, feminine part of her still found that look of effortless privilege so…so… Well, so attractive.

''Sure you don't need any help?'' Conner asked, and she

flinched. On the surface his question was perfectly polite, but she knew what lay beneath it. She had seen the weary resignation on his face when he told her there'd never been a job, and she knew what he must be thinking. Here's some good-time girl who fell into a gold mine.

Just like her mother…

"No," Lucy answered abruptly, heading back toward her room for the stack of sweaters. "We're fine." She didn't need to remember her mother right now, not with such a humiliating parallel staring her right in the face. When she'd begun supporting herself halfway through high school, she had vowed that Lucy Velardi would either pay for her own dance lessons or go without. That she would never, *ever* depend on the generosity of men with expense accounts and wives back home.

Until all of a sudden she'd let herself move in with a celebrity golf pro who spent money like water.

But at least Kenny wasn't married.

Oh, God, *was* he?

He could have lied about that, too, Lucy realized with a sickening lurch in her stomach. They hadn't spent much time discussing family, which at the time had suited her fine, but surely he would have mentioned a wife.

Wouldn't he?

After all, he had mentioned a "big-time responsible" brother and a mother "who about died when my brother got divorced," and *he* was the one who'd blithely suggested a quick wedding at the courthouse when the pregnancy test turned blue.

So she hadn't fallen in love with a married man, Lucy decided, standing up straight and surveying the room one last time. Just a scumbag…which was Shawna's description of the man who'd never once called to ask whether Lucy had given birth to a daughter or a son. The man who probably still hoped she'd gotten rid of his baby.

A hope which justified her refusal to ever contact him

again. Although if she had, maybe she would've been warned about the arrival of his brother...a beautifully mannered attorney who probably suspected her of using Kenny for whatever she could get.

"He's not thinking that," she knew Shawna would protest, but Shawna hadn't seen the grim set of his jaw when she announced that Kenny had already paid her. Maybe she was overly sensitive at times, but there was no mistaking the rueful look on Conner Tarkington's face.

Shouldering the diaper bag and wrapping her baby in the pile of sweaters on top, Lucy headed for the front door and found Conner just coming inside with his keys in hand. "That's the last of it," he told her, holding the door for them with the kind of reflexive grace she supposed Cinderella's prince might have shown. Then he stopped, as if only now realizing she was on her way out. "Lucy, where's your car?"

That was a question she hadn't expected. She'd been more prepared for a request to examine her bag for stolen silver, although that might be a little crude for someone as well-bred as this man. But instead, he was looking at her with startled concern, as if he couldn't imagine leaving the house without a car waiting in the driveway.

"I don't need one," she said, balancing Emma against her shoulder with one hand while extracting the house key from her purse and holding it out to him. If she could just maintain this confident tone of voice, just let him report to his brother that Lucy Velardi was doing fine... "Tomorrow I'll come get the rest of our stuff."

"You—" He glanced from the key to her, then at the sleeping baby, and the frown in his dark blue eyes deepened. "Is somebody picking you up?"

What, all of a sudden he was worried about them walking in a neighborhood like this one? She'd never lived anywhere as luxurious as this secluded enclave of golf villas, not since leaving her mother and Mr. "I'm In Charge Here" the year she'd turned sixteen. "No, we're going right down the street," Lucy said, nodding toward the distant lights of Hayden Road, where the donut shop stayed open around the clock.

"At this time of night?" Conner sounded horrified, and he still wasn't taking the key she held out. "I'm not throwing you and a baby out in the street!"

Maybe not technically, but from the moment he'd broken the news that the Tarkingtons had never requested a house-sitter, there was no other choice. Still, he looked troubled by the realization that she and Emma were actually planning to walk away. "You're not throwing us out," she told him, setting the key on the stucco wall that bordered the porch. "We're leaving."

"Lucy, wait a minute. I didn't mean for—" With a swift gesture into the house, he pushed the front door open wider. "Look, there's plenty of room. Why don't you stay the night, and in the morning I'll take you wherever you want."

That was an unexpectedly generous offer, and it was silly to argue with him when the two-mile walk seemed longer and heavier every minute. Still, her pride wouldn't allow a complete surrender. "In the morning, I can get the bus."

He gave her a slight smile, as if conceding that she could take care of herself just fine. "All right. But I'll tell you the truth," Conner said, reaching to pick up her discarded key and dropping it on the table just inside the door. "I really don't want to stay up all night worrying about you. And Emma."

Oh.

Well...

When he put it that way, Lucy decided, staying one more night in the Tarkingtons' home seemed like a pretty reasonable choice. And it would certainly make things easier than waiting with Emma at the donut shop. All she needed to do was return to the guest room where she'd spent the past eight months, and remember that nobody could lose their independence by accepting only one night of hospitality.

"All right," she said, stepping back inside as Conner turned off the porch light and checked the front door dead-bolt…the same rituals she'd performed every night since returning here alone in March. "Thank you."

"No problem." He started down the hall toward the master bedroom, then turned back. "You can lock your door if you want," he suggested, and as his dark gaze met hers she realized with a sudden, startling flicker of warmth that they both knew how very little space lay between their bedrooms. "But just so you know, I'm going right to sleep."

"Good night," was the only response she could think of, and as soon as she delivered it Lucy ducked into her own room to catch her breath. Lock her door? As if she hadn't learned a long time ago to protect herself from whatever she had to? It was sweet of him, in a way, to act like she *needed* such a promise—like she was some blushing virgin who'd never dream of spending the night in a stranger's house—but she knew perfectly well that a stranger as respectable as Conner Tarkington would never approach her door.

Still, his attempt at reassurance was endearing. And somehow, oddly satisfying. Because it showed that, at least on some inner level, he was as aware of her as she was of him.

Not that anything would come of such awareness, she reminded herself after phoning Shawna and canceling the request for a place to stay. A blue-blood lawyer would probably never look beyond the surface of a woman he viewed as a gold digger…and it wasn't like she wanted him to! No matter how ruggedly attractive Conner Tarkington might be, no matter how unexpectedly *nice* he might be, she wasn't letting herself wonder about him.

But as she put Emma to sleep in the blanket-padded bureau drawer on the floor beside her twin bed, she had to remind herself with increasing severity that she was *not* going to think about this man. About his intriguing combination of challenge and compassion. About the same compelling gaze and instinctive self-assurance that had drawn her to Kenny in the first place.

No, she wasn't letting herself make such a mistake again. Ever. Because she now understood the danger in noticing the raw, elemental appeal of a man like that.

It had been far too easy to fall in love with a Tarkington. And it had cost far too much.

Coffee.

He needed coffee.

Conner opened his eyes and felt a moment's disorientation at the sight of the white stucco ceiling before remembering where he was. The Scottsdale vacation villa, right…which would explain why this room seemed so much lighter than the oak-paneled office where he'd woken up too often lately, before vowing to limit his workdays to twelve hours or less.

Still, there was always coffee in the kitchen at Weller-Tarkington-Craig, where the more ambitious junior partners arrived by dawn. And judging from the light on the ceiling, it had to be past dawn. More like—he blinked at the watch on his bedside table—seven-thirty in the morning?

God, had he really slept that late? There was no excuse for it, not on his first day of setting up The Bryan Foundation. Even though he'd pushed himself harder than usual these past few weeks, completing and reassigning cases to cover his leave until January fifteenth, sleeping until seven-thirty in the morning was unforgivable.

He'd better get that coffee fast.

It didn't take long to shower, shave and dress for a day with no appointments, and by seven-forty Conner was heading for the kitchen—when the lusty squeal of a baby woke him more effectively than a jolt of caffeine.

A baby…?

Emma, he remembered.

And Lucy.

He found them in the living room, where Lucy was just bundling her daughter into a quilted carrier. "You must've been wiped out, to sleep through all the noise this morning," she observed, picking up her own denim jacket with the same easy grace he remembered from last night. "Emma's been up since five."

Con vaguely remembered hearing an infant's shrill cry sometime during the night, but the sound must have been absorbed into some dream. Still, it had made him wonder again why Kenny had chosen someone with a baby to keep him company during the Phoenix Open.

Although the baby couldn't be more than a few weeks old, so she wouldn't have been around at the time.

And Kenny had probably been dazzled by Lucy's sparkling energy, which Conner had to admit was even more enticing after a full night's sleep. This morning she wore her wild curls pulled severely off her face and a conservative white shirt tucked into khaki slacks, as if dressed for a job interview, but there was still no hiding her vibrant, vivid beauty.

"No kidding," he muttered, wondering if she was seriously planning a job interview at this hour of the morning. "I guess *you* didn't need coffee to wake up, huh?"

Lucy grinned apologetically as she shouldered the pink diaper bag resting on the table beside the front door. "There isn't any coffee," she told him. "I quit drinking it while I was pregnant, and the past week I've been getting it at the diner."

Oh, hell. "Where's the diner?"

"Emma and I were just on the way there," she answered, which made him remember that she'd mentioned a weekday shift someplace. "The bus comes at eight, so—"

"I'll take you," Con offered, bracing himself for more time with the baby. "As long as I can get a cup of coffee there."

Starting coffee was her first task of the day, Lucy assured him, because she had the place to herself for lunch setup until the owner arrived at nine. So within a remarkably short time he found himself at the polished plastic counter of an old-fashioned diner, taking his first, sustaining gulp from the thick white mug she handed him.

"You're a lifesaver," he told her as she poured another mug for herself and pulled a handful of flimsy paper placemats from under the counter. "I have to remember to pick up some coffee on the way home."

"Next best thing to a baby when you need to wake up," she agreed, deftly spreading placemats from the far end of the eight-seat counter to his side, where the baby carrier rested. "Isn't it, Emmie?"

The baby responded with a perfectly timed coo, jubilantly waving her fists from the depths of her carrier. It was easier than he'd expected, Conner realized, watching Emma's look of rapt attention—a wide-eyed fascination he hadn't remembered from last night. "She's a morning person, huh?"

"Yeah," Lucy agreed, tweaking her daughter's fist with a smile of pure enjoyment, "and I don't know *where* she gets that." She picked up her coffee, then rested the mug on the counter so she could look at both the baby and him as she took her first sip. "I've always been a night person, and her dad…" She shrugged, as if Emma's dad was the type who had never watched a sunrise. "Well, you know Kenny."

Kenny?

Conner almost choked on a mouthful of coffee. That piece of news, delivered so offhandedly that Lucy evidently viewed it as common knowledge, explained a lot. His brother's abrupt departure for Asia, Lucy's haunted look when she mentioned that Kenny had already paid her, and most of all the reason she'd been offered this house-sitting job in the first place. But for Kenny to install her in the family home and then just walk out…

"Does he *know* about Emma?" Con demanded.

Lucy's eyes darkened with what looked like a flash of hurt. "I haven't talked to him since March," she answered flatly. She picked up the baby, who was still waving both fists, and cradled her gently against her shoulder without meeting Con's gaze. "He didn't want her, and I don't want him involved."

But if Kenny had said he didn't want Emma, which wasn't hard to believe, then he'd obviously known about the baby. And while it was bad enough to walk out on a woman, it was something else altogether to ignore a child.

You did the same thing, remember?

"Well, even so," Con observed, moving from the shaky ground of threatening emotion to the reliable bedrock of fact, "he's got some responsibility, here."

It wasn't until Lucy's posture stiffened that he realized he'd struck another sore spot…either that, or a source of fear. Not that Kenny would ever demand visitation rights, but maybe Lucy didn't realize that.

"Not actually *raising* Emma," he hurried to explain, "but at least paying his share."

The explanation didn't seem to make much difference in the rigid set of her shoulders. "I don't want that, either. Just leave it alone, all right?"

"But…"

She turned the baby even closer to her, so that Conner could see nothing of his niece but a soft pink blanket, and glared at him. "Emma is *mine,* and I don't need anyone else getting involved!"

Making things better would be a serious challenge, he realized, considering that no one except himself was unhappy with the status quo. Kenny obviously hadn't cared to follow up on his child, and Lucy just as obviously didn't want any assistance.

In fact, she seemed almost panicked at the very idea.

"All right," Con said. A courteous withdrawal was always a safe delaying tactic, and it might take a while to locate Kenny on the Asian tour. Meanwhile, he would have to arrange for child-support payments until his brother showed up. But before he could find an acceptable way of phrasing such an offer, Lucy surprised him once again.

"I mean it," she insisted, facing him across the counter with such intensity in her gaze that he wondered for a moment whether she had guessed his plan. "As far as Kenny's concerned, I could've gotten rid of her and he'd be fine with that. So he's got no business in Emma's life—and neither do you."

"All *right,*" Conner repeated, more loudly this time. "Lucy, I hear you. I won't fight you for the right to change her diaper."

For once, he saw, he'd hit exactly the right note, and he was rewarded with her sudden, sheepish smile. "Okay, then," she said, giving Emma another gentle squeeze before returning her to the baby carrier, taking another gulp of coffee and picking up a handful of flatware. "I didn't mean to jump on you like that. I just…"

"You've just got this thing," Con finished for her, "about taking care of yourself."

She regarded him thoughtfully for a moment, as if searching for some trick in his statement. But she evidently didn't find anything to disagree with, because she gave him another smile…the kind, he imagined, that would make anyone within view feel suddenly lighter. More energized. "Exactly," she said, laying a white-handled spoon, fork and knife on the first placemat to his left. "So, what are you doing today, anyway? Playing golf?"

It was a reasonable question, Conner acknowledged, gulping the last of his coffee a little faster than he'd meant to and forcing himself to concentrate on business instead of her smile. Why else would a Philadelphia lawyer spend the holiday season alone in Scottsdale, if not to soak up the sunshine on a resort course?

"No," he answered, moving to the coffee machine to refill his mug and gesturing a warm-up offer at her. "I came here to get some work done." Not to mention a fierce desire to escape the memories of Christmas at home. "I figured I'll turn the dining room into an office for the next six weeks. What about you?"

She looked surprised at the question, which reminded him that she was already planning today's move—a move she'd better forget, Conner realized, because he couldn't very well throw his brother's baby out of the family home. No, Lucy and Emma were entitled to stay there, assuming she wouldn't mind sharing a roof with Kenny's brother.

"I'm going to find an extra job," Lucy answered, sliding her mug down the counter for him to refill without letting their fingers touch. *Just as well. You're not going there.* "This time of year, everybody's hiring."

She sounded remarkably confident, which made him guess she was no stranger to the process of job-hunting. And of course that made sense. A dedicated career woman wouldn't have time to follow a pro golfer—even one as entertaining as Kenny—from party to party. No matter how earnestly he might have promised to love her forever.

Damn, Lucy deserved better than that....

"So as soon as we find a place," she continued, accepting the freshened coffee he slid back to her with a nod of thanks and gathering another set of flatware, "I'll come get the rest of my stuff out of your way. I'll call first and see if you're home, or out on... What kind of work are you here for?"

"A foundation," Conner said, forcing his attention toward business as he returned to his seat. She obviously didn't think Kenny's family owed her a place to stay, but he couldn't turn his back on a baby. "My partners talked me into taking some leave from the law firm, so I can get it done before I go back in January."

"A foundation?" she repeated, looking so bewildered

that he wondered whether Kenny had mentioned *any*thing about the past two years. "Like for charity?"

"It's a memorial." The words came harder than he expected, but he knew better than to let the guilt over Bryan linger. No, he had to focus on what he could do right now. "There's a lot of work involved up front, and that's what I'm starting today."

Or at least, that was what he'd planned to start today. But first, Con knew, he needed to figure out some way of making things right for his brother's child.

Which, given Lucy's determination not to accept anything from the Tarkingtons, might present a problem.

"Foundations give money to people, right?" Lucy asked, returning to the flatware bin at his end of the counter and setting down her coffee a safe distance from Emma's carrier. "How much work does it take for you to write checks?"

Not nearly enough, which was why he'd set himself the task of creating The Bryan Foundation in the first place. Only by using every skill he possessed, not just every dollar, could he say that he had come to terms with his son's death. That he was ready to move on with his life.

A life with no more false promises. To himself, or to anyone else.

"First," Conner explained, "I have to organize the groundwork. Today I'm calling a temp agency…" And then, with a sudden jolt of triumph, he flashed on a solution to the problem of Lucy's pride. "I've got to find someone who can help with the clerical stuff," he told her in the same cordial tone he'd use with any potential employee. Thinking of her as an employee should make it considerably easier to keep his mind on business…and that was the only responsible choice he could make. "Typing envelopes, copying proposals, that kind of thing."

Lucy was watching him warily, but there was no mistaking the interest on her face—so he might as well finish the offer.

"Is that," Con asked her, "something you could do? Whenever you finish here?"

She hesitated. "I've done office work, sure. But I already know about the Tarkingtons and phony job offers."

"This one's real," Conner retorted, trying not to show any annoyance. Such caution was understandable, considering what Kenny had pulled. "If you don't want the job, that's fine, but I've got to hire somebody. And I'd rather it was someone I know."

He'd intended all along to hire someone for a few weeks of office work, and maybe she saw the truth of that in his eyes, because she frowned in concentration. "How much would it pay?"

"Not that much," he answered slowly. If he tried to offer her something too generous, she'd go back to insisting she didn't need *any* help and probably wind up in some fleabag apartment. "Minimum wage. But I'd like to get someone who can be on call if the job runs late, or stay as long as it takes...." Then another brainstorm struck. "So of course I'd throw in the guest room."

Lucy stared at him in disbelief. "You're making this up."

"I'm not my brother!" Which was a stupid reaction, Conner knew. It was pointless to feel any flicker of hurt, because he shouldn't care what this woman thought of him. "I'm offering you a straight, up-front deal," he concluded. "You take care of the office work, and you and Emma can stay at the house until January fifteenth."

It wasn't going to be an easy sell, he knew as soon as Lucy folded her arms across her chest. "Why?" she demanded, glancing from him to Emma. "Just because she's your niece?"

Because taking care of family was the kind of habit no one ever outgrew.

Because, like it or not, he'd spent a lifetime cleaning up after his brother.

Because if he turned his back on yet another responsibility, Conner Tarkington might as well check out.

"That's partly it," he told Lucy. After all, his responsibilities now included his brother's baby. And as long as he didn't allow himself any distractions from Bryan's memorial, he could handle six weeks with a woman who made him feel more alive, more aware than he'd felt in a long time. "But I also want to get this foundation up and running, and I'll need some help to get it done by January. So do we have a deal?"

She met his eyes, and the gaze lingered for a long moment before she drew a deep breath and reached forward to offer a handshake he wouldn't have dared to suggest himself.

"All right," she said as Con accepted her small, strong hand and felt the warmth of her skin radiate through every cell of his body. "Yes. We have a deal."

Chapter Two

They had a deal, Lucy reminded herself two days later as she inserted another sheet of letterhead into the printer and watched The Bryan Foundation logo slide toward the tray. She gave Conner neatly typed letters, he gave her a paycheck and a place to stay. That was all.

Their deal didn't require him to act like family, to enjoy playing with Emma instead of keeping a careful distance whenever the baby was awake. It didn't require him to act like anything more than a housemate who traded cooking and grocery-shopping duties with her, and who didn't go beyond the light conversation they shared during breakfasts and dinners at the kitchen counter. It didn't even require him to answer a simple question like, "Why do you call this The Bryan Foundation?"

But every time she remembered his response to that question—"It's a long story. Do you have the investor list?"—she found herself gritting her teeth. If he didn't even want to tell her how he'd named a foundation which provided after-school care for children, there was obviously never going to be much of a friendship, here.

Not that she cared, Lucy reminded herself as she glanced at the baby carrier, where Emma seemed enchanted with the pulsing concerto she'd put on the CD player. Not that she even *wanted* to be friends with Conner Tarkington. It was just hard to share a house and a dining-room office with someone who stayed so remote all the time…except for that one, never-mentioned flash of awareness between them, the night he'd mentioned locking her door.

Then she heard the front door slam, which meant he was back already. "Lucy, can I Fed-Ex that proposal tonight?" Conner called, and she hastily turned her attention to the page emerging from the computer printer.

"They close at five-thirty," she told him, and as Con came into the office he glanced at his Rolex watch.

"Damn, I guess not."

But he said it calmly, the way he said everything else. Wednesday evening, when she had whooped with exhilaration over finally getting the new fax machine to send pages, he had barely nodded. And yesterday afternoon, when the computer swallowed the addresses she wanted and Lucy had burst into tears, his only response had been a quiet suggestion that she call someone to recover the data.

It was probably that very lack of emotion which made the man so incredibly good at business, Lucy suspected. And while she couldn't help wishing he'd let himself relax once in a while, she had to admit there was something impressive about his detached professionalism, his innate confidence that things would go exactly the way he wanted. No one who dealt with Conner Tarkington would ever have to worry about him changing his mind or backing out of a promise.

She could handle her end of their deal just as professionally, she knew, the same as anyone he might have hired from the temp service. Although, Lucy admitted, as the CD player in the living room began a lush violin solo, maybe a temp wouldn't answer phone calls while dancing to the Tarkingtons' music collection....

Conner reached for the message slips she handed him, then halted momentarily as the violin's melody soared. "Thanks," he said, but in his voice she could hear a thread of tension. "What's that?"

"I can turn it down," she offered. Maybe Con was one of those people who couldn't think with noise in the background, but the sound wasn't loud enough to disturb Emma. "Or do you just not like music?"

He hesitated, and she saw his knuckles whiten as he tightened his grip on the messages. "It doesn't bother me," he muttered. "It's just... Do you have anything else?"

"Practically everything," she told him. "You should know, it's your family's collection." But now that she thought of it, Lucy realized, over the past few days she hadn't noticed him anywhere near the cabinet of jazz, big band, classical and contemporary CDs in the living room. "Are you sure you don't mind music?"

Conner squared his shoulders, picked up the portable phone from the dining room table and then met her gaze straight on. "I've been on the board of the Philadelphia Orchestra First-Nighters," he answered gruffly, "for the past six years."

That didn't really answer her question, but she sensed there was no point in asking anything more. Whatever bothered Conner Tarkington about music, it wasn't something he intended to share with her.

"Good for you," she told him instead, and noticed the slight relaxation of his neck muscles...as if he hadn't expected such matter-of-fact acceptance of that curious tension. "That's one more nice thing," she offered, "I can tell Emma about her family."

If he appreciated how easily she'd switched the conversation to neutral ground, he didn't show any sign of it. "What, the Tarkingtons?"

"Well, you know, kids need to hear good things about where they came from." Which meant never saying their father had been a scumbag...not that she could say such a thing to Conner, in any case. He seemed like the kind of person who believed in family loyalty, and that was all the more reason to remember her vow of speaking well about Emma's dad. "I already saved the articles that talked about Kenny in the Phoenix Open."

Crumpling the message slips onto his side of the desk, he set the phone down harder than necessary. "No kidding."

"For when she's older, I mean." Emma would grow up hearing only the best about a talented golf pro who needed to travel the world...the same reassuring generalities Lucy'd heard about a guitarist who had played twenty-six years ago at some festival in Santa Fe. "She needs to know I—" Lucy swallowed, wishing the statement didn't take so much effort. "I fell in love with him the first time we met."

Conner stayed very still for a moment, then flexed his shoulders under the white broadcloth shirt that made him look like an ad for some old-money tailor. "Right," he said abruptly. "I figured that." With a quick gesture, he grabbed his stack of letters from the printer and sat down across from her at the dining room table. "So how come you won't take any help from him?"

She'd been prepared for doubt, but not for such a challenge. "We had this conversation already," Lucy protested, trying not to notice the hard muscles of his shoulders as he reached across the table for his pen. She didn't *want* any more Tarkingtons in her life, but sometimes watching Kenny's brother made it difficult to remember that.

"You want Emma to have the best of everything, right?" he persisted, picking up his monogrammed silver pen as if it were an ordinary felt-tip. "You want her to hear good stories about her father...."

"She will!"

Con drew the first letter into position and fixed her with a challenging gaze. "So why do you want your daughter to have stories, but not child support?"

He made it hard to argue with him, Lucy realized, hard to think why he might be wrong. But he was wrong about Emma needing anything from Kenny's family. "Because," she answered, "I can support her myself."

Conner signed the letter with his usual swift, almost illegible scrawl, and folded it into the envelope she'd left beside him. Only then did he offer a flat objection. "Not like the Tarkingtons can."

Maybe not in terms of money, but… "It's not about money, all right?" she protested. It was about love, about family, about building a home where children were cherished. "If Kenny doesn't care about her, then why would your family? I mean, from what he said, it doesn't sound like you're all that close."

Con closed his eyes for a moment, as if weighing a series of potential arguments and rejecting each one. "We aren't," he admitted finally. "But it's not like we fight or anything. I mean, we get along whenever we see each other."

"When was the last time your whole family saw each other?"

His expression didn't change in the slightest, but she saw his shoulder muscles tighten as he signed the next letter. "My mom's wedding, I guess," he answered while folding the pages. "She remarried a few years ago."

Kenny hadn't mentioned that, although if he'd tried to share life stories about their mothers she would have quickly changed the subject. "Is your dad…" she began, and Con answered before she could finish the question.

"He died when I was twelve."

She had learned firsthand how amazingly hard it was to lose a parent, but there was a world of difference between such a loss at twelve and at twenty-three. "Oh, Conner, I'm sorry.'' Lack of family was even worse at this time of year, as the calendar moved from November to December. ''So on holidays, you... What are you doing for Christmas?''

''Nothing.'' He must have heard how stark that answer sounded, because he offered a quick amendment. ''Working. But you don't need to stick around.''

Darn right she wasn't going to stick around—she'd already made her plans for the holiday. But nobody should be alone at Christmas! ''Emma and I are spending the day with Shawna and Jeff,'' she offered. ''You're welcome to come, if you'd like.''

Although he smiled in response, she suspected Conner had no intention of accepting such an invitation. ''Well, thanks,'' he said noncommittally, handing her the stack of envelopes. ''Anyway, these need to get out.''

Okay, fine. Maybe he really *didn't* want anyone in his life, even during the holidays. After all, not everybody enjoyed the kind of close relationship that Lucy wanted for herself and Emma. Yet still, it troubled her that Conner seemed so detached from not only his family, but from the rest of the world as well. Because, although she'd taken calls from acquaintances suggesting a round of golf, a lunch or dinner when he had the time, even a *Riverdance* performance that Lucy would have shrieked to accept, he declined them all with impersonal courtesy and concentrated on his work.

Even on Saturday, which appalled her. ''It's the weekend!'' she protested when she found him at the computer shortly after sunrise the next morning. ''Don't tell me you work Saturdays, too.''

He gave her an unapologetic glance. ''Yeah, pretty much. But if you need the weekend off, take it. I just need to finish some planning while there's nobody calling in.''

Her own plan was to take Emma shopping—well, window-shopping, because she couldn't justify buying any gifts—but even so, they spent a pleasant few hours strolling the shops at Scottsdale Fashion Square. When they came home and found Conner still in the office, Lucy gazed in disbelief at the untouched stack of folders beside him. This was getting way out of hand.

"Conner," she announced, tweaking the lid of his laptop computer, "it's time to take a break. I mean it. Come to the park with Emma and me."

He looked at her strangely for a moment, as if returning from an impenetrable gulf of time or space. "Uh…" he mumbled, glancing at his watch. She saw the look of surprise dart across his face, then felt a rush of triumph when Con slowly rose to his feet. "Yeah, okay," he answered. "Thanks."

Conner knew she was right. He needed a break. He'd spent the past three hours engulfed in memories, engulfed in guilt, and that was a dangerous habit even without any scotch in the house.

But even so, it took him a moment to save the document on his computer screen, to flex the stiffness from his shoulders and to return his full attention to the present. Saturday afternoon. Scottsdale. A trip to the park.

With Lucy…

"We can walk there," she told him. "It's right up the street, and it's really nice out."

She must have been out walking already, he noticed, because her cheeks were flushed with color. But the weather was evidently warm enough that she hadn't taken a coat, so he followed her and Emma outside in his long-sleeved rugby shirt and inhaled the fresh December air.

"Thanks," he told Lucy again, stretching his arms behind his back and feeling the muscles shift into place. Her invitation was all the more welcome because he'd spent the past week maintaining a formal distance between them, and yet here she'd taken it on herself to offer a gesture of friendship. "I needed to get out for a while."

"Darn right," she agreed, tucking a baby blanket between Emma and her loose green sweater, then flashed him a challenging glance. "Don't you ever do anything besides work?"

"Not lately," Con said, wishing he could set aside his sense of responsibility for the next hour or two. But that wouldn't be fair to a woman who'd already been abandoned by his brother, and Lucy didn't seem inclined to pursue the question. Instead she transferred Emma to her shoulder and pointed toward the west.

"The park's right across the street, practically. They have a lake, and a soccer field…Emma's never been, but I think she'll get a kick out of it. Last week I saw a bunch of kids playing there."

It seemed wildly optimistic to believe that Emma would enjoy playing with other kids—she couldn't be more than six weeks old—but he wasn't going to mention that. Instead he observed, "She might need a few more years before you give her a soccer ball."

Lucy grinned at him. "Did you ever play soccer, growing up? Or was your whole family into golf?"

Her quick pace was a pleasure to match, and already her sparkling energy seemed to have jump-started his own, which was happening far too often lately. "Kenny was the golfer," he answered, hoping the conversation would stay on sports rather than on the Tarkingtons. "I mostly ran track."

"What did your mom do?"

It took him a moment to remember. "She played tennis."

"How about your dad?"

He drank.

"Golf," Conner said, choosing the simplest answer. After all, his dad had still been a member of the Philadelphia Cricket Club when he wrapped his car around a Schuylkill River boathouse at ninety miles an hour. "He would've been proud seeing Kenny make the tour."

"I bet he would've been proud of you, too," Lucy observed, pushing a stray cluster of dark curls behind her shoulder. "I mean, you're a lawyer and everything."

"Well, everybody in the family's a lawyer." This was a safer line of conversation, one he'd used with dozens of women over the years. He had discovered during his first semester at Cornell that there was something appealing in the notion of eldest sons carrying on the family tradition, which made it useful for impressing women without moving beyond the surface.

Not that he cared about impressing Lucy....

The hell he didn't.

"Do you miss it?" Lucy asked, and it took him a startled moment to realize she must be asking about his practice.

"Yeah, it'll be good to get back." His partners had already covered for him longer than he had any right to expect, but they'd agreed to another six weeks of leave. And by the time he returned with The Bryan Foundation up and running, Conner knew, he'd be able to live with himself again. Next year, he could face the holiday season with his soul intact. "But I have to get the foundation started."

She wrinkled her forehead, as if calculating feasible workloads, which reminded him once again that this vividly emotional woman was a lot smarter than he'd expected. "Couldn't you start your foundation and do your lawyer stuff at the same time?"

Even if he'd been willing to face another Christmas in Philadelphia, that would have required more time than he possessed. At least he'd learned that much from the therapist his partners had insisted on, after discovering he'd spent eighty-two consecutive hours at his desk.

"No," Con answered, letting her precede him out the community gate and trying not to let his eyes linger on the naturally sensual way she walked. "Only so many hours in a day."

"And *some* of them," Lucy announced with a nod at the

grassy park across the street, where clusters of people were enjoying the afternoon sunshine, "you have to spend enjoying."

He knew that, Conner reminded himself, with a twinge of envy at how easily she moved from business to pleasure and back again. He tended to forget the importance of taking time to play catch, feed the ducks, all those things the people across the street were doing. All the things he could do once the foundation was complete. "Yeah, you're right."

"I don't want to sound like I'm bossing you around," she said as they waited for a break in traffic. "But working as much as you do...I don't think it's very good for you. I think you need to take more breaks."

When was the last time, Con wondered, anyone outside the firm had worried about him like that? All this time he'd been keeping his distance from Lucy, she must have been noticing far more of his habits than he realized. And it was endearing that she cared enough to try and straighten him out.

That she saw him as...well, as a friend.

"You're right," he said again, letting his mind explore the concept of friendship and realizing that it could work out fine. Just because she loved his brother was no reason they couldn't be friends. "Once the foundation's up and running, I'll make more time for fun."

Lucy shifted Emma to her other shoulder as a distant group of golfers strolled toward the adjacent course. "I bet you'd enjoy playing golf if you ever got back into it," she offered, evidently guessing how quickly he'd always neglected his periodic vows to relax more often. "Kenny said you guys used to play together."

Back in college, yeah, when he was still trying to get his brother through high school. "Well, it was a way to keep an eye on him."

"Really?" She slowed her steps, regarding him with what

looked like fascination. "Did you kind of take over, after your dad died?"

He'd taken over even before that, in a way, but it wasn't until the death of his father that his mom had completed her escape into the haze of prescription drugs. "Yeah, pretty much," Conner replied. He had learned early on that the agency who replaced the Tarkingtons' constantly quitting housekeepers never challenged a new request, and that no one ever questioned his scribbled initials on whatever papers his mother let pile up on the desk.

But that wasn't a story which needed sharing, and Lucy seemed more concerned with crossing the street than his response. Until they reached the opposite sidewalk and she glanced at him with open curiosity. "I'll bet having you around made things easier on Kenny, didn't it?"

Things had always been easier on Kenny, though. Con had recognized even as a child that everyone—including himself—enjoyed his brother's carefree attitude, the happy-go-lucky charm which proved their family was as normal as anyone else. While Conner had been silently acknowledged as the one who kept things running, Kenny seemed to have a gift for attracting fun and friendship and love.

He was just that kind of person.

And you're not.

"I don't know," Conner muttered, "I probably wasn't anyone's dream of an older brother. I was always throwing my weight around—do your homework, don't stay out too late—that kind of thing."

"That sounds more like a dad or a mom," Lucy observed, surprising him with the accuracy of her perception. It wasn't like any big secret, of course—there was no reason *not* to explain the Tarkingtons' sordid family dynamics—but the habit of making his life sound normal must be more deeply ingrained than he'd realized, because he automatically chose an evasive response.

"My mom was pretty easy on us," he said lightly, and

Lucy gave him a teasing smile. As if she sensed the growing companionship between them.

"So she didn't mind if you spent all day playing golf, huh?"

"No, not really." When she'd completed her recovery a few years ago, Grace Conner Tarkington had apologized for being so uninvolved with her sons, as if their inability to love might somehow be her fault. But he couldn't remember whether she'd mentioned their frequent escapes to the golf course. "Anyway, that was only on weekends."

Lucy glanced around the park, evidently seeking a spot near children whose voices might attract a baby's interest, then started toward a group playing Frisbee in a nearby clearing. "So what kind of things did you do during the week?"

Good, they were finished with the family history. And she still sounded genuinely interested, Conner realized. Not in whatever trauma he might have suffered, the way the shrinks had been, but simply in his everyday life. "You mean, besides school?"

She spread her baby blanket on the grass and set Emma down on it, then brushed her hands against her jean-clad hips and cocked her head at him. "School, or whatever. I'm just trying to picture you, when you were little."

It was a little unnerving how flattered he felt by her forthright interest. By the way she kept her eyes focused on his, waiting for an answer he didn't even know how to give. "Well…"

"You know," Lucy explained, "what you did for fun." As if spotting an example, she gestured at the teenager attempting to throw a bright orange Frisbee with an elaborate, under-the-knee move. "Did you go around collecting golf balls?"

Golf— She was asking about *Kenny,* he realized with a sudden jolt of embarrassment. Of course she wanted to know about the childhood he'd shared with his brother.

Because Lucy loved his brother.

Before he could stammer a response, the orange Frisbee came sailing right toward them, and he instinctively grabbed for it. Caught it on the downward arc, then steadied his balance. Glanced around for the kid who'd thrown it, took aim and flung it back.

"Good one!" the teenager's buddy called, and sent another shot his way.

He could deal with a Frisbee a lot easier than anything else, Conner thought, and already Lucy was moving Emma toward a nearby olive tree as if acknowledging the newly expanded playing area. So he caught the second throw as well, returned it with the same lofty spin as the first, and in no time was part of a three-way circle that soon expanded by a couple more teenagers and a dad with some kids.

This was mindless activity, nothing but working his body, watching the angles, running and catching and throwing whatever came his way, but it offered the same distraction as his computer. A refuge from thinking, a refuge from feeling, and that was all he could ask for right now.

"Feelings are our—"

No, forget it.

The game began moving faster, tighter, and he found himself making higher catches, more demanding throws than he would have attempted at the start. But by now he was in the rhythm of motion, the simple exhilaration of calling on his muscles and feeling them respond. And when the kid beside him missed a Frisbee that skittered to the ground near Lucy, his first reaction to seeing her fling it back was an instinctive admiration—damn, she was good! Even as he watched, one of the teenage girls moved over to where she sat with Emma and gestured an invitation to switch places, and in another minute Lucy was part of the circle as well.

She was *good,* Conner realized, sending her a tougher throw than he'd aimed at the previous girl, and feeling a surge of pleasure as she caught it deftly and, without ever moving too far from Emma, sent it skimming across the circle. The way she moved, the way she threw herself into the game, laughing, so alive, so...

God, I want her.

The raw heat of recognition startled him, even as he realized that it was nothing new. He'd been wanting her for days, but had never let himself feel it so intensely, so acutely—until now, with the vigor of the game pulsing through his veins, with the pleasure of her company still heightening his senses, with her sparkling energy almost radiating across the circle to him.

Lucy had a gift for enjoying the moment, he realized, watching as she applauded a successful catch by the kid beside her and beamed at Emma's sitter, who was entertaining the baby with a bright red balloon. A gift for reaching out to friends, as well, but right now she was so happy, so vibrant, so gut-wrenchingly beautiful that he found himself staring at her without a single conscious thought in his head. With nothing but the raw, pulsing desire for—

Don't go there.

But he'd already shot way past friendship, Con knew as the orange Frisbee came his way again—there, up, another step, grab it—and he almost missed the catch before flinging himself sideways for a perfect, last-minute save. Lucy grinned at him, a smile that might have been simple congratulations but which he suddenly suspected, with a flash of heat that left him reeling, meant that they'd shared the same primal awareness.

The same ache of need.

Now wasn't the time for reasoning, not when the other Frisbee was coming right toward him—easy, up a little, there, coming, got it, go! But when he fired it back across the circle and saw Lucy still smiling at him, still watching him with that curious new light in her eyes, he knew that reason didn't matter. Nothing mattered right now except moving, straight toward her, forget the game, forget the park.

And to his exultation, she seemed to feel exactly the same way. As soon as he approached her she backed out of the circle…then welcomed him with a hug that could have been sporting, could have been the same congratulations she'd offer any teammate, but…

But there was more than congratulations going on, more than celebration. More than sharing the fun of a game, more than simple enjoyment.

Because when he kissed her, she kissed him back.

As eagerly, as joyously as if she'd been waiting all day, all her life for this fierce embrace. He had never imagined such a flash of heat could rise so intensely, sweep in so fast, but it was happening now with staggering power, with astonishing force. He ran his fingers down her spine and heard her gasp, drew her hips closer and felt himself shudder as she deepened the kiss, buried his hands in her hair and abandoned all thought, all reason, knowing they were soaring together into something that could sear their very souls—and just as the thought took shape in his mind, Lucy pulled away.

"Conner," she gasped, "we have to stop."

They had to stop, Lucy reminded herself as she struggled against the wave of dizziness that had all too swiftly replaced the pressure of his body against hers. She couldn't let this happen, no matter how much she might have wondered what Conner would feel like, whether his body was as hard as his gaze, how his lips might taste if she—

She couldn't do this.

But when she heard the growl of "Why?" it took her a moment to realize that the question hadn't come from her.

"Why?" Conner repeated, gazing down at her with such unabashed desire that she felt herself starting to sway toward him again. Even though she couldn't. Hugging a teammate was one thing, but this... She couldn't.

"You're my boss," Lucy whispered, although that was the least important reason. But she couldn't think well enough right now to explain why falling for another Tarkington would mean the end of her battered self-respect, why she couldn't let herself lose control again.

"Lucy," he began, and then suddenly the pleading in his eyes gave way to a harder, darker expression. "I know," he said abruptly, squaring his shoulders and taking a step back from her. "We can't do this."

The swiftness of his acknowledgment hurt, even though it was what she'd wanted, and she found herself staring at him with the hope she might witness another, equally sudden change of heart.

But that wasn't happening, she realized. Instead, she saw on his face the same uneasiness she'd seen the first night they met. When he'd found her in his family's home and made it clear—without so much as a word of discourtesy—that he knew Lucy Velardi was a gold digger.

"Because of what happened with Kenny," she guessed with a sinking sensation in her heart, and his gaze turned even darker.

"Right."

"But I—" Lucy faltered, then forced herself to remember what mattered most. Emma deserved to know there had been *some*thing between her parents, regardless of how quickly it had faded. And that meant she could never deny that, for a few giddy weeks, she had loved her child's father. "I'd never loved anyone," she pleaded, "the way I—"

"I know. You said that." Conner shoved his hands in his pockets, casting a quick glance behind him as one of the Frisbee players shouted in exultation, and then seemed to recognize a source of inspiration. "This was just," he said slowly, as if seeking some reason for an otherwise inexplicable kiss, "just…the game, that's all. People get carried away when they're winning."

It wasn't like anyone could win a game of Frisbee, but Lucy seized the flimsy explanation with relief. "That's it, exactly," she agreed, noticing that her daughter was still engrossed in the teenage sitter's balloon. At least, during that passionate lapse of responsibility, she hadn't fallen down as a mother. She had remembered that Emma mattered most. "That's all it was."

"Right." Conner sounded equally relieved, which bothered her. But after all, she reminded herself, it wasn't like she *wanted* him to blame anything beyond the excitement of the game. It wasn't like she wanted to throw away her carefully salvaged independence. "So we ought to head back to work."

Work. Right.

"Sure," Lucy agreed, although she hadn't planned on working today. "I mean, if you need me for any—" *Anything* wasn't the right word, she realized, because that could imply more than office duties. "I mean, *do* you—" Then she broke off, recognizing how difficult it would be to phrase the question correctly. And for the first time since he'd let her go, she felt a tremor of dread.

That kiss was going to be hard to forget.

Maybe Con knew that, too, because he was already shaking his head at the idea of spending time in the office together. "It can wait until Monday," he said gruffly. "Nothing urgent."

"Okay, then." She had faced other awkward situations before, but never had she come up against one like this. How on earth could she survive five more weeks in the same office, the same *house* with this man? "Let me just get Emma."

Emma's sitter offered to let them keep the balloon, which Conner tied onto her ankle, and the baby's rapturous interest in her new treasure provided sufficient material for conversation on the way home. But by the time they arrived at the front door, Lucy could tell they were both feeling the strain of keeping up a casual dialogue. Conner immediately headed for his computer, then hesitated a moment, and she saw his shoulder muscles tighten before he turned to face her with a troubled expression.

"Lucy," he said, "I just want to make sure you know…I mean, back at the park…" He looked more uneasy than she'd ever seen him before, but drew a deep breath and finished in a rush. "I was out of line. That's not going to happen again."

She already knew that, had known it ever since he backed away from her with such disconcerting swiftness. But she had to give him credit for such flawless courtesy, pretending that a blue-blood lawyer would even consider repeating such a mistake.

"Right," she murmured. Normally they might shake hands to seal the agreement, but touching Conner now was out of the question. "It was just the game."

"Yeah, that's it." He looked over his shoulder at the computer still waiting on his desk, then gave her what was probably supposed to be a comforting smile. "So, everything's all right."

But it wasn't all right, Lucy knew. She spent the rest of the day avoiding any glance at the office, and took a sandwich to her room before their usual dinnertime, but she knew this self-imposed distance wasn't working. She was getting too close to Conner Tarkington. She was remembering too often how the crackling barrier had shattered for that dazzling moment in the park. And if she couldn't control herself any better than she had at the instant when he'd kissed her, well, she needed to get out of here.

Plain and simple. She had to get out.

Getting out the next morning was easy, because Shawna had invited her to string popcorn for the community Christmas tree at her grandmother's senior center. It was a tradition Lucy appreciated all the more this year, since she desperately needed a few hours away from Con's resolutely impersonal gaze.

She arrived early, relieved that the church shuttle driver hadn't minded picking up passengers for the trip back to Mesa, and grateful that she and Emma had made it through breakfast with Conner while maintaining a conversation that would have sounded normal to anyone else. She could get through five more weeks under his roof if she had to, Lucy told herself, and she *would* have to unless Shawna could come up with an idea.

"I guess you could move out," her friend suggested when Lucy finished the story, then wrinkled her forehead as she dropped another popcorn chain into the collection bag. "But I can't really see why you want to. Couldn't you just…enjoy him?"

"Oh, right, go from one brother to the next," Lucy protested, relieved that Shawna's grandmother had taken the baby for a walk outside. Emma didn't need to hear any of this. "Shawna, what kind of person would that make me?!"

"Not your mother," came the swift reassurance. "Because you *loved* Kenny—at the beginning, anyway. I was there when you met him, remember? It was instant, for both of you."

That was true. They'd met in one of the Phoenix Open party tents, where she'd been working the afternoon-drinks shift, and had hit it off within the first thirty seconds of laying eyes on one another. "He was…" Lucy let the memory resonate, wishing it would rouse more than a faint sense of nostalgia. "Well, he was fun."

Shawna twisted her thread into a knot and bit the end off, shaking her red-beaded braids back behind her shoulder. "So you loved Kenny, and you like this guy. Why can't you just enjoy each other while he's here?"

Because she knew better than to make the same mistake twice. "I like him too much," Lucy explained, remembering how carefully they'd maneuvered around the coffee-maker this morning and how quickly he'd cut off her attempt to explain about Kenny. "Anyway, he already said it was a mistake. He doesn't want to get involved with a gold digger."

"He couldn't call you that!" Shawna sounded fiercely certain. "Lucy, you're not *asking* him for anything."

No, of course not. But that hadn't stopped him from offering to make her life easier. "He already wants to take care of me," she muttered, remembering his repeated mentions of child support. "I mean, like a family honor thing. But I don't need any help...especially from someone like him."

Her friend glanced up from knotting the thread with a small frown. "He's paying you, isn't he?"

"Well, minimum wage." Which she could justify accepting, because he'd have to pay anyone else the same amount. "And free rent." Which was harder to justify, except... "I could make more money somewhere else, because weekday-lunch people don't tip much. But I'd still have to find a sitter for Emma."

"You know Gram would love to take care of her," Shawna offered, nodding at the patio where her grandmother was showing the baby a bright ribboned wreath. "She's said that all along."

That was true, and it was a relief to know Emma would be in good hands once she started waitressing full-time again. "I know," Lucy agreed, glancing out the window at her daughter and Gram, "and I'll plan on that in five more weeks."

Five weeks is too long!

The thought startled her with its desperate intensity, but she recognized the raw truth of it. She couldn't spend another five weeks working in the same house, living in the same house, with Conner Tarkington.

Who had delighted her yesterday with that first glimmer

of an easy camaraderie between them. Whose powerful hands and searing mouth had invaded her dreams last night. Who had promised she'd never need to worry about him touching her again.

"I have to get out of there," she blurted, and saw from Shawna's startled glance that there must have been a note of panic in her voice.

"Well, then," her friend advised, reaching for the bowl of popcorn, "just tell him you're moving out. You've almost got enough saved up, right?"

Not enough for the trailer park where she could feel safe letting Emma play outside. Even with what Conner was paying her, the electricity and security deposits there would take another month. But the sooner she moved out, Lucy knew, the sooner she could put the memory of that kiss behind her.

And while it would be wretchedly irresponsible to abandon free rent until she had at least another three hundred dollars saved, she needed to earn the money fast.

"I need an extra job," she announced, feeling a rush of relief at hearing the words aloud. Even making such a declaration was already a step toward independence, toward regaining control of her life. "Maybe something on weekends."

"I know we're looking for more catering people at Joseph's," Shawna offered, sliding a piece of popcorn onto her chain. "All those holiday parties up in Carefree and Paradise Valley, and you don't have to drive there yourself. You just get to Joseph's, and the van takes everybody."

She could manage that easily enough, and she still had the traditional white shirt and black slacks she'd worn for catering jobs in the past. "But Emma—"

"Gram would be happy to baby-sit, remember? You know you can call her anytime."

"All right, then," Lucy decided, closing her eyes for a moment against the memory of Conner's promise never to touch her again. "Because I can't keep wanting him like this. I've got to get out of there—fast."

Chapter Three

He had to get over this fast, Conner warned himself as he rounded a curve on the Scottsdale Greenbelt running trail. He had no business coveting Lucy. After all, he couldn't keep a promise of love any better than Kenny could. But it was taking far too long for him to get this craving out of his system.

She kissed you back, remember?

Which made things worse. If she'd flinched or slapped his face, it would be a lot easier to put the whole afternoon out of his mind. But Lucy had responded with the same genuine passion she showed for everything else in life...with the dazzling enthusiasm that had intrigued him from the first night they met...with the same unabashed honesty that enabled her to explain a moment later that Kenny was the man she loved.

She hadn't lingered over the vast differences between a man who offered nonstop excitement and a man who offered stolid responsibility. She hadn't needed to. Because she'd made it clear that wanting Con was a mistake—

So forget it.

Running should help, Conner knew. This was the fourth day he'd taken off at lunchtime to run the nearby greenbelt. At least that afternoon of Frisbee had shown him how badly he needed the distraction of movement, but it was ludicrous that in four days of carefully cheerful companionship, he hadn't quite been able to get Lucy Velardi out of his mind.

The way she'd closed the lid of his computer and insisted he come to the park.

The way her entire body had stilled as she whispered, "I loved him."

The way she'd smiled when he helped Emma with that balloon—a balloon the baby had enjoyed so much that Con intended to replace it the next chance he got. Emma was a cute kid, he'd noticed over the past few days, always fun to watch while he waited for his pages from the printer. And watching her was a lot safer than watching her mom. This morning he'd enjoyed letting the baby grip his finger until Lucy whisked her off for a feeding.

And damn it, he was thinking about Lucy again!

Hell, anybody would think he loved her. But he knew better than to believe that, Con acknowledged as he caught sight of the splashing fountain ahead. Conner Tarkington might be capable of any number of things, but wholehearted love wasn't one of them.

He'd learned that two years ago, when Bryan…

No, he wasn't thinking about Bryan now. It was pointless. He was already atoning as best he could, and he didn't need those agonizing memories of the holiday season two years ago to know he was incapable of loving anyone the way they deserved.

Which meant he needed to get this longing for Lucy out of his system before he forgot what the mother of Kenny's child meant to him—a family responsibility, nothing more.

Con splashed a handful of water across his face and picked up his pace, vowing to keep his mind on the well-worn track of caring for Tarkingtons. As long as he stayed focused on the foundation, he could make it through the next five weeks. Bryan's memorial was what mattered, his responsibility was what mattered, and he was never going to neglect a responsibility again.

Especially to a child.

Which was why he'd tracked Kenny down in Hong Kong a few days ago. His brother would check in on Thursday, the hotel had announced, so Con was planning to call him tonight while Lucy put Emma to bed. There was no sense confronting her with the possibility that Kenny could have forgotten her name.

"Lucy Velardi?" his brother repeated blankly when Conner reached him that evening. "Who—oh, yeah. You're in Scottsdale now, right? Did she, uh…"

"She had your baby," Con told him. "A girl, named Emma." Lucy was bathing her in the kitchen sink right now, while he used the phone in the hall to keep his conversation private. "So it's time to start taking some responsibility."

"Yeah, well, last spring I sent her a check," Kenny offered. "I know I said I'd marry her, but—"

But instead he'd walked out? Con felt his entire body tighten with fury. "You *what?*"

"It wouldn't have worked! She was okay with that," his brother added defensively. "I just didn't think she'd keep the baby.… Look, I'll pay a settlement or something, but it's not like I really wanted a kid in the first place. And things are kind of tight right now, so… How much does she want?"

Right to the bottom line, Conner observed. For all his freewheeling charm, Kenny was still a Tarkington at heart. "She doesn't know I'm calling."

"What?" His brother sounded incredulous. "You just de-cided to... Whose side are you on?"

He had always sided with Kenny, even while dealing with half a dozen disappointed women whose dreams of marry-ing money had never materialized. But none of them had ever borne Kenny's child, and Lucy wasn't even *looking* for money. "I'm thinking," he told his brother flatly, "about the kid."

"The— Aw, hell." During the pause, he could almost hear Kenny realizing what time of year this was. "Look, I'm sorry about— Are you doing okay?"

The sympathetic question caught him off guard, but Con managed to swallow the unexpected rush of feeling in his throat. He didn't need feelings. He didn't *have* feelings, no matter what the therapists said. "I'm fine," he answered hoarsely. "Just taking some time to set up the foundation." And even though it was frustrating to quit after twelve hours of work each day, so far he'd stuck to his self-imposed limit.

Which was a lot tougher than he'd expected.

"Oh, yeah, Mom mentioned the foundation thing." Their mother was the clearinghouse for family messages, although Conner suspected she talked to Kenny in Asia far more of-ten than himself in Philadelphia. "Anyway, about Lucy's kid...I'll come up with something. Just buy me some time, okay?"

Lucy had called this one correctly from the start, Con reflected, remembering how much easier it was to breathe when he kept his focus strictly on facts instead of feelings. She'd insisted all along that Kenny had no interest in fa-therhood, but that was still no reason to ignore his own responsibility. While he wouldn't mention this conversation to her, he wasn't about to forget another child.

"All right," he told his brother, "but just so you know, I'm not letting this go."

"You haven't changed, have you?" Kenny muttered. "Still trying to make sure everything's fair and square."

"Somebody has to, dammit!" Conner snapped, just as Lucy emerged from the kitchen with Emma wrapped in a fluffy towel. "Look, I'll talk to you later."

She made no pretense of having missed his outburst, but at least she didn't ask who he'd been talking to before slamming down the phone. Instead she gave him a look of frank curiosity and asked, "Somebody has to what?"

Minimizing bad news had always been part of his responsibility, both while growing up and while married to Margie. "Take care of the finances," he replied, hoping he sounded indifferent enough that she would drop the subject altogether.

Apparently the strategy worked, because Lucy rested Emma on the sofa and rubbed the baby's damp hair with the top of her towel before turning to another topic. "I meant to tell you, Shawna called a little while ago. She said they— You still don't need me to work weekends, right?"

The last thing he needed was more time with Lucy. "No."

"Okay, good," she said, rewrapping the towel around the wriggling baby. "So I'll get Shawna's grandmother for Saturday—her name's Lorraine, she's really sweet. But I'll tell her you're working, so she won't distract you or anything."

A whole platoon of sweet grandmothers would be far less distracting than a woman he couldn't let himself want. "No problem," Conner answered, wondering why she felt obligated to notify him of a visitor. "You don't need to clear it with me if you want to have someone over."

"Well, she'll be spending the day here," Lucy explained, picking up Emma and starting toward her bedroom, "because they won't let her baby-sit at the senior center."

Wait a minute, this grandmother was a *baby-sitter?* "How come you need a sitter?" Con asked, following her as far as the door.

She didn't seem to notice that he'd never come this close to her vanilla-scented room before. Instead she addressed him over her shoulder as she transferred the cooing baby from her fluffy towel into some fuzzy, footed sleepers. "That's what Shawna called about. I got a job at the same place she—"

"Lucy, you've *got* a job!"

"Not on weekends," she said simply, fastening the sleepers over Emma's diaper. "And I need the money."

Oh, hell, he'd messed up. He should have called Kenny sooner, arranged for some kind of child support before she had to take a second job. "Look, if you need—" he began, and she interrupted him in a rush.

"I don't need anything from you! I take care of myself, remember?"

From the steel in her voice, he knew this was an argument he couldn't win. At least not yet. "So…"

"So, Lorraine will be here Saturday," Lucy concluded, nestling Emma in what looked like a bureau drawer lined with blankets. My God, his niece was sleeping in a *drawer?* "But I'll tell her you're working, so she won't get in your way."

And she didn't, Conner acknowledged on Saturday after four hours of listening for any fussing from Emma and hearing nothing at all. This pudgy, white-haired grandmother seemed like a nice lady, although he wished she had come bearing gifts…like a crib, or a car seat, or any of the other things Lucy would never accept from a Tarkington.

But the sitter did such a great job of keeping Emma out of his way that by midafternoon—with only four hours left on his workday limit—he found himself almost missing the baby. And when he moved into the kitchen for coffee and insisted that she and Emma weren't in the way, he was pleased that Lorraine took him at his word.

She didn't seem to realize that he had very little experience with babies, because when she shifted Emma for a better grip on Conner's finger, she smiled at the baby's rapt expression.

"Looks like she wants *you* to hold her," Lorraine said, moving his coffee out of the way and handing him the baby as easily as if she were handing him a dinner plate. "There you go. Isn't she just the cutest thing?"

Emma felt so incredibly fragile that he was uneasy about breathing, but she didn't seem to mind his lack of skill at holding a baby. In fact, she nestled into his embrace so warmly that for a moment Conner let himself imagine that she felt safe, comfortable, cared for....

That Emma felt loved.

"I'm going to run to the rest room," Lorraine told him, and he nodded without taking his eyes off the child in his arms.

He had to give her back, of course. He wasn't capable of caring for a baby for more than two or three minutes, but it was surprisingly sweet to pretend that he knew what he was doing, and that this little bundle of life welcomed the assurance of his heartbeat against her own.

Still, he handed her back to the sitter without trying to prolong the moment, and hastily retreated to his work. It had been a fluke, that's all, enjoying that sense of protecting a baby. But two hours later, when he heard Emma wake up from her nap with a hearty cry, he closed the lid of his computer and followed the sound.

"Somebody needs a clean diaper," Lorraine observed, lifting the baby onto the dresser Lucy kept covered in blankets. Then, apparently taking it for granted that Conner had arrived with assistance in mind, she nodded at him. "Want to hand me the pins? We've got the old-fashioned kind, here."

He could do that, Con decided. There was a pile of diaper pins right there on the dresser, and it couldn't be that hard to offer one whenever the expert held out an expectant hand. Still, he was amazed at how deftly Lorraine folded the cloth under Emma's squirming body and tucked it into a neat triangle shape. "You're good at that."

''Years of practice,'' she told him, then set the baby down again and whisked off the just-applied diaper. ''But anybody can do it. I'll show you.''

Conner gulped. There was no way to refuse that offer, even though he hadn't quite planned on learning such a skill. But within a few minutes he realized that the baby-sitter was right.

''I can do this,'' he acknowledged, lifting the freshly diapered baby into his arms and marveling at the knowledge that he, Conner Tarkington, had completed the entire task himself.

Maybe he couldn't *love* a child, but he could sure take care of her.

''Of course you can.'' Lorraine gave him a cheerful smile as he nestled Emma into the crook of his arm. ''Babies are easy as pie.''

''It's easy,'' Lucy muttered to the low-hanging desert moon as she skirted an ocotillo cactus behind the festively lighted hacienda, circulating yet another tray of chorizo-stuffed tarts. ''I used to do this all the time.'' For the past week she'd kept telling herself how easy it was, how she used to sail through the workday after dancing all night, but the pep talks were starting to wear thin. Still, it shouldn't take too much longer to get back into the swing of things.

At least she hoped not.

''Oh, the chorizo!'' a woman exclaimed, and Lucy turned with a practiced smile to offer the tray. Tonight's guests were a cordial group, celebrating somebody's fortieth anniversary, and it was encouraging that most of them looked old enough to go home early. With any luck she'd be finished by ten, the Joseph's van would already be waiting to shuttle everyone back to the restaurant, and she could get enough sleep that Emma wouldn't need to wait more than thirty seconds while she dragged herself awake for the two o'clock feeding.

But first she had to circulate these tarts. Then the jalapeño crackers, the miniature tacos and another round with the chorizo.

Working inside would be more fun, she knew, because the hosts had set up a dance floor in the great room, and she'd enjoyed the music whenever she returned to the mansion-size kitchen to refill her tray. On her last trip they'd been playing a song she loved, a song she'd danced to a hundred times on the radio, and she had entertained herself by peeking at the couples out there. Some of them were good; some of the younger men were the kind she'd have chosen for herself if she had her pick of partners.

I'd rather have Conner.

The thought startled her—what was she doing, envisioning him as any kind of a partner? Lucy hastily returned her attention to the hors d'oeuvre tray. She wasn't going to think that way, she told herself as she offered tarts to a cluster of people by the pool. Not when she'd finally made it through almost an entire day without remembering their kiss in the park.

Not now that she was finally regaining her independence.

She'd held the thought of independence like a talisman, every time she handed Emma over to Lorraine and changed from her diner clothes to her catering uniform. With every hour of evening and weekend work, she was closer to acquiring the money she'd need to move out before Christmas. And with every hour of circulating trays, directing guests to the bar and collecting crumpled napkins from the patio planters, she was proving that Lucy Velardi could pay her own way in life.

That she didn't depend on anybody's goodwill. Especially not a "gentleman's."

It had surprised her, Lucy remembered as she returned to the kitchen, the first time her third-grade teacher addressed the girls and boys as "ladies and gentlemen." She had always thought the term applied solely to those friends of her mom who visited at random hours and occasionally presented her with a pack of gum or a comic book.

Those gentlemen who had made it clear, through years of gifts and favors granted or withheld, that nobody mattered more than the man providing the money.

But by now she had moved beyond the humiliation of depending on *any* gentlemen. Which was why, Lucy reminded herself as the party wound down and the crew supervisor directed her to collect all the glassware left outside, she needed to pay Lorraine as soon as she got home. Before Conner could offer his help and whip out a checkbook, the way he'd done a few nights ago when he dismissed the sitter twenty minutes early.

Lorraine wouldn't have left, of course, if she hadn't trusted him with the baby, so Lucy had decided she wasn't going to fuss about Con sending the sitter home. But she drew the line at letting him pay someone she'd hired herself. As long as she and Emma were living under his roof, she needed to guard her pride.

Still, she admitted while she finished her share of the cleanup, pride was costly. It was costing her tonight, in aching muscles and growing fatigue, but the power of independence was worth it. And when she finally made her way to the desert-landscaped front yard to wait for the shuttle, with her first week's pay voucher safe in the pocket of her black slacks, Lucy felt taller than she'd felt in a long time.

Since Conner Tarkington had revealed that she'd spent the past nine months living off his brother's made-up job.

"Lucy," she heard someone call from the curb, "your ride's here."

Her ride? There was no sign of the shuttle, but—

Oh.

Parked beside the sprawling desert lot next door was Conner's million-dollar rental car.

What on earth?

From the ease with which he moved to open the passenger door, looking as richly comfortable as ever in his Irish fisherman's sweater and jeans, she realized it couldn't be an emergency—Emma must be safe at home with Lorraine— but even so, she felt uneasy at how quickly the heat of anticipation flared inside her.

She shouldn't be *this* pleased to see him.

So she slowed her steps, walking with deliberate leisure past the clumps of mesquite and the low adobe wall that separated the hacienda from the adjacent desert, and made a point of turning to wave good-night to her fellow crew members when she heard the Joseph's van arriving.

It wasn't like she expected a ride home, she assured herself as she sauntered toward Conner in the remarkably bright moonlight. Or even *wanted* one. It wasn't like she'd asked for his help.... Had she?

No, Lucy decided, he probably just needed some typing done and couldn't afford to wait.

Which meant her pride was safe.

"Ready to go?" Con asked her, looking as if he hadn't minded waiting while she took her own sweet time approaching his car. "The caterer said we'd find you here, and I figured we'd give you a ride home."

We? Then, as she followed his glance to the back seat, she saw what looked like a brand new car seat, with Emma asleep in a cocoon of blankets.

Her first instinct was joy, the same joy that always surged through her at the sight of her daughter after so many hours apart, and as she gathered the dozing baby into a heartfelt embrace, she momentarily forgot her concern over where a new car seat might have come from.

"You brought Emma," she marveled, nuzzling her daughter's forehead with a familiar rush of delight. The baby felt perfect, sweetly warm, with just the right amount of padding for a night as pleasant as this one. Which of course made sense, because Shawna's grandmother knew how to keep babies comfortable. But… "Where's Lorraine?"

"I sent her home," Con answered as easily as if reporting that he'd made a pot of coffee for breakfast. "She said it was silly for her to take your money when you already had someone at home all day."

Someone at home… "*You* were taking care of Emma?" Lucy demanded, reeling against the mixture of disbelief and the sweet sensation of this beloved child nestled comfortably in her arms. "All *day?*"

"Just since lunch." Maybe the horror in her voice had already reached him, because he was starting to sound a little defensive. "Lorraine was talking about the swap meet in Mesa, and I told her to take off early. Don't worry, I paid her for the rest of the month."

The rest of… No, he couldn't have. But it almost sounded as if… "You fired my sitter?!"

"I didn't *fire* her," he replied as she reluctantly returned Emma to the new car seat, which looked five times more expensive than the one she'd earmarked at the thrift store, and nestled her amidst the familiar blankets. A sleeping baby didn't need to hear what Lucy already suspected would turn into a shouting match. "Lorraine said you should call anytime you needed her," Conner continued, following her as far as the sidewalk beside the open-doored car. "But for now, I can handle things on weekends and at night."

Lucy glanced at the car door, calculating the safe distance between herself and Emma, before turning to face him with her hands on her hips. "I don't believe this," she told him. "You *decided,* all on your own, that you're paying off my sitter and taking care of my daughter?"

Conner looked genuinely surprised at the anger she felt crackling from every pore of her body, as if he had no idea how incredibly presumptuous he'd been. "What…?" he began. Then, when she gestured impatiently toward the car seat, a sudden recognition flashed across his face. "Are you worried because I bought her a present?"

He had no business talking about "worry" as if she were some overprotective mother. "I'm *worried*," Lucy snapped, "about you making decisions for me!" She glanced over her shoulder to make sure the catering crew was gone—she didn't need anybody watching this scene—then stepped forward so she could look him directly in the eye as she delivered her warning. "I don't want you doing that. *I* take care of paying for Emma, I take care of myself, and—"

"What is it with you taking care of yourself?" Con interrupted, glaring right back at her without retreating one inch. "Why can't you ever let anyone help you?"

He was wrong about that, because only tonight she'd accepted Rico's offer of a hand with the glassware. "I let people help me all the time!"

Conner let that declaration hang between them for a moment, echoing in the desert silence, before he answered very softly.

"Not me."

Not him...

No, Lucy admitted with a sudden sensation of tightness around her heart, he was right about that. But she *couldn't* accept anything from this man, not after falling into Mom's appalling habit once already. "You're Kenny's brother," she explained, hunching her shoulders as she shoved her hands in her pockets.

He nodded, watching her with a troubled expression. As if he knew there was something missing, and couldn't quite grasp it. "And that's a problem," he prompted, "because..."

Could he really not know? "Because I expected Kenny to take care of me, all right?" Lucy cried, swallowing back the tears that always threatened to spill when she remembered that shattering day at the courthouse. "It was stupid,

I knew better, but for once in my life I thought fine, take it easy, go ahead and let a man look out for you, and—''

She couldn't even finish the sentence, the tears were so thick in her throat. But Conner evidently didn't need to hear any more because, very gently, he finished for her.

''And it hurt like hell.''

That pretty well summed up her experience with Kenny, except for the joy of having Emma. But the anguish of knowing she'd let herself relax her long-held vow of independence, only to wind up with a golf pro as indifferent as any of her mother's gentlemen...

Conner had it right, Lucy acknowledged as she wiped her hands across her face. It hurt like hell.

''I'm not letting that happen again,'' she insisted, rubbing her tear-dampened hands across the back of her slacks and taking a deep, restoring breath. ''I'm *not*. If I ever give up my independence, if I let someone else take care of me, make decisions for me, only to have him walk out, I—'' She broke off, unable to think of a bad enough conclusion. ''I can't do it!''

''I know,'' Con answered gently, then guided her with a light touch on the shoulder to the low adobe wall that bordered the sidewalk. ''Lucy,'' he said, waiting until she sat down before seating himself a few feet away, ''I swear, I wasn't trying to take over your independence. I was just trying to...to take some responsibility.''

That sounded better than taking over her life, but it didn't change a thing. ''And I don't want you doing that!'' she reminded him. She couldn't let herself depend on anyone, not after that fiasco with Kenny. ''*I* am responsible for myself and my daughter, and—''

He closed his eyes for an instant, then raised his hand to interrupt her. ''Lucy, wait a minute. It's...taking responsibility...it's something I've always done. I *have* to.''

In his voice she could hear both passion and an edge of pain, but that didn't make sense. ''What do you mean, you have to?'' Surely not even Conner Tarkington could believe he was responsible for the entire world. Unless maybe… ''You have to take responsibility for everyone who works for you?''

''For everyone in my family,'' he corrected her on a ragged breath. He started a gesture of explanation, then cut himself off and stared at her with a look of raw determination. ''That's what I do.''

All right, maybe technically she and Emma qualified as family, but this man should really be focusing his efforts closer to home. Finding someone *else* to take care of. ''You know, Conner,'' Lucy suggested, gazing just beyond him at a lone saguaro surrounded by mesquite, ''you ought to have a family of your own.''

''I had one.'' And when she stared at him in the vivid moonlight, at the sudden overwhelming tightness of every muscle in his body, she realized for the first time where that edge of pain and passion must have come from. ''Bryan,'' he said gruffly. ''My son.''

If he hadn't heard the words still echoing between them, Conner thought, he wouldn't have believed he'd just told Lucy about Bryan. God, where had that come from? Why, out of all the people he knew who would offer a simple ''sorry to hear that'' and move on, had he spilled it to her?

Maybe, he realized as her eyes widened with the shimmer of held-back tears, because of the compassion that was already softening her voice.

''You had a son?'' she whispered.

Con dug his heels into the ground, forcing some balance against the rigid tension in his spine. If he could just keep his voice from breaking…. ''He died two years ago.''

She closed her eyes for a moment, and he could see in her body the same look of heaviness, the same anguished weight he felt in his own. But she didn't seem to be fighting it…instead she let her shoulders slump, as if no one could withstand such pain. "That's why you named it The Bryan Foundation," she said softly. "It's for him."

"It's not enough," Con muttered. Nothing would be enough to make up for his failure. "But it's all I can do."

Lucy evidently recognized the truth of that, because—unlike the therapists who insisted it was more important to grieve than to focus on building a memorial—she didn't attempt to challenge the statement. Instead she asked softly, "What happened?"

He could tell her this part. He had told it often enough that by now he knew the only way to get through it was to talk without stopping. "I didn't pick him up from school on time," Conner began, "so he started to walk home. And right before I caught up with him, he got hit by a car." Keep going. Almost through. "I came around the corner, and…there was Bryan. In the middle of the street, with his leg twisted under him. He was still bleeding, but he was already dead." That was it. That was enough.

She didn't need to hear the worst part.

The part for which he could never forgive himself.

But she reacted as if she *had* heard the worst part, drawing her hands up to her mouth. "Oh, Conner," she murmured, twisting her fingers together. "Oh, no."

"It was my fault," he concluded tightly. "My responsibility. I didn't live up to it, and…that's never going to happen again."

Lucy shifted on the adobe wall, wrapping her arms around her knees as she regarded him with a thoughtful gaze. Then, very softly, she echoed what he'd told her a moment ago. "And it hurt like hell. Only worse," she concluded, before straightening her posture to face him directly. "You do know it's not really your fault, right?"

"Yeah, all the therapists said that, too." They'd said often enough that anyone could get wrapped up in work and lose track of the time. But they hadn't heard what Bryan told his classmate, Neil, after waiting half an hour for a ride that never came. They hadn't heard Neil quoting, in a matter-of-fact voice that sounded curiously like Bryan's, *"My dad doesn't care about me."*

They hadn't heard the same thing repeated in the devastating aftermath of their son's funeral, by a mother who had lost her only child. By the woman Conner had vowed to love and cherish for a lifetime...before realizing that whatever it took to sustain that kind of love was somehow missing from his heart.

He had cared for Margie, certainly, gone through all the right motions. He had made sure she and Bryan lacked for nothing, providing the mansion, the club memberships and the private school as a matter of course. He had even made a point of spending two nights a week with his family, while building a dazzling reputation at Weller-Tarkington-Craig, and had taken pride in avoiding his father's mistakes.

No unexplained absences. No broken promises.

And above all else, no drinking.

Until after the funeral, when Margie confronted him with the stark accusation that Conner Tarkington was simply incapable of loving anyone...and he had realized she was right.

"I figured you knew that already," Lucy said, startling him. "I mean, of course they're going to make sure you know car accidents aren't your fault."

She was talking about the therapists, he realized, feeling as if he'd just been yanked from the cemetery in Philadelphia to the Arizona desert with two years still scattered in shards around him. Those same therapists who had warned that work could be as big a crutch as alcohol.

"Right," Con muttered, "I heard that from a bunch of people." He could recite it by heart, along with all those other phrases that were supposed to ensure a healthier, happier life. Listen to your body. No pain, no gain. Feelings are our friends.

"But I'll bet you didn't believe 'em," she observed, surprising him once again with the accuracy of her perception. She cocked her head, as if considering his situation, then conceded, "I probably wouldn't either. I mean, I believe it about *you*. But I wouldn't believe it about *me*."

"You'll never have to," he said, wishing his voice felt normal. This woman would never fail her child the way he'd failed his own. "You'd do anything for Emma."

"Well, sure," she agreed, "same as you'd do for Bryan." And then, evidently seeing the shadow of guilt in his eyes, she hurried to confirm the assurance. "Look what you're doing now, setting up this whole foundation as a memorial...."

"It's not enough," he repeated. It would never be enough, and he would have to live with that for another forty or fifty years. "But it's all I can do." He paused, struggling for a breath over the unexpected tightness in his throat. "It's all I can do."

"Oh, Conner..." Swiftly, Lucy moved to his side, reaching for his clenched fists with the same wholehearted warmth he'd seen her lavish on Emma. She took both his hands in hers just as gently, just as fiercely, as if all her energy belonged to this nurturing intensity, this protective comfort.

You don't deserve this.

Conner hastily drew back, startled by how much he wanted that comfort. "I'm okay," he said hoarsely, trying to regain some vestige of balance. Some sense, some order, some reason amidst the tornado of emotion, the flood of yearning that had swept through him in less time than it took for Lucy to stand up.

"You sure?" she asked, watching him with almost maternal concern. "You want some coffee or anything? I'll be glad to make it for you the minute we get home."

He must look pretty bad, Con realized with a tremor of embarrassment, if she thought he needed such tenderhearted care. Here was this woman who'd loved his brother, ready to get him whatever he wanted.... "No, thanks," he managed to answer, although his voice still didn't feel quite normal. "I'm fine."

Maybe he sounded more convincing than he felt, because she followed him back to the car, chattered about nothing all the way home and tucked Emma into bed before joining him in the living room. Then she turned off the evening news, plopped down on her side of the sofa and shifted the cushions behind her, as if settling in for a cozy chat.

"Okay," she said gently. "Let's just talk for a while—I'm still all wound up from work. You don't mind talking, do you?"

For some reason, he couldn't tell how he felt about that invitation. Sitting here talking to Lucy, who had startled him with the intensity of her compassion and with his own reaction to it, sounded incredibly tempting...and strangely frightening.

But there was nothing to be frightened of, Conner reminded himself. She wasn't going to accuse him of anything he didn't already know. And considering how clear she'd made her preference for Kenny, she certainly wasn't going to want anything he couldn't give.

No, she didn't expect anything like love. No matter how deftly, how sweetly she'd touched his soul back there in the desert, right now she was simply offering him the warmth of companionship. Of comfort. Of conversation.

He could do this.

"Tell me about Bryan," she suggested, and he felt his heart lurch with a thud of dismay.

He couldn't do this.

But Lucy, maybe thinking he simply didn't know where to start, offered a prompting question. "How old was he?"

He could answer that one, Con realized with a rush of relief. "Eight," he told her. "He'd just turned eight."

"Did he look like you?"

"Yeah, he did." Everyone had said so, from his mom

and Kenny to Margie and her parents. "Except he had freckles, like Margie." It was funny how clearly he could still see that freckled photo on his desk, even though it had disappeared almost two years ago. Someone must have moved it, knowing that, after the funeral and the divorce, he no longer had any claim to his son. *Or* his wife.

"Is she…?" For the first time, Lucy faltered. "Uh…"

Anyone could probably guess what had happened—after all, nobody would stay married after such a tragedy, especially when there hadn't been much of a relationship to begin with. "We split up after the funeral," he confirmed. The divorce might have been a relief, but he couldn't quite remember. That whole holiday season was still a fog in his memory, and last year's was even darker.

And the best thing he could hope for this year was to make it through Christmas in one piece. Which would be a lot easier, Conner realized, if he cut this conversation short.

"Thanks for listening," he said abruptly, standing up and moving to check the lock on the front door. Even if Lucy wasn't ready to call it a night yet, he needed to make sure the house was safe before leaving her alone in the living room.

But she stood up as well, pushing her sofa cushion back into place as she murmured, "Kenny never mentioned any of that."

"Well, it's over now." He flicked off the switch for the porch light and turned back to face her in the deeper shadows. "Except for the foundation."

"I'm so sorry," Lucy concluded, still regarding him with that look of luminous compassion as they started toward the hall together. "If anything ever happened to Emma, I don't know what I'd do."

"You'd get through it," Con told her, waiting until she'd opened the guest room door before adding, "better than I did."

She didn't ask for details, only gave him a troubled glance

and turned away. But as he retreated to the darkness of his own room, he knew why Lucy would get through the loss of a child so much better than he had. It was because she would never have to face the most devastating realization a parent could endure.

"You'd get through it," he murmured in the silence, "because you'd know…" He swallowed hard, then finished on a ragged breath. "No matter what happened, you'd know you could love."

Chapter Four

Two in the morning.

He might as well give up on falling asleep, Conner decided, squinting at the red numerals on the clock beside his bed. It wasn't going to happen. And he'd wasted enough time telling himself to relax, to listen to his breathing, to tighten and release his muscles one by one…because none of the therapist's tricks were doing the job tonight.

So try something else.

He found a clean shirt and yesterday's jeans, which had survived an entire afternoon with Emma, and made his way to the office before remembering the danger of using work like a drug.

No, forget that.

The sight of his car keys on the table inspired him. A drive would clear his head, get him back into a rational frame of mind, better than another marathon session at his desk. And since he hadn't heard Emma yet tonight, it wouldn't be long before she woke up hungry. Which meant that unless he wanted another gut-churning conversation with Lucy, he'd better get out of the house.

Scottsdale Road was quiet for a weeknight, especially since the bars had closed only an hour ago. Con drove through the Old Town area with galleries and stoplights every few blocks, past the silent shops and hotels farther north, and finally wound up heading for the Carefree Highway, where he could forget about stoplights and speed limits for a few liberating miles at a stretch.

This, he told himself as he shifted into gear and sped through the vast darkness of the desert night, was what he needed to restore his balance. This was the way to clear his head.

To put that conversation with Lucy behind him.

What the hell had gotten into him, anyway, telling her about Bryan in such excruciating detail?

Okay, maybe he owed her an explanation of why family responsibilities mattered to him, but he'd gone way beyond that. Beyond the standard phrases he recited whenever some returning client or acquaintance asked about his son.

She was just so damn easy to talk to, Conner reflected, downshifting for a curve in the road ahead. So genuinely interested, so wholeheartedly compassionate, that he'd let himself forget the boundaries of their relationship. Let himself forget that *he* was supposed to be the one taking care of *her*.

Not the other way around.

That was the mistake keeping him awake tonight, he admitted as he eased off the gas pedal. He needed to remember that Lucy Velardi was his responsibility, and nothing more.

But, considering how fiercely she'd reacted to his gift of a car seat for Emma, living up to that responsibility was going to be a bigger challenge than he'd anticipated.

Conner gripped the steering wheel and sped into the curve, gritting his teeth as he remembered her anguish over

Kenny. The kind of tears that could only come from genuine heartbreak.

Until tonight, he had never quite grasped how deeply she'd been hurt—although he should have recognized it, since she felt things so much more intensely than most women he'd known. And, considering what it must have cost her to lose the man she loved, her passion for self-reliance made sense.

Still, that didn't mean Con could abandon all responsibility for his brother's baby. No matter how much Lucy insisted that she could take care of herself and Emma, no matter how horrified she'd been at the idea of him filling in for the baby-sitter, he needed to make things right.

To find some way of helping her besides looking after her baby, while she worked those ludicrously long hours at the diner and catering service.

And to make her accept it without any sacrifice of pride.

It took him nearly two hours of driving, following the Black Canyon Freeway north and then looping back toward Scottsdale, before he came up with a plan that might work. He was slipping, Conner knew—it shouldn't take him that long to identify a solution to some basic financial problem. But what could he expect, when he was going around blabbing about emotions to some woman who loved his brother?

Taking responsibility for the family, he resolved as he turned onto Scottsdale Road, would put him back on track. It had to. And while Lucy would resist any obvious effort to make her life easier, at least he'd identified a way to make things right.

With a mental outline of his plan ready to put into action, he managed to grab a few hours of sleep upon returning home. When he woke to find Lucy and Emma already gone, Conner set out for the diner where they spent most mornings on the preopening shift, preparing for the lunchtime crowd. He found Lucy keeping one eye on the baby carrier while slicing bread at the coffee counter, but when he knocked on the window she hurried to let him in.

"Good morning," he said, noticing with a pang of concern that she looked more tired than usual. How many hours had she worked yesterday before he kept her awake listening to his problems? Not that she'd ever admit to feeling worn out.

Sure enough, she poured him a mug of coffee with a smile that almost hid the faint circles of weariness under her eyes. "Did I hear you," she asked as she handed it across the counter, "coming home incredibly early this morning?"

Damn, he thought he'd been quiet enough to let her get some sleep. "I was just out driving around," Con answered, and she glanced at him curiously. "Thinking about some work for the foundation."

Her eyes darkened with concern, as if she suspected there was more to the story. "Are you...okay?"

"Yeah, fine." But after what he'd dumped on her last night, she probably couldn't help worrying about him, and she didn't need anything else on her mind. Conner took a gulp of coffee and squared his shoulders as she resumed slicing the loaf of dark bread. "Look, I appreciate your listening to me last night, but that's... Well, that's over with."

She reached for a roll of plastic wrap and smoothed Emma's sleep-tousled blanket before returning her gaze to him. "Conner..."

"No, I'm over it." The last thing he needed was Lucy worrying about him. "I've got my life back together. All I need to do is set up the foundation."

She covered the bread with plastic wrap and regarded him thoughtfully. "So that's what you were driving around thinking about? The foundation?"

"Yeah." And he couldn't ask for a better introduction to his plan, Conner realized as she gestured for him to bring the baby carrier while she headed toward the kitchen with the bread. "I've figured out this new mailing campaign, but I'm going to need a lot more help in the office."

She reacted exactly the way he'd expected, with an immediate frown of suspicion. "Are you trying to come up with some way of offering me more money?"

He evaded the question with a wry smile. "You've made it pretty clear how you feel about that."

"Because I've already *got* a job," she continued, opening the refrigerator and emerging with a giant sheaf of lettuce. "Three of 'em—yours, and this one, and the catering."

"I know." He parked Emma's carrier on the floor and watched her sleep while Lucy started tearing off leaves. She was knocking herself out with those three jobs, moving slower after every late night, yet she wouldn't accept such an observation from him. "I'm not saying you have to quit your other jobs and work more hours for me. You're taking care of yourself and Emma as it is."

She looked slightly mollified, which meant he was on the right track. "All right, then. Just so we're clear."

Good time, Con decided, to return to the front counter and retrieve his coffee. Leave her alone for a moment, with the reassurance that he wasn't trying to undermine her pride. He refilled his mug and headed back to the kitchen, where she was stripping the last few leaves off the lettuce core.

"I can hire somebody else to help me," he told her as if there'd never been a break in their conversation, "no problem. But it'd make things easier if I got someone who already knows the system."

"Me, right?" She set down the lettuce core with a loud thunk and turned to face him, her hands on her hips. "Conner, you're not gonna talk me into… How do I know this isn't some make-work charity job?"

"This is foundation business, for God's sake!" It was easier than he'd expected to hit just the right note of annoyance. After all, no matter what his reason for launching a handwritten mailing campaign, it would benefit the foundation in the long run. "That's something I take seriously."

From the sudden stillness of her slender body, he could tell she wasn't going to argue with him about The Bryan Foundation. Not after what he'd told her last night.

"The job's yours if you want it," Conner concluded, shifting his gaze to Emma and hoping he'd handled this right. All he could do now was segue into the wrap-up. "But if you don't, I'll just hire a full-time secretary to write these letters." He turned back to Lucy and spread his hands in a gesture of relinquishment. "Your call."

She was silent for a moment while she wrapped the lettuce leaves in a damp towel, and he could almost see the battle between pride and practicality whirling inside her. "So, if I took the job...would that pay the same as what I'm making here and with the catering?"

"Probably a little more," he said, making a mental note to check on salaries in the Phoenix area. He couldn't offer more than a regular secretary would earn, no matter how much he wanted to make things easier for her and Emma. "But I won't kid you, Lucy. It's a lot more work."

She straightened her posture, and he made an effort to keep his expression relaxed. To keep from blurting out the advantages of a job that meant more time at home with Emma. And she must have recognized that for herself, because she said slowly, "As long as it's a real job, I'll take it."

"Okay, then," Conner said, and gulped the last of his coffee to make sure she wouldn't see any sign of relief on his face. "How soon can you start?"

He hadn't exaggerated the amount of work, Lucy realized the next day as she started what felt like the fortieth letter on the list. Conner must be writing to every school principal in North America, thanking them for their input on childcare programs, and he wanted every note written by hand.

"People feel better getting a real letter," he explained, "not some computer thing." And his purchase of five thousand notecards embossed with The Bryan Foundation logo had confirmed that this was definitely more than a make-work job.

So she'd felt safe committing to a full-time schedule for as long as the work lasted. Which, given the magnitude of his address list, would definitely be through Christmas. She would miss Van and Mary Ellen, who ran the diner, but they had accepted her resignation with flattering regret. And as for the catering jobs, she wouldn't miss anything except the occasional surprise of great dance music.

Which was nothing compared to the pleasure of spending every evening with her daughter, and of getting enough sleep to handle midnight feedings without a moment's delay.

"Lucy," she heard Conner call as he came in the front door, "is Emma awake? She's got to see this."

She glanced up from her work as Con brought a bright yellow balloon into the dining room, where he attached it to the carrier handle and grinned at the baby.

"How 'bout that?"

To her surprise, Lucy felt a sudden tightness in her throat. There was no reason to get choked up over such a simple gift. Which might be, she realized as Emma gazed in fascination at the bobbing yellow globe, why Conner had chosen it.

Maybe he'd finally come to realize how she felt about accepting gifts from gentlemen.

But nobody could quibble over a balloon, and the fact that he'd remembered Emma's enjoyment of the first one was enough to make her swallow hard.

"That's sweet of you," she told Conner, who looked slightly abashed as he reached for the stack of messages she'd piled in his box.

"I just figured she'd enjoy it," he muttered. "How are the letters coming?"

All right, back to business. Which was just as well, because no matter how often she remembered his insistence on taking care of everyone around him, there was still something disturbingly attractive about this man.

The way he moved, maybe. With that innate sureness of his place in the world. Or maybe it was the way he watched her, as if fascinated with the way *she* moved. Or his way of thanking her for letters with the same courtesy he showed his law partners on the phone. Or the way he grinned at her when he produced the first cup of coffee from the new coffeemaker, as if inviting her to share a moment of triumph. Regardless of what lay behind it, though, there was definitely something appealing about Conner Tarkington.

"The letters are coming fine," she answered hastily, sliding the next envelope into place for a perfectly centered address line. "And you've got some calls. I wrote them down over there."

"Thanks, Lucy."

She wasn't going to let this man's Prince Charming style of courtesy affect her common sense, Lucy reminded herself. As soon as she had the money for a move-in deposit, she'd be out from under his family's roof. Meanwhile, she could manage as many hours in his office as she had to, by focusing strictly on the work before her and forgetting anything more personal.

Conner obviously felt the same way, which she should be glad about. He had kept to himself more than usual over the past two days. And his emotional distance made it easier to ignore the occasional warmth of awareness that still flickered between them whenever she forgot to maintain her guard.

But her guard was firmly in place now, and she slid the note into the envelope with a firm gesture as he finished scanning his messages. "I'm almost done with the *Bs,*" Lucy announced.

"Great. I'll get those to the post office tonight."

She'd had time to consider his project, though, while writing the same text over and over. "You know what I was thinking?" she offered, adding the newest letter to the stack. "If you want to know what makes a good after-school program, you ought to talk to some actual schoolkids."

The idea had delighted her when she thought of it—not only because Conner could use some input from the people he most wanted to help, but also because it would draw him back into a world beyond foundation taxes and board of director consultations. Nobody could spend time with children and maintain that kind of emotional detachment.

Which was probably why he dismissed the suggestion as soon as she finished it. "I don't know any schoolkids."

"You don't know these people, either," Lucy reminded him, gesturing to the lists in front of her. "But that doesn't stop you from writing to them."

He gave her a dark look. "You're thinking I should go interview kids on a school playground someplace? Because—"

"I'm just saying," she interrupted before he could fire off half a dozen objections, "if you want to know what matters to somebody, the best way to find out is to ask them."

Maybe she'd made her point well enough for today, because Conner turned aside to give Emma's balloon another tweak that set it bobbing again. "I'll keep that in mind," he said just as the baby screwed up her face. Then he gave her an appraising glance. "Meanwhile, I think it's time for a new diaper."

He was absolutely right, Lucy could tell. "I'll get her," she said, but even as she scooted back her chair Conner reached into the carrier.

"No, it's okay," he said, lifting the baby onto his shoulder. "Come on, Emma."

He looked completely at ease, she saw with a mixture of guilty appreciation and amazement. Of course he'd taken care of Emma when he sent Lorraine home early, but she had never imagined him heading off for a diaper change with the relaxed attitude of someone handling a routine task.

Yet he seemed to find it as routine as checking the answering machine, Lucy realized over the next few days. He never interfered when she was already feeding or bathing Emma, but he never hesitated to offer a hand when the baby was nearby.

"You're good with her, you know that?" Lucy told him on Friday morning as she watched him blot the spit-up milk from Emma's chest. After a ten o'clock feeding, her terry-cloth sleepers were frequently stained, but Conner didn't seem at all perturbed.

"She's pretty easy to handle," he answered, taking the new set of sleepers she handed him from Emma's top drawer. "Thanks."

But she was the one who should be thanking him, Lucy knew. Conner was going well beyond the call of duty when it came to helping with the baby, and even though he seemed to enjoy it, she should still find some way of repaying him.

Because accepting any favors from this man was dangerous.

She needed to give him something in return, Lucy decided as she watched him deftly slide the new garment into place. Not the kind of gift you'd wrap in a box, because his caring for Emma was more of a service than an object. No, she wanted to find some kind of gesture…something that would matter to him the way Emma mattered to her.

Something that would keep them on an equal level when it came to exchanging favors.

And in the split second it took for him to fasten the last snap of Emma's sleepers, she realized what she could do.

"Conner," she asked as he lifted the baby off the toweled dresser, "would it be okay with you if we had some music playing in the office?"

He shot her a startled glance. "Music?"

"You know, just in the background. Something to listen to."

Con shifted Emma onto his shoulder and headed back toward the dining room. "You can listen to anything you want."

She already did, when he wasn't around. But ever since that day when he'd insisted that music didn't bother him, that he even belonged to some symphony board, she'd hesitated to subject him to an obvious source of discomfort.

Now that she knew about Bryan, though, the discomfort made sense. There was nothing like music for stirring up emotions, and anything that roused the feelings he'd shut down after the death of his son would naturally bother this man.

So, if she could restore the kind of emotions he'd cut himself off from, she would be giving Conner Tarkington a genuine gift.

"Okay, then," Lucy said, following him as far as the CD cabinet in the living room. She grabbed a handful of discs and some old cassettes without even looking at the titles, then spread them across the office table while he nestled Emma in her carrier. "Which ones do you like?"

"It doesn't matter," he said, fastening the safety strap without so much as a glance at the music choices. "Play whatever you want."

"Which ones *don't* you like?"

For the first time he seemed to realize she wasn't about to give up the topic, because he turned away from Emma with an uneasy look. "Lucy…"

"Great radio themes of the 1950s?" she offered, gesturing to one of the tapes she'd pulled from the bottom of the cabinet. "Duke Ellington?" That had been a favorite of Doug from Detroit, one of the gentlemen she'd actually gotten attached to. "Or how about some mariachis?"

To her surprise, Con smiled at the sight of a group wearing the traditional fiesta garb. "I remember that one," he said, picking up the cassette with a faint glimmer of nostalgia in his eyes. "First time we came out here, my mom got this idea to have a Mexican party. Because we were only about four hours north of the border."

Every winter, the city was deluged with tourists expecting the combined charm of Old Mexico and the Wild West, and it was easy to imagine Mrs. Tarkington as the type Lucy had seen at half a dozen catered parties. "Did you all wear sombreros?" she asked.

His smile deepened, making her wish he'd let himself relax more often. When his face softened its usual tight lines, the man was an even greater pleasure to look at. "No, it was just a regular party. With Mexican food, I guess. Probably some kind of decorations, like from a bullfight or something. And the mariachi music."

Maybe the goofiness of such a theme explained why the memory had stayed with him. "That sounds like more fun than I'd expect from the Tarkingtons," she remarked, resting the cassette on top of the ones surrounding it. "At least from your parents."

Conner shrugged, but already she could see his expression growing more remote as he touched a key on his computer. "Well, coming to Scottsdale was always supposed to be a vacation. We quit doing that after my dad died."

"You don't talk about your family much," Lucy observed.

"Not much to say." He took his seat again, moving the laptop closer to him, then glanced back at her. "You already met Kenny."

Yes, but there was more to his family than Kenny. "What about your mom?"

He didn't shrug, this time, but he might as well have. "We're not that close."

She had gathered that already, since there hadn't been a single phone call from the same woman who used to call Kenny nearly every Sunday. "But she lives in Philadelphia the same as you, right?"

"Oh, sure. We get together every now and then." Conner sounded as matter-of-fact as if he were talking about a college roommate he saw once or twice a year. "But she's got her life with Warren—he's a judge, good catch on the social circuit—so she's happy."

Maybe, Lucy thought, there was something worth pursuing in her quest to help this man regain his emotional balance. Maybe a closer relationship with his mother would help him through the loss of his family. "How often do you talk to her?"

"I don't know, maybe once a month. I saw her before I came out here," he said, then glanced at the stack of cassettes and returned his gaze to Lucy with the same cool regard he might have offered someone who challenged him to a duel. "Anyway, go ahead and play whatever music you want. It's fine with me."

Mariachis were fine with him, Conner decided two days later, watching Lucy sort through the music section of the bookstore where his Christmas-gift order had finally arrived. So was jazz guitar. So was whatever he'd found her dancing to last night when he came back from an investor meeting.

It was only the swell of a symphony that could tighten his throat to the point where he had to stop breathing, start counting multiples of fourteen, start doing whatever it took to jolt his brain into resuming its customary control.

"How about this one?" she called, holding up the CD from a Broadway musical he'd never listened to, and he nodded. Broadway musicals were fine with him. Anything she wanted to claim with the store's reward-for-purchase program was fine with him, as long as it didn't remind him of the former family housekeeper.

"Good choice," Conner answered, shifting the stack of gift books for his clients from one hip to the other. "Ready to go?"

"Wait, there's still another section."

With Emma still dozing on her shoulder, Lucy could probably browse for hours—or at least until time for the next job—so he deliberately turned his attention to the classical music section. It was stupid, avoiding memories of those long-ago Sunday afternoons with the housekeeper, Mrs. Henderson, who had insisted that no one should ever waste a symphony ticket. Memories had nothing to do with actual feelings, and looking at CDs had nothing in common with actually listening to the kind of music that turned you inside out.

That turned your body and soul into fire and air.

Mrs. Henderson had taken him to nine performances during the two years she'd worked for the Tarkingtons, and from the very first afternoon he'd been astonished at what grown-ups playing instruments could do. They could make you feel lighter, like you were flying over mountains or shrinking into nothingness, make you forget whatever was happening at home, make you so free and so wide and so close to pure happiness that it almost hurt to know the sensation could never last.

But the sensation returned every time he visited the symphony, and it was all the stronger after the ten-year gap between his father's death and the evening when he'd accompanied some blind date to a Brahms concerto. By then he knew better than to linger in his seat after the houselights came on, knew better than to let himself stay engrossed in the rapture of flight, but even so he could recapture that sense of soaring with every performance he attended. Under controlled circumstances, there was nothing like the sheer, liberating wonder of emotional release.

"Would you rather get one of these?" he heard Lucy ask, and hastily jerked his attention back to the music section where a staggering array of choices lay before him. "Really, you should get to pick. You're already doing me a huge favor."

She had asked him this morning, after a frantic call from someone at the catering firm, whether he could possibly take her to one last job today "because they need someone so badly, they're willing to pay double." And Conner had agreed, suspecting she'd take the assignment whether he helped her or not, and knowing he could manage to entertain Emma for two hours at the park alongside some VIP reception. "I needed to get out for a while, anyway," he answered, reaching for her Broadway CD and adding it to his stack of books. "No problem."

"It's just, the kind of money they're paying…" Her voice trailed off, then she straightened her posture and looked at him directly. "I'd like to get Emma something for Christmas."

So she was knocking herself out on what should have been a restful Sunday afternoon, after five straight days of nonstop letter-writing, to provide her daughter with whatever gift a baby might want. She would never, ever let him make things easy on her, but she'd work eight days a week on Emma's behalf.

"And you'd hit the roof," he muttered, "if I tried to give her something. Wouldn't you?"

"You already bought her the car seat," she answered immediately, shifting Emma to her other shoulder and starting toward the front register with the complimentary-disc certificate. "*And* the balloons."

It was time they got moving, he saw, if they were going to make it to the Phoenix Indian School park by two-thirty. Still, a car seat wasn't much of a Christmas present, and

Lucy deserved whatever he could offer under the guise of holiday tradition. "I haven't gotten *you* anything yet," he observed, and she stopped right in the middle of the bookstore aisle, turning to face him with a warning stare.

"Don't. I mean it. Because I don't have anything for you, and—"

"Lucy, you don't have to get me anything!" He'd never expected a gift from any of his co-workers at Weller-Tarkington-Craig. "Seriously. You don't."

"Okay, then," she said briskly, heading for the checkout counter and handing the certificate to the nearest clerk. "And the same goes for you."

He couldn't very well argue the point, not without hurting her pride. "Got it," Conner conceded, adding his books to the pile and reaching for his wallet. "No Christmas presents. Although if you wanted to make the first pot of coffee for New Year's, I wouldn't turn it down."

She grinned at him which meant he'd hit the right note by referring to their ongoing argument over who should start the coffeemaker each morning.

"I'll remember that." Then, watching the clerk scan the first of his books under the price reader, she gave him a more sober look. "You know," she murmured, "what I'd really like from you?"

There was a raspy tremor in her voice, and he wondered for a moment whether his heart had actually skipped a beat or whether such a thing was even possible. "What?"

Lucy glanced down at Emma, then met his gaze again. "Call your mother."

Of all the requests she might have made, he sure hadn't expected that one. But what *had* he expected? Con asked himself. No matter how roughly sensual she might've sounded just now, this woman didn't want someone like him...even if Kenny hadn't broken her heart. He had no business fantasizing about what she might have murmured instead. Especially in a public bookstore.

With a baby right there in her arms.

"Maybe it's just the time of year," Lucy continued, evidently not noticing the train of thought he had no business pursuing, "but I've been thinking more about families lately. And I bet your mother would be really happy to hear from you."

His mother. Right.

"I talked to her the other day, did I mention that?" Conner managed to say in what felt like a normal tone of voice. Grace Tarkington Reed had called to report that they were visiting her husband's brother in Gstaad next month, and asked him to close up the Scottsdale house when he left. "They're not coming out here after all."

He probably should have mentioned it sooner, he realized, in case Lucy had been looking forward to meeting Emma's grandparents, but she didn't seem affected by the news one way or another. Instead she replied simply, "All the more reason you should call her."

The clerk interrupted to take his credit card and wait for a signature, but Lucy wasn't finished.

"It's just," she continued, "with Christmas coming... I don't know, I think people who have families should appreciate them."

Conner signed the charge slip and returned the card to his wallet, glad he could honestly say that he'd already placed orders for his mother's, stepfather's and brother's holiday gifts. "I do," he said, picking up the holly-sprigged bag of books that represented the last of his shopping. "What about your family?"

He regretted the challenge as soon as he delivered it, because her eyes darkened as she turned away from the counter. "My mom died three years ago this September," she said, preceding him down the checkout aisle past a half dozen other clerks and book buyers. "Lung cancer, and it... I'd give anything to see her again."

"I'm sorry," Conner blurted. Not only for her loss, but

for the fact that until now, he'd never even asked about Lucy's family. "You were pretty close, huh?"

She waited for him to open the exit door to the parking lot, which was clogged with early Christmas shoppers. "Not until the last few years," she said, tucking the baby blanket more snugly around Emma's rosy face as they made their way to the car. "We fought a lot while I was growing up, because I didn't like how she always gave in to the Boyfriend Of The Month. After I'd been on my own for a while, we started getting along better."

Boyfriend Of The Month? If Lucy's mother sparkled with the same looks and personality as her daughter, she'd probably had no trouble attracting men, but monthly boyfriends seemed a little irresponsible for a woman with a child. Unless Lucy had been raised by her father instead. "What about your dad?"

"I never met him." She sounded surprisingly nonchalant about it, but he couldn't help wondering whether that had affected her desire to give Emma a father. "It was always just Mom and me…and whoever was paying the bills. Making everybody depend on him, calling the shots, and breaking her heart when he left."

God, no wonder she was so determined to pay her own way. Conner opened the back door for Emma's car seat, trying to frame a coherent response, and saw Lucy stiffen at the sight of his expression.

"I know what you're thinking," she snapped, clutching the baby more tightly against her. "My mother was a great example of how *not* to live, but even so, she—"

"I wasn't thinking that."

"Oh." She took a shaky breath, then bundled Emma into the car seat and gave him an apologetic smile. "Okay. Never mind."

Switching the conversation was probably the most diplomatic thing he could do, Con decided, but as they drove to the catering job he found himself wondering what it had been like for Lucy to grow up with a mother who evidently lived off men. Her fierce passion for independence made a lot more sense now, if her mom had insisted on letting boyfriends dictate the terms of their life.

Still, he knew none of that would affect his responsibility for Kenny's baby. It only gave him a clearer idea of how difficult arranging child support would be.

Especially when Emma's mother would rather work herself blind than accept a simple Christmas present from a man with money.

"You can drop me off at the side," Lucy told him as he slowed near the park entrance, looking for the VIP reception tent. The park was already jammed with people for some monthly pops concert, but apparently the corporate hosts offered their hospitality only during intermissions. "And then I'll meet you out front after the second break."

"Sure." He could take Emma for a walk in the park while they waited, take advantage of the desert weather. "We'll just wander around here, and see you then."

"It's okay if you want to stay," she told him while unfastening her seat belt. "The public can go everywhere but the VIP tent. But I ought to warn you, there's gonna be music."

Even though she spoke lightly, he could see the note of caution in her eyes—almost as if she suspected a local performance in the park might be too much for him. What the hell was she thinking, that he was some kind of fragile flower? "I can handle it," Conner snapped.

"Okay," she said, reaching back to give Emma a farewell caress before getting out of the car and then gazing wistfully at her daughter. "You enjoy wandering around with Conner, sweetie. Mommy's off to work."

Once again, his heart twisted at her unconscious gallantry. "Lucy," he said, leaning across the seat to address her through the open door, "I think you're about as different from your mother as it's possible to be."

He saw a sudden rush of moisture in her eyes, and she gave him a tremulous smile. ''Thanks,'' she murmured, then swallowed hard. ''I need to remember that. Anyway, I'll see you around four-thirty.''

''Right.'' Emma would probably doze in her car seat for most of the two hours, he figured as they drove off. At least that would give him time to find a parking space, after which they could wander around the park.

And listen to whatever music was playing, because it wasn't like he had a problem dealing with concerts in the middle of Phoenix in broad daylight. It wasn't like he had anything to be afraid of.

He could handle it just fine, Conner repeated to himself an hour later, as he sat on the grass with Emma in his lap and listened to the opening of a piece he'd last heard in Philadelphia seven years ago. When Bryan was only a little bigger than this baby—at least, that seemed about right. He couldn't remember for sure, but—

Don't go there.

No, he wasn't thinking about Bryan.

He was just listening to the music.

Feeling the sun on his shoulders.

Breathing in rhythm with the woodwinds, letting the strings carry him aloft....

Not too far, however. Not too high.

The violins were soaring, though, and he could feel his soul clamoring to respond. Which wasn't an option. Better to concentrate on something else—numbers, maybe. Hard facts. Tangible sensations. Something like that.

He could handle this just fine, Conner assured himself as the flutes joined the shimmering violins. All he had to do was focus on the grass beneath his hands. The pressure of Emma's tiny feet against his knee. The red bandana someone had tied on a tree branch. The kid laughing as his dad lifted him onto his shoulders.

No, don't look.

You never did that with Bryan.

Forget it. Just listen to the music.

But the music was pulsing harder now, making his heart pick up speed. Making his throat tighten, even though there was nothing to feel here. He didn't *have* feelings, he didn't need feelings, he wasn't feeling anything at all.

Never had, never could, never would.

"My dad doesn't care about me."

Conner lurched to his feet and grabbed Emma. There was no point sitting here listening to some orchestra, not when they could be moving around. Not when there were kids and bandanas and woodwinds choking his veins, cutting off his air and his heart and it wasn't like he had a heart, anyway, but he had to get out of here, get Emma back to the car and get himself back together, whatever it took, just get Lucy a ride home—leave her the cab fare, just get out of here, that way, the VIP tent, catering people everywhere, a bartender staring at him, a twenty-dollar bill, there, and Conner thrust the money blindly at the bartender.

"Tell Lucy I had to leave," he stammered, and ran for the parking lot.

Chapter Five

Even from the back of the VIP tent, Lucy could tell there was something wrong. Conner looked almost desperate, as if he were on the verge of losing his innate, impeccable control. And when he muttered something to the bartender and took off, she immediately set down her tray and hurried after him and Emma, catching up with them before they made it halfway to the parking lot.

"Conner, are you all right?"

He turned to face her, and she bit back a gasp. His skin was pale and splotched with red, his hands were shaking and he was breathing in short, unsteady bursts. "I'm fine," he said.

If he truly believed that, she'd hate to see when he *wasn't* fine. "You look awful," Lucy told him, instinctively reaching for her daughter. "Let me have Emma."

To her relief, he nestled the baby in her arms without so much as a fumble. "Here," Conner said raggedly. "You keep her. I'm getting out of here."

"Not like this!" Nobody who looked the way he did should be walking around alone, much less heading for a car. "Wait a minute," she ordered. Balancing Emma against her shoulder, she untied the catering apron with her other hand and dropped it onto the grass, where someone would surely find and return it. "I'm going with you."

"Lucy—"

"You're not driving right now," she protested, moving to block his route toward the parking lot. Someone as well-mannered as this man wouldn't shove her out of the way, and she could stand here as long as she had to. "I don't care how fine you feel, you're not driving home."

"I'm not staying here." With an abrupt gesture, he dismissed the entire city-block park. "There's kids all over the place...."

All right, maybe it was seeing the kids which had thrown him off balance, reminded him of his son. "We're just gonna walk," Lucy told him, linking her arm through his and feeling a burst of relief when he didn't attempt to pull away. Keeping her voice as relaxed as if she were dealing with a customer who'd drunk too much, she guided him toward the desert-landscaped courtyard far away from the concert crowd. "We'll get your car later. Right now we're just walking, see?"

Conner was still edgy, almost shaking, and she could feel the heat of his skin throbbing against hers. "I shouldn't have been there. Everybody there loves their kids enough, and—"

"And you loved your son," she said gently.

He drew away from her, shoving his hands in his pockets as if any kind of touch was too much to bear. "No," he muttered. "I didn't."

There was no mistaking the raw pain in his voice, but surely he couldn't believe—

"I didn't even *know* him!" Conner burst out. "Eight years in the same house, I never once—" He broke off, swallowing hard, then turned to face her. And although his body was rigid with tension, his eyes were so bleak it frightened her. "There's something missing."

All right, maybe she'd feel the same way about herself if Emma were killed. But no one deserved such crushing guilt for one late pickup, no matter how tragic the result. "Everybody in the world," Lucy offered, "forgets things once in a while."

"No, it wasn't just forgetting. It was more…" He halted, gesturing as if looking for the right phrase, then shook his head. "I should've seen it. With Margie. But I thought I could do it."

He still wasn't making sense, but maybe talking would help him. "You thought…" she prompted.

Conner took a deep breath, then finished the sentence she'd begun. "I thought I could love," he said flatly, "like anyone else. All right, so that was a mistake." He started walking again, and she had to hurry a few steps to catch up with him. "But even while we were married, I still didn't get it."

From the bitterness in his voice, she suspected his guilt had extended from the death of his son clear into the end of his marriage. One thing at a time, Lucy decided, and divorce was probably easier to talk about. "A lot of people," she reminded him, "don't stay in love with the same person their whole life."

"Yeah, but they knew how to love 'em, make 'em feel wanted, in the first place. Whereas here *I* am—" He raised his hands, palms up, as if any observer could tell what was wrong with him simply by glancing his way. "It was bad enough doing that to Margie, but at least when she married me, she had a choice. Bryan didn't have any choice!"

His voice cracked, and she interrupted with the only reassurance she could think of. "Conner, nobody gets to choose their parents." And in any case, he must have been a wonderful father…a man like him would make a point of caring for Bryan at every opportunity. "Besides, I'll never believe you didn't love your son."

He slowed his pace and looked at her, as if seeing her for the first time since they'd started walking toward the courtyard. "You couldn't believe it," he said slowly. "You're not that kind of person."

It hurt, watching him in such pain, and she had to swallow back the tears in her throat before stepping in front of Conner to address him face-to-face. "I'm the kind of person," she told him, "who sees you bringing home balloons for Emma."

Glancing down at the sleeping baby, he shook his head. "That's not the same thing."

"It's close enough for me," Lucy protested, but she could tell he wasn't truly hearing her. "Con, will you listen for a minute?" Maybe the only way to make him pay attention was to stop this mindless pacing, so she gently placed Emma on her blanket beneath a tree and rose to face him again.

"There isn't—" he began, and she cut him off by bracing her hands against his shoulders.

"Stop," Lucy said. "I mean it. You've got to quit beating yourself up."

He drew a ragged breath, and she was suddenly aware of the warmth of his body, the hard surface of his chest so close to her. But this wasn't the time to draw back—not now that he was finally listening.

"I mean it," she repeated. "Conner, you're a good person. You *are*."

For a moment it felt as if the noise of the park had abruptly halted, as if the sunlight had become more intense, as if everything hung suspended in time, but then he let out a shaky breath and drew her closer to him.

And the world swiftly tilted into a new and more challenging rhythm as she felt the warmth of his body against hers.

Comfort, that's all this was, Lucy told herself wildly. She

was just comforting a friend, but already this felt like something more than reassurance, something far more than friendship. And all of a sudden it didn't matter, anyway....

Right now, nothing mattered except this man.

She wrapped her arms around him, glorying in the feel of his broad shoulders, the crisp sensation of his collared shirt, the tantalizing play of muscles in his back. Oh, and the pleasure of his hands on her shoulders, the joyous strength of his solid embrace, the surprising comfort of his touch...

It shouldn't feel this good.

This was simple comfort, she reminded herself again, nothing more. But somehow that was hard to remember, with her body exulting and her heart practically shouting and every fiber of her shimmering on the edge of exuberance from the sheer, wild happiness of holding this man.

Feeling his heartbeat against her skin. Breathing in the scent of him, the familiar mixture that tantalized her senses. Nestling into his embrace with the exquisite sensation of coming home. Feeling her heart swell with the crazy, soaring certainty that she belonged with him, now and forever, wanting him, loving him—

Lucy opened her eyes.

This was dangerous. This couldn't really be happening.

She couldn't be falling in love.

But neither could she back away from Conner just yet, not when he needed someone to hold him, needed the comfort of a hug. And he *did* need it, she could tell from the choked sound of his breathing, from the way he'd abandoned his habitual control and let himself take such desperate refuge that all she could do was shelter him, welcome him, care for him the way she'd care for anyone who needed all the nurturing she could give.

As long as she kept her eyes open.

As long as she remembered the cost of losing her heart.

As long as she didn't let herself get swept up in that first, dizzying sensation of rightness, of wonder, then there was nothing to worry about. She could hold him for as long as he needed to let his breathing even out, to let the incredibly tight muscles in his back and shoulders begin to relax.

She didn't need to think about anything else right now, Lucy assured herself over and over as she waited for him to stop shaking, to start regaining his customary calm. She could stand here holding him, keeping an eye on Emma, not letting herself worry about anything except Conner, for as long as he needed to get himself back together.

Because it wasn't like she loved him.

Not really. Not this man.

He was her boss. He was Kenny's brother. He was compulsively responsible, and he already thought his mission was to take care of her and Emma exactly the way her mother's boyfriends had done, providing gift after gift until gradually they were running the show, calling the shots.

No, the man in her arms was the last man in the world she would *ever* fall in love with.

But even so, when he finally let her go and straightened up with a deep sigh, her entire body felt the sense of loss far more acutely than any sense of relief. As if she had needed that long embrace, that sustaining warmth, every bit as much as he did.

Except she didn't, Lucy knew.

So she shoved her hands in the pockets of her black catering slacks and forced herself to look him straight in the eye.

"No more beating yourself up, okay?" she ordered, trying not to notice the broad planes of his chest where she'd let herself feel the rhythm of his heartbeat against her skin. "You're a good person, Conner Tarkington."

He flexed his shoulders, as if returning his focus to the real world, and regarded her with an expression of mingled fascination and caution.

"So are you, Lucy Velardi," he said softly, and for a long moment he held her gaze in silence before speaking again. "So are you."

She was a good person, Conner told himself for the fifth time since sitting down to the usual Monday morning session with his tax attorney. A far kinder, more generous person than he'd realized over the past few weeks. A better friend, a better listener. All along he'd known she was easy to talk to, but yesterday...

"Coffee, Mr. Tarkington?"

He jerked his attention back to Joel's secretary and managed a cordial refusal while the attorney spread his revised contracts across the conference table. This was not the time to continue daydreaming about Lucy.

But the image of her stayed fresh in his mind, as heartening as her absolution for a failure he would never overcome. She had told him he was a good person, flat out, right there in the park while he was still reeling under the impact of a virtual collapse. As if she saw more good in him than anyone else ever had or ever would.

Which was all the more reason, Conner reminded himself while listening to Joel's analysis, to live up to what she expected. To quit pretending that, for a minute or so when he'd let himself enjoy the softness of her in his arms, she had felt the same flare of heat, the same spark of recognition, the same urgent and compelling joy.

It was only his imagination, he knew, because all the way home she'd kept up such a cheerful flow of chatter that there was no mistaking her intent. She was putting a barrier between them, a barrier as sweet-natured and bright as Lucy herself, but still a reminder that no matter how supportive she might be to a friend in need, this woman had already given her heart to someone else.

"Your board will want to look it over, of course," Joel announced. "But you see how this is set up."

"Right." He saw all too clearly how she'd fallen in love

with his brother, how she'd suffered the heartbreak of learning the man she wanted was incapable of loving her. So what the hell was he doing, wishing she'd repeat the same mistake with *him?* "I'd say it looks pretty clear."

"Any questions, give me a call."

Joel couldn't answer the question plaguing him this morning, though, Conner knew as he headed back to his office at home. Nobody could tell him how to make Lucy happy, how to give her the kind of love she deserved. Yet she'd abandoned her job for him yesterday without a second thought, she'd listened with wholehearted compassion while he'd practically fallen apart in front of her, and then she'd taken him in her arms and gently put him back together as if he deserved that kind of loving care.

And all he could do for her in return was…was…

"You know what I'd really like from you?"

That moment in the bookstore burst into his mind with startling clarity, just when he needed it most.

"Call your mother."

He would do that tonight, Conner resolved, turning down the winding street that led to the neighborhood entry gate. Put together a mental checklist of things to chat about— maybe the trip to Gstaad or the opera board—and then, while Lucy was giving Emma her bath, he would pick up the phone and call Philadelphia. Tell Lucy about it afterwards, put it in the most positive light he could. Give her the satisfaction of feeling like she'd sparked a mother-and-son reunion between two people with nothing in common except a name.

Well, a name and a certain amount of determination. He had to give his mom credit, he admitted as he punched in the entry-gate code, for overcoming twenty years of prescription-drug dependence and marrying someone as decent as Warren. The judge probably would've been a great stepfather if he'd come along sooner, but Conner had managed well enough on his own.

At least for himself, because he'd learned early on not to expect more than his parents could give. And as for Kenny, well...his brother had somehow managed to find affection wherever he turned, so their mom had nothing to worry about there. If nothing else, his frequent requests for loans gave her the chance to feel needed.

To feel like, even if her value as a mother was twenty years late in coming, she finally mattered to her son.

But tonight, Con resolved as he parked his car and braced himself to walk in on Lucy and Emma with no more than a friendly hello, tonight he would give her that same sense of mattering. Not by asking for anything—because, really, there was nothing he needed—but at least he could offer some conversation.

So after dinner he took the phone to his room, where he could stay clear of the bathtime activity, and called his mother's Philadelphia home.

It took a while for Hughes to summon Mrs. Reed, and Conner found himself gazing out the window at the last streaks of sunset above the McDowell Mountains...until his mother came on the line and he automatically squared his shoulders.

"I was just thinking about you," he explained by way of a greeting. Lucy could have come up with something a lot better, but since when did he need any help with opening remarks? "Thought I'd call and say hi."

"Well, how nice." Grace Conner Tarkington Reed's voice was as exquisitely modulated over twenty-five hundred miles of phone lines as it was across a dining room table. "Your package arrived this morning...we're going to wait and open everything on Christmas."

Of course she'd assume he was calling to check on the courier service, Con realized. Nobody in the family ever called simply to say hello. "That's good," he answered, remembering that he still hadn't swung by the post office to collect a package from Philadelphia. Warren occasionally surprised him with sports memorabilia, the type of thing a longtime judge would select for an attorney's office, and he'd have to phone his thanks before they left for Gstaad. "I'm doing the same thing."

Maybe his mother knew how he dreaded the thought of Christmas, when every wreath and snowman and caroling angel reminded him of the grim period surrounding Bryan's death, because her response sounded concerned. "Is everything going all right? The foundation and...everything?"

"It's coming together." She deserved whatever assurance he could give regarding The Bryan Foundation, since she'd agreed to sign over Con's entire share of the Tarkington family trust as soon as he'd announced his mission. "I've started a mailing campaign, touching base with schools all over the country."

"You're good at that kind of thing," his mother observed, which gave him a curious feeling of pride. Parental approval shouldn't mean so much to someone his age. "I'm sure your partners will be glad to have you back at the firm."

"Well, there's only a month to go." He heard Emma break into a lusty wail in the background, and hastily moved to close the bedroom door—his brother's indiscretions had always horrified their mom, and Kenny might have delayed telling her about an unexpected child. "So, are you getting packed for vacation?"

But Emma's cry must be more piercing than he'd realized, because instead of answering his question she asked one of her own. "Did I just hear a baby?"

Oh, hell. Once again, he was covering for his brother. "I'm in Scottsdale," he improvised, glancing at the barely lit mountains in the distance. "Babies all over the place." Too late, he realized that his mother's phone would display the number of the vacation villa. "Or, well, actually—"

"Conner," she interrupted as though she hadn't even heard his attempt at evasion, "do you have guests visiting?"

Dammit, why hadn't Kenny mentioned the baby yet? How hard would it be to pick up the phone and announce that he'd fathered a child?

"Uh," Con faltered, trying to calculate how long he could dodge the question and how long he might have to sustain a lie, "actually, they've been here a while."

When his mother spoke again, there was a subtle note of anticipation in her tone. "I'm not sure how to ask this, but…is there somebody new in your life?"

Somebody new meant someone eligible for the kind of marriage he'd shared with Margie, whose family had known his for three generations. "Not really, no. She's just helping me out with the office work."

"At this time of night?" It was barely eight o'clock in Philadelphia, but Arizona office hours were over by now as well. "I…see."

"Mom," he protested, leaning against the bedroom door so he could watch the last of the light outside, "it's not like that. Lucy needed a place to stay, and—"

"And you invited her to stay at our house?"

"She was already here!" Big mistake, Conner realized as soon as he said it, but now there was no way out except straight through. All right, time for damage control. "Kenny moved her in last spring, before he left for Asia—"

"Kenny left a *baby?*"

Emma chose that moment to start crying again, and he closed his eyes against a sinking sensation. There was no plausible way to defend his brother's decision, and all he could do now was try to make things right.

"He's gonna take care of things," Con promised desperately. "I already talked to him."

But his mother didn't seem interested in how that could happen. Instead she asked, "How old is this baby…boy, or girl?"

"Uh, a girl." A girl who was bawling her head off out

there, making him wish he knew some magical cure for the normally contented infant. "She's about two months old."

"So I have a granddaughter?" That wasn't distress in his mom's voice, he realized even as he moved from the door to the window again. That was fascination. "I can't believe it! Why didn't Kenny say something?"

Anyone who knew Kenny should be able to figure it out, but that wasn't the most diplomatic response. "He's not really thinking long-term dad. But—"

"But he'll have to!" And that was joy, pure and simple, something he couldn't remember ever hearing from his mother. "Conner, don't you realize? I'd given up on any more grandchildren from you, but Kenny's never had the chance to be a father."

The sudden weight in his chest surprised him, coming out of nowhere. Almost as if he'd been punched in the gut.

"He needs to come out there right away," she continued, evidently unaware of any tightness of breath on the other end of the line. "I'll talk to him."

"Mom," Con managed to say, "I already talked to him. He's not interested."

"He will be," she answered blithely. "Of course if he hasn't seen the baby, he can't imagine what it's like to have a child. But after he's seen her, it'll make all the difference in the world."

All the difference in the world. Kenny becoming a father to Emma.

Kenny coming back to Lucy.

Breaking her heart all over again.

"And I'm sure the baby's mother will understand why someone who grew up without a father just didn't feel ready at first," she continued. "Don't get her hopes up yet, though, because it might take a while to reach him."

But Conner had already reached him, and Kenny had refused to get involved. Yet things might be different this time.

Because if the person who controlled Kenny's trust fund wanted a grandchild…

It wouldn't make any difference in the long run, he knew, because Lucy would continue refusing any involvement with the Tarkingtons. But while she could easily stand up to his mother, facing Kenny was a whole different situation. "Uh, Mom—" he began, and she interrupted with another exclamation of delight.

"I can't believe it, a granddaughter! I've got to tell Warren."

There was nothing he could say. And evidently his mother recognized the same thing, because already she was plunging into a flurry of farewells.

"Conner, thank you so much for calling. And isn't it wonderful you decided to visit Scottsdale this year? Because now you can get things ready…you know, for when Kenny arrives."

Conner looked uneasy, Lucy noticed as soon as he approached the kitchen where she'd started wiping down the sink after getting Emma into bed. Either because he couldn't shed the memory of yesterday's hug any better than she could, or—more likely—because he wanted to request that she keep the baby quiet during his phone calls. But Emma had never been so disruptive before….

"I don't know what happened," she told him, wringing out the washcloth she'd left draped over the faucet. "She's fine now, it was just a bad night. But next time I'll wait until you finish your calls."

"No, that's okay." He hesitated, looking even more uneasy, and she realized as he took a seat at the breakfast bar that Emma's shrieking wasn't the problem. "It's just… Well, there's something… I was just talking to my mom."

"You called her? That's wonderful!" And here she'd been worried about disturbing his work. Still, making contact with his family should be cause for celebration rather than concern—unless maybe his mother had announced some health problem. Lucy shook the water off her hands and reached for Emma's discarded bath towel. "Is she okay?"

"Oh, yeah." Conner fidgeted, flexing his fingers against the edge of the counter. "Yeah, she's fine."

"I bet she was happy to hear from you." Although from his edginess, it seemed likely they hadn't shared an especially joyous connection. Maybe his mother was the same as him when it came to showing emotion, and no matter what he tried to tell himself afterwards, that had to hurt. "Even if she didn't get all gushy on the phone," Lucy offered while wiping down the sink, "moms love hearing from their kids."

He shrugged, dismissing the issue as if it had nothing to do with him one way or another, but the tension was still evident in his posture. "The thing is," he said, shifting his gaze from the edge of the counter to her, "Kenny might be coming out here."

From his look of concern, it was clear that the news worried him, but she couldn't quite see why. Pro golfers always came for the Phoenix Open at the end of January, and she and Emma would be gone by then. So it wasn't like anybody needed to worry about an awkward reunion.

"I mean," Con continued, still watching her with a troubled expression, "within the next week or so."

That put a different spin on things, Lucy realized with a pang of dismay as she headed for the laundry alcove with her damp towel. It wasn't like Kenny wanted to see his daughter, or else he would have called a long time ago, but now Conner's uneasiness made sense. A man who cherished family responsibility would naturally want to accommodate his brother.

"So," she finished for him, avoiding his sympathetic gaze by hanging the towel on the line overhead, "you'll need the guest room."

She heard a sudden crash as he shoved back his seat, and looked up to see him headed straight toward her. "I don't give a damn about the guest room!"

"But—" she faltered. But why was he so upset?

"I was thinking," Con said more quietly, "about you."

Oh. She felt a purely feminine thrill, somewhere deep inside her, even as she hurried to remind herself there was no reason for it. She had to remember his concern was for the mother of his brother's baby, not for her, but even so, the words were sweet.

"Kenny coming back," he began, bracing one hand against the wall of the laundry alcove as she fumbled to open the dryer, "is like… See, he's probably going to show up saying he wants to get to know Emma."

Lucy tightened her grip on the dryer door, wishing she could concentrate on something other than Conner standing so close to her. Kenny's intentions should be far more important, especially if that meant a chance for Emma to meet her dad. But somehow she couldn't imagine him wanting to know the baby.

"*Does* he want to meet her?" she asked, trying to focus on her daughter's welfare as she reached for a handful of clean blankets.

"I don't think so," Con said grimly, then lifted his hands in a gesture of resignation. "You know Kenny. I could be wrong."

"Well, if he wants to see her, I'll deal with it." She couldn't deny her baby a visitor, as long as she made it clear that there was no point in expecting him to stick around. Emma would never suffer the humiliating disappointment of seeing a man who'd cared for her take off without warning, but in any case, it wasn't Conner's problem. "Don't worry about me and Emma."

His response came so fast and so vehemently that she nearly dropped the dry laundry on the floor. "I'm worried," he snapped, "about you getting hurt!"

"By Kenny?" It was sweet of him to be concerned, but he didn't realize the impossibility of such an event. "That's not gonna happen," Lucy assured him, setting aside her freshly washed blouse and spreading the baby blankets on top of the dryer. "It can't."

"The hell it can't. You don't realize—"

"Look," she interrupted, turning to meet his angry gaze, "I don't *care* about Kenny, all right?" Even though Emma would hear only good things about her father, there was no longer any point in trying to hide the truth from Conner. "He's a scumbag, and—"

"A what?"

She gulped. That wasn't something to tell a Tarkington. "I'm sorry," Lucy blurted, hastily turning away to fold down the ironing board. "I know he's your brother. He just…isn't somebody I want in my life, that's all."

For a long moment, the only sound in the laundry room was the clatter of the ironing board and the hiss of the slowly heating iron. When he finally spoke, Con sounded quietly incredulous.

"But you loved him."

It was easier to admit the truth when she didn't have to meet his gaze, and she kept her attention resolutely on the wrinkles in her white catering blouse. "For a few weeks," she muttered, "that's all. Emma doesn't need to know that, all right? She ought to grow up feeling like…well, like her mom loved her dad."

His expression was confusing, a mixture of what looked like compassion, disbelief and hope. "But you don't anymore?"

"Not in a long time," Lucy admitted. There was no sense in trying to maintain the story of loving Kenny if all it did was make Conner worry about her. "Last winter, for a few weeks, but that was it."

"Oh." He reached for the blankets on the dryer, looking suddenly younger than she'd ever seen him. "So," he said, folding the first one into a rough square. "Well. Okay, then."

Whatever had upset him so badly, he seemed considerably lighter now. And that made her feel better about yesterday's hug, because it didn't seem to have left any awkwardness on his part.

"I'm glad," Lucy told him, lifting her hand to gauge the heat of the iron, "you called your mom. That was a nice thing to do."

He grinned at her, and again she was struck by the difference in his demeanor. For once, Con looked almost carefree. "Early Christmas present," he said lightly.

It was exactly what she'd asked him for yesterday afternoon, but she hadn't expected such a fast response. And it was only fair to return the favor. "Tomorrow," she promised, "I'll make the coffee."

"Tomorrow…" Conner finished folding the next blanket, then stacked it on top of the first. "Let's take the day off."

This, from the man who'd spent every minute of the past three weeks organizing a foundation? She smoothed her blouse onto the ironing board, wondering whether she'd heard him right. "What?"

"We've been working like crazy," he said, as if she might not have noticed until now. "Let's just take a day off."

There was something infectious in his eagerness, Lucy realized as she started on the first side of the blouse. Something that made her more than ready to skip a day of letters. "Go play Frisbee?" she suggested, before remembering with a jolt of embarrassment how their last excursion had ended. "I mean—"

"Something fun," he said, either not noticing her blush or doing a good job of ignoring it. "Come on. My treat."

Oh, no. She wasn't letting him pay for this day of freedom. "Conner—" she protested, but he cut her off.

"Look, I owe you for keeping after me about calling my

mom." He waited until she looked up from the ironing board, then fixed her with a sober gaze. "Give me a chance to say thank you."

She couldn't very well refuse an invitation like that, could she? And a day off sounded wonderfully tempting.

"We'll take Emma with us," Con said, and her last doubt vanished like the wrinkles under the iron.

"Okay, then," Lucy agreed, shaking out the blouse and turning it over. "Sure. This'll be fun."

"Tomorrow, then." He smiled at her as he picked up the last of Emma's blankets, and she felt her heart skip a beat.

"I'm looking forward to it," she managed to answer, and Conner's smile deepened.

"So am I," he said, then turned away with the stack of blankets for Emma's room. "See you in the morning."

Chapter Six

She was up before dawn the next morning, a little surprised at how the prospect of a day off had kept her in such a state of anticipation all night. Emma's bright yellow socks seemed just right for such a festive occasion, and Lucy wished she had something in her own wardrobe that Conner hadn't already seen.

Which was silly, she warned herself, settling for her comfortable green sweater and well-worn jeans. It wasn't like she wanted to impress him, show off her almost-back-to-normal figure with the kind of outfit that would make any man look twice. Because this wasn't like a date or anything. He'd said himself it was simply a thank-you for suggesting he call his mom.

Still, she lingered at the bathroom mirror, trying her hair in a ponytail and then a baseball cap and finally a loose shower of curls, before remembering that it didn't matter how she looked.

This was a day off work, nothing more.

Even so, she felt a fresh surge of anticipation when Con came into the kitchen looking ready for adventure in a red golf shirt and casual khaki slacks she'd never seen before. Apparently he hadn't changed his mind about business taking second place, and that must be why he looked so much more carefree than usual.

Today was going to be fun.

Lucy handed him a mug of coffee, which she'd just finished making, and he took it with an appreciative smile.

"Kind of nice not having to fight over whose turn it is. Thanks, Lucy."

"I *told* you I was gonna make the coffee," she reminded him.

"You did," he agreed, taking a quick gulp and ignoring the fruit bowl that sometimes provided their breakfast. "And I told *you* we're taking the day off."

If he wasn't even going to sit down at the breakfast bar to drink his coffee, he must be as eager as she was to get started. "Emma and I are ready to go," she announced, and he picked up the baby carrier with his free hand.

"Okay, then. C'mon, Emmie, let's hit the road."

Lucy grabbed the pink diaper bag, which was already stuffed with a day's worth of baby gear, and followed him out to the car. "What did you have in mind?" she asked, storing the bag on the floor of the back seat while he buckled the safety belt of Emma's car seat. "Or do you want some ideas?"

She had debated last night whether to offer suggestions of fun activities—tourists frequently asked their waitress for recommendations on "where the locals go"—but suspected Conner would automatically take on that responsibility himself. And she was right.

"I was thinking about that," he told her as they drove toward Scottsdale Road. "It'd be nice to get out on the water, and there are boats at Tempe Town Lake."

This man was full of surprises, she realized, and a day

on the water sounded wonderfully different. Even though the artificial lake was only a few miles down the road, it hadn't registered on her mental list of tourist attractions. "I've never been on a boat."

He slowed for a stoplight and shot her a concerned glance. "Are you afraid of water?"

It wouldn't even occur to someone like him, who traveled all over the place for exotic vacations, that a lifetime in desert cities didn't offer much opportunity for boating. "Of course not," Lucy retorted, straightening the neckline of her floppy sweater. "I'm not afraid of anything."

Conner regarded her with curious appraisal. "Nothing at all?"

Turning out like her mother, maybe, but she wasn't going to let that happen. And besides, he was talking about physical fears—of which there was only one.

"Well, spiders," she admitted, glancing over her shoulder at Emma in the back seat. "It's stupid, I know it's not like a spider is gonna attack me in my sleep or anything, but if I even see a picture of one I get all creeped out."

"Yeah?" He sounded more understanding than most men, who either chuckled indulgently or tried to explain why spiders weren't dangerous—the way Kenny had, she remembered, when a horror-movie preview made her shriek. "I guess everybody's got something like that."

"What about you?"

He hesitated, fixing his gaze on the stoplight until it turned green and he hit the gas pedal. Then, as they shot through the intersection, he muttered, "Flying."

A man like him? "I thought you'd done a lot of that."

"I have," he said, easing into a steadier speed. "Like you said about the spiders, it's not really rational." He adjusted the sun visor on his window, glancing at Emma in her car seat, then shook his head and shrugged. "It's just something I don't like much."

That was probably putting it mildly, she suspected, considering his habit of denying emotions. "But you do it anyway," Lucy observed. After all, he'd flown out here from Philadelphia, booked a round trip to Seattle for right after New Year's, and last week he'd gone to L.A. for a two-hour meeting with some investor.

"Not much choice," Con answered. "It's not a big deal, it's just…" He trailed off, then shot her a glance that looked almost embarrassed. "I've never mentioned that to anyone."

But he trusted her, which was sweet to know. "I won't tell anybody," she promised, and he gave her a slow smile. "I know."

With anyone else, she would have responded with a touch, a pat on the shoulder, some kind of acknowledgment. But that would be a little too intimate, a little too risky, for people who were supposed to be simply enjoying a day away from the office. Lucy straightened her posture and shifted in her seat, reminding herself once again that this man was her boss and a Tarkington and everything else she needed to avoid.

"Well," she said hastily, "when it's time to go back to Philadelphia, you could always drive instead of flying. Get one of those red convertibles, like in a movie."

Conner shot her a speculative glance. "I can see *you* doing that."

So could she, and it was a tantalizing picture. Almost up there with finding a winning lottery ticket, or dancing for an applauding crowd. "I'd do it in a minute," she said. "Drive through California, New York, Minnesota, all of it. With the top down, the whole way."

He nodded, as if envisioning the same bewitching image of coast-to-coast freedom, then smiled at her again. "You see the fun in everything."

Which was a skill *he* needed—although he'd done a great job in planning for this day off. "Well, yeah," Lucy agreed, resolutely turning her thoughts away from the urge to touch him again. ''And a boat ride sounds like a lot of fun.''

Apparently other people felt the same way, because when they arrived at the lake there were already half a dozen families with children scattered around the grassy park and waiting in line at the boat-rental booth. But Conner didn't seem to be in any hurry to join the line. Instead he set a leisurely pace, stopping to show Emma the skateboarders and cyclists along the waterside walkway, and when a boat that looked like a long canoe appeared on the far side of the lake, he pointed it out with a touch on Lucy's shoulder.

''Sculling, see? I used to do that, back in college.''

It was a casual touch, the kind she'd exchange with Shawna or Jeff without even thinking about it. But even so, she had to catch her breath before responding, ''I thought you said you ran track.''

From the flash of pleasure on his face before he glanced back at the rowing team, she could tell he was flattered that she'd remembered a casual comment from two weeks ago. ''You've got a good memory,'' Con replied. ''Track was in high school.''

Better not to think about him running, the way he'd done those times when she saw him coming in with his gray T-shirt plastered to his body. Better to think about…oh, high school. ''Did you go to one of those snooty places where everybody wears a tie?''

''Not on the track.'' It wasn't until she saw the glint of humor in his eyes that she realized he was teasing her, and she faked a punch at him. ''I'll bet at your school,'' he said, lifting Emma to his shoulder, ''you were a cheerleader.''

''Me? No.'' Cheerleaders were the girls who could afford those red-and-white uniforms, who didn't have to polish the dance studio mirrors and floor during after-school practice sessions. ''But I would've liked it.''

He regarded her thoughtfully, keeping an easy grip on the baby. ''You would've been good at it.''

"Well, thank you." She would have been, Lucy knew, but being a cheerleader required staying in school. "Maybe Emma will be." Emma would see the wisdom of waiting to graduate with her classmates instead of rebelling against a punitive curfew set by the gentleman who'd replaced Doug from Detroit. Emma wouldn't be stupid enough to hang out with a shoplifting crowd in the first place, much less leave home to avoid any more lectures from the Boyfriend Of The Month. And Emma would *never* have to make her way in the world while struggling to earn a diploma five years late.

Which was not something Conner needed to hear about.

"Maybe she *will* be a cheerleader," he agreed, following the baby's gaze to a cluster of children by the water's edge. "Or maybe she'll be a sea captain. What do you think, Emma? You like the look of that?"

This was a side of Conner Tarkington she'd never seen before, Lucy thought as she watched him turn the baby for a better view of the boats at the dock. He was more at ease today, more lighthearted than she would have thought possible. And when they headed for the ticket booth and the clerk asked whether they'd prefer the tour boat or a pedal boat, it took her less than a moment to decide that time alone with him would be a far more entertaining way to enjoy the day.

"Let's not do the tour," Lucy told him. "Let's do it ourselves."

He shot her an appraising glance, but she couldn't tell whether he was questioning her pedaling ability or her intentions. "You're up for that?"

"Sure," she said brightly. After all, this was only one day. No matter how attractive Conner Tarkington might seem right now, tomorrow they'd be back to their usual routine. All she needed to do was hang onto her common sense for another few hours. "This'll be fun."

It *was* fun. Pedal-boating was easier than riding a bike,

and although Con ordered her not to overdo it—"one person
pedaling is all we need"—she enjoyed using her body for
something other than letter-writing or housework. Emma
seemed enchanted with the view from Lucy's lap, with the
ducks diving for food beyond the white-striped sailboats,
with planes from the nearby airport taking off directly over
their heads and fishermen reeling in their lines on the shore.
The bright December sunshine was perfect, just right for a
day on the water. And Conner…

Conner was a different person today. Still as ruggedly
good-looking as ever, still as careful about shielding Emma
from the shifting sun, but there was a vigor in him she had
never seen before. A playful sense of enjoyment, as if for
once in his life he was fully aware of the present moment.

And very aware of her.

He wasn't flirting, exactly—anyone listening might assume they were nothing more than housemates—but there
was an undercurrent flowing between them that made every
word, every gesture, every glance seem more significant.
More fascinating.

More enticing.

It had started the first night they met, Lucy knew, but she
hadn't expected that ongoing warmth to grow steadily hotter, steadily more intense, as they drifted on the water and
traded desultory bits of conversation. But today there was
something different in the air. Something different about the
way he listened when she spoke, the way he let his gaze
linger on her, the way he reached so often to almost touch
her before catching himself and drawing back.

And she suspected the difference came from their conversation last night, when she'd told him about Kenny. She
could see how someone like Conner, who valued family
responsibility above all else, would never let himself want
a woman who loved his brother.

But today…

Another plane soaring overhead distracted her, and she

hastily returned her attention to the baby in her lap. No matter what she was thinking about Con, she had to remember that Emma mattered most.

"See up there?" she asked her daughter, holding her for a look at the rapidly vanishing flash of silver. "That plane is full of people going to...places like Philadelphia. Even some really brave people," she added with a smile for Conner, "who don't like to fly."

He reached his hand into the water and flicked a few drops at her, as if to acknowledge her compliment without taking credit. "It's not that big a deal."

Maybe not, but the fact that he'd trusted her enough to tell her about it was. And she might as well say so, before they returned to their usual cordial distance tomorrow. Lucy took a deep breath and turned to face him.

"I feel...well, honored," she said, "that you told me something you don't tell most people."

He didn't glance away, as he normally would after such a straightforward statement. Instead he met her gaze without speaking for a moment, then said slowly, "I've always thought you're easy to talk to."

The awareness between them seemed to take on a new pulse, and she felt a flutter of uneasiness at how much she was enjoying this man. At how quickly a simple day away from the office could take on such captivating dimensions.

At how very close she was to forgetting all common sense.

"Maybe," she said a little breathlessly, "we ought to give back the boat." After all, the rental contract was only for an hour, and they'd probably been out here a lot longer than that already. "I wouldn't mind stopping for lunch."

Conner evidently understood how she felt, because he turned the steering lever to aim them back toward the dock. "Good idea," he said. "Except the ducks have probably gotten all the fish already."

It was such an unexpected response that Lucy laughed.

"You know," she told him before she could think better of it, "you're more fun than I expected."

He didn't seem to take offense, probably because someone as dedicated to business as this man wouldn't expect to be viewed as the life of the party. "You've got this idea about lawyers being stuffy, right?" Con observed, then flashed her a quick grin. "Once in a while we surprise people."

"I like surprises." This felt dangerously close to flirting, she realized, but as long as they both knew they were heading back to the dock there was really nothing wrong with it. They could enjoy a little more back-and-forth humor, a little more of this intriguing awareness, before they called it a day and returned to work tomorrow.

Because they both knew today was an exception.

"I like surprises, too," Conner told her, maneuvering the boat next to the dock. Waving off the approaching attendant, he extended his hand so she could disembark with Emma safely in her arms, and she let herself enjoy the sensory memory of his touch lingering far longer than necessary as they made their way down the walkway. "So, for our next surprise…"

Even on a day like today, lunch was about as safe as you could get. Nobody could forget their common sense while sitting on a park bench across from a hot-dog vendor—like that one with the bright red umbrella. "It's my turn," Lucy announced, "to pick what we do next."

He followed her gaze to the vendor's umbrella, then turned back to her with a smile.

"Your turn, Lucy. Surprise me."

She was a fountain of surprises, Conner realized that evening as they lingered over Mexican food at a *tacqueria* he would've dismissed as a hole in the wall. Lucy had sworn there was no better place for homemade tamales, and as soon as their order arrived he had realized she was right.

It wasn't just her expertise with university-district restaurants that surprised him, though. All day long she had delivered punch after punch, catching him off guard over and over again with her incredible gift for making the most of an ordinary moment.

The way she'd coaxed the hot-dog vendor into holding Emma while she dived into his ice chest for cans from the very bottom, then touched the coldest one to Conner's forehead.

The way she'd plunged right into the fight between a pair of squabbling kids by the jungle display at the zoo, asking whether it was safe for her to step inside and turning them into confederates as they earnestly explained the danger of marauding lions.

The way she'd cocked her head at the distant sound of a street-corner jazz trio while they wandered through downtown Tempe, impulsively breaking into a dance step and drawing him and Emma into it with a swift touch of her hand on his shoulder. Mill Avenue was no place for dancing, he knew, but something about Lucy made him wish he could waltz her up and down the street like one of those old movies.

It shouldn't surprise him that she was so good at turning a simple day off into a joyous event, Con admitted now as she finished the last of her iced tea and set down the dark blue glass with her lips still parted and moist. Lucy had impressed him all along with her capacity for enjoying whatever situation arose, for living fully in the moment at hand. But never before had she turned that exuberant vitality in his direction, the way she was doing now.

Touching him as easily, as naturally as she'd always touched Emma. Watching him with frank appreciation when he rose halfway out of his seat to catch the waitress's attention, and smiling with unabashed pleasure when he met her gaze and held it.

Held it.

Held it until the waitress arrived with their check, and Lucy pouted at the interruption.

She wasn't teasing him on purpose, Conner thought as he reached for his wallet. He didn't have the sensation of watching a calculated performance, the way he sometimes felt when a law clerk or secretary made it clear that any advances would be welcome. No, Lucy wasn't putting on any kind of a show.

She was simply enjoying herself, enjoying *him,* and that made the game even more entertaining.

Made the anticipation even more captivating.

But he couldn't really let himself anticipate much more, not with Emma growing fussy on Lucy's lap. The baby was probably on sensory overload by now, after a day of nonstop activity, and even though she'd napped in the carrier occasionally it was clear that her bedtime couldn't be postponed much longer.

"I guess," Lucy said, confirming his thoughts, "we'd better get her home."

"Yeah." Conner glanced at the check…one more example of Lucy's consistency in choosing activities that would keep the budget to a minimum, which he'd already decided not to argue about. She hadn't argued about his paying, which was a refreshing change, and in turn he had refrained from suggesting dinner at the kind of place he would normally choose. "Emma's been a trouper."

She responded with a look of pride, snuggling the baby closer as he pulled a twenty from his wallet and set it on the check. "She's never had a day like this before."

"Me, neither." Con stood up, then saw her look of amazement. "Well, I mean…"

"You don't spend nearly enough time having fun," Lucy told him, tucking the baby's blanket snugly into place and weaving her way through the mismatched tables out to the dimly lit parking lot. "Oh, listen."

He could hear the same music they'd heard earlier, but it

was closer now. Apparently the group had moved into one of the open-air bars that lined Mill Avenue. "Dancing all night long, huh?"

She nodded, gazing toward the lights in the distance so wistfully that it twisted his heart, then turned away and nestled Emma into her car seat. "Here you go, sweetie. We'll be home in no time."

Within fifteen minutes, Conner realized, the day would be over. A lot sooner than he would've liked, but nobody could haul a baby into the nightspots marked by those beckoning lights. Even so, he found himself moving more slowly than usual as he opened the car door for Lucy, and when she turned to him as he started the ignition, he found himself hoping for a reprieve.

"This has been wonderful," she said simply. "I wish we didn't have to call it a day."

He wished the same thing. Even another few hours with this woman would be more fun, more enlivening, than anything he'd experienced in a long time. "Same here. But I can't see Emma on a dance floor."

Lucy smiled slightly, but he could see the rueful agreement in her eyes even while he shifted into gear. "No, she needs to go to bed."

Ordinarily he'd suggest hiring a sitter, but it was hard to imagine someone turning up on such short notice. "Too bad Lorraine isn't parked right behind us," he muttered, and Lucy's face lit up.

"Jeff and Shawna live five minutes from here! You know, my friends who— Lorraine is her grandmother. I bet they'd watch Emma for a while."

Conner reached for the car phone and handed it to Lucy, feeling a new surge of anticipation in his veins.

"Call them."

Shawna cheerfully agreed to keep Emma until ten-thirty, when she had to leave for the closing shift at work, and within half an hour they were making their way onto the dance floor at some club Conner doubted he would've found on his own. But Lucy, who was now wearing her friend's sparkly black top and pants, seemed to know where to find the best music as easily as she knew how to celebrate everything else.

It didn't matter that he wasn't much of a dancer, Con realized as she drew him with her into the pulse of the music. It didn't matter that she wanted nothing to do with the Tarkingtons, that in four more weeks he'd be back in Philadelphia, that neither of them had planned for anything beyond a day off work. All that mattered now, here, tonight, was that for a few hours they could share the raw excitement of moving in rhythm, the smoky sensuality of a saxophone solo, the ragged satisfaction of knowing that until the band returned for the next set, they'd be back at their table swallowing melted ice cubes and watching each other with the usual barriers completely gone.

Because tonight, for the first time, he was seeing Lucy at her natural, instinctive best. She was no longer holding back the full force of her radiant sensuality, the way she'd done over the past few weeks, and every time she touched him, shook back her hair, took a swallow of his drink, it was getting harder to remember that technically, this woman was someone he needed to take care of.

That such a responsibility didn't add up to a night—or a month of nights—together.

"You're looking sober all of a sudden," Lucy told him, dipping her fingers into the last of her melted ice and laughing as she drew a cool trail across his forehead. "I bet you're trying to figure out how to save our table if I'm in the bathroom and you're getting the drinks."

It took him a moment to make sense of her words, the sensation of her fingers on his skin was so distracting. "The drinks can wait," Con assured her, and she stood up with such vibrant energy that he felt his mouth go dry.

"I don't want to wait."

Did she even know what she was saying? "Lucy…"

"This is just such *fun*," she told him, almost glowing as she rested her hands on his shoulder to keep him from getting up. "I've never seen you like this before."

He'd never felt like this before, Conner knew. "You make me…different."

"I like you different," Lucy said, then turned away and flashed him a quick smile over her shoulder as he stared at the smooth expanse of skin from her neck to her waist. "I'll be right back."

Right back, and he still didn't want to let her go. He had to, though. He had to quit fantasizing about anything more than another few dances.

Because if they went beyond that…

No, he was going to be fair to Lucy if it killed him. No matter how much she might be enjoying him tonight—and she was, he could tell with every primitive instinct in his body—she deserved someone who could love her. Love her for real, for good, for well beyond a night or a month or even a year. And that was something he flat-out couldn't do.

But she knows that.

He'd told her so already, Conner remembered with a sudden flash of recognition, when he'd admitted the other day at the park that he couldn't love anyone enough. She *knew* that, and yet here she was acting like it didn't matter at all.

So it wasn't like she wanted anything serious from him, he realized as he gulped down the last of the melted ice from his glass. No, it was more like she wanted the same thing he did.

Fun. Heat. Exhilaration. Just plain, no-holds-barred sex.

The kind you didn't have to think about. The kind you could just enjoy, with all the wholehearted exuberance that Lucy brought to everything she did.

He wanted that.

He wanted her.

And the want spiraled even higher as he saw her coming back toward him. She looked so good, so ready, so incredibly alive that it was all he could do to stand up and—

And freeze at the sound of his watch alarm beeping a twenty-minute warning.

Emma.

They had to pick up Emma.

They had to pick up Emma, Lucy knew as they drove in heated silence toward Shawna's, because the baby mattered more than anything else she might want.

But, oh, she wanted Conner.

She should be glad he'd set the alarm on his watch, even though the clock in the ladies' room had indicated another half hour before the final deadline. She should be glad that Conner took such responsibility seriously, glad that he valued Emma so much.

And besides, half an hour wasn't nearly enough.

But if only Shawna didn't need to leave for work, they could have taken off for another few hours and finished what they'd been building up to all day.

If only they could have found someplace nearby.

Someplace they could get to very, very fast.

The back seat of the car, even, but she couldn't let herself think that way. They had to put Emma first, they had to take Emma home, and at home there was no place to go. The guest room was Emma's sanctuary, and the master bedroom was the one she'd shared with Kenny—and she couldn't very well expect Conner to put that out of his mind.

"We'll make it," he muttered, glancing at his watch.

They would make it to Shawna's in plenty of time, yes, and she had better get used to the idea that nothing else mattered.

"Good," Lucy managed to answer. "That's good."

The silence still felt electric, though, as if the air between them were tingling with sparks that would only grow hotter if they spoke.

Speaking to Shawna didn't seem to make any difference in the pulsing sparks. She was aware of Conner saying all the polite things, while her friend bundled up the sleeping baby with the assurance that everything was fine, but she still found herself floundering for words.

Words would only get in the way of sensation, and she couldn't quite let go of this shimmering sensation humming through every fiber of her body.

Until she took Emma in her arms and felt her heart lurch with the joy of this soft, sweet bundle nestled against her. This, *this* was her life. Emma was worth anything, any amount of frustration, and she held the thought fast as Conner drove home with the same uneasy silence still tingling between them.

But when he paused at a stoplight and reached to tweak the baby's fingers, she saw on his face the same recognition. The same rock-bottom acknowledgment.

Emma mattered more than anything else.

Oh, he knew. He understood, Lucy realized. He might be as frustrated as she was, but even so he recognized the same thing she did.

It was that recognition which prompted her to offer him the privilege of tucking the baby into her nest of blankets as soon as they got home, and Conner responded with such a look of wonder that she felt her heart swell. He knew how much this child mattered, knew what it meant to put Emma above all else, and for that alone, she could love this man.

At least with her heart.

Because that was the only choice left tonight, Lucy reflected ruefully as she watched him smooth the pink blanket over Emma's tiny feet. She kissed her daughter's forehead while Conner turned out the light, then followed him to the doorway of her room.

"Well," she said, trying to come up with a suitable closing for a day of revelations and settling for the most conventional, "thank you. It's been a really, really good day."

"Yeah." He looked down at the floor, shoved his hands in his pockets and returned his gaze to her. "Yeah, it has."

They still had to check the answering machine, turn out the porch light, lock the front deadbolt, but the day was as good as ended. She knew it, he knew it, and there was no sense complaining about it. But even so, she couldn't help admitting, "I wish it wasn't over."

Conner stared at her in silence for a long moment, and she felt the heat between them crackling even higher. Then he said fiercely, "It's not."

And pulled her into his arms.

She felt herself reeling under a wave of sensation as he drew her against him, lowering her lips to hers for a kiss that electrified them both.

It was hard.

It was hot.

It was hungry, and it exploded between them with such force that she heard him gasp, heard herself moan, then knew nothing but heat, nothing but yearning, nothing but the sheer, raging glory of kissing this man. Feverishly, hungrily, jutting her hips to meet his, tasting the rough contours of his mouth, feeling the warmth of his hands as he ran them down her back and pulled her nearer, tighter, so close she could almost feel the pulsing rhythm of his heartbeat against her own.

"Conner..." she whispered, and heard him growl in response.

This wasn't a good-night kiss. This wasn't a kiss between friends. But this was what she wanted—his strength, his heat, his ardent demand of more, closer, harder, yes! She heard herself moan again, as if from a distance, and the sound raised the last fragile flag of awareness that she couldn't quite let go.

''We can't wake up Emma,'' she gasped, and Conner reached with one hand to tug the bedroom door shut.

''We won't,'' he promised, and kissed her again. Harder this time, exactly the way she wanted—all of him, all here right now, with all the fire he normally kept under control flaring hotter, rising higher until she could barely remember what she'd worried about only a moment ago. Emma, yes, but they would hear Emma if she cried, and with a giddy sense of exuberance she let the worry melt away.

Let herself celebrate the sheer, primal glory of feeling this man against her. Wrapping his fingers in her hair. Deepening the kiss, fumbling with the knotted bow behind her neck as she worked her hands inside his shirt—oh, he was so much warmer, so much harder than she'd guessed, with his muscles straining under her touch—until she felt the ties of her blouse give way and the fabric slither down to her waist. Then, before she could even wonder whether she looked all right, Conner whispered her name, and in his voice was a note of awe.

Slowly, very slowly, he moved his fingers down her skin in a caress so exquisitely sensual it left her gasping, writhing against him, wanting more of his touch, yes, his tongue, more, his mouth against her—

''Yes,'' she pleaded, and he paused only long enough for her to yank the shirt off over his head before returning to his leisurely exploration with a thoroughness that made her ache for more. She wanted him, all of him, *now,* but still this tantalizing slowness was so sweet that she felt herself reeling between pleasure and desperation…because still, still he was taking his time.

Lingering, sustaining, drawing out each enticing stroke and each coaxing touch until she cried out in a mixture of joy and frustration. She needed him to keep going, needed him to stop, needed him to fill the yearning inside her, because she couldn't take any more of this, couldn't bear for him to stop, and in a frantic rush she grabbed for whatever she could unfasten at the waist of his khaki slacks. There, a button, work it however she could, and already she could feel his response, harder, more—

"Ah, Lucy," he muttered, and with a sudden move he lifted her into his arms, still teasing her with the rough attention of his lips and the sweet demand of his tongue. Moving with exquisite slowness yet without a moment of hesitation, he carried her down the hall to his bedroom…where he didn't even bother to turn back the plaid comforter, but nestled her atop it and watched while she kicked off her shoes. "You don't have to worry," he said hoarsely, "about taking care of the furniture."

Once again, the comment was so unexpected that she laughed. How could he do that, make her laugh right in the middle of this frenzied longing, make her fly so rapidly from passion to practicality to joyous, searing need? But then, this was Conner, and Conner could do anything he set his mind to.

Or his body.

Or hers…

Oh, definitely hers, Lucy thought with each new spasm of pleasure. He knew just where to touch her, just when to draw back, just how to show his appreciation for each new wonder that sparkled between them. That lifted them into giddy swirls of sensation, breathtaking flight, soaring beyond anything she'd ever dreamed possible. This man was more than she'd dared to imagine, and she'd imagined a lot over the past few hours—but never with the kind of rapturous intensity that vibrated between them now, as he drove her into new heights of elation and she finally responded with a cry of satisfaction which had never filled her so thoroughly before.

It was different this time, Lucy realized as he joined her at a crest that lasted until they lay spent and entangled in each other's arms. Different, she realized again at midnight when they woke from a sated doze and ascended to another peak of excitement that left them both gasping for breath. Different, she decided as they drifted into a sweetly contented slumber, because this time she knew the truth.

She loved this man. In spite of everything that made him wrong for her, she loved him with all her heart.

And, even though he had promised nothing except safe sex, Conner couldn't have fulfilled her so completely if he was as incapable of love as he claimed.

He might need time to acknowledge it. He might not yet have realized that his heart worked just as well as his enticingly powerful body. He might need time to recognize that they brought out something special in one another.

But she could wait.

Lucy nestled more comfortably into his protective embrace and gently rested his hand against her heart.

She could wait for as long as it took.

Chapter Seven

It took a long time to wake up from this kind of dream, and Conner was in no hurry. The dream of Lucy beside him, beneath him, welcoming him, urging him.

God, if only this were real.

Maybe it is.

The suspicion grew as he felt himself stirring to wakefulness with the scent of her still surrounding him, and he remembered with a rush of amazement that last night hadn't been a dream. That Lucy was actually in his bed, here and now, after a night that still seemed beyond the realm of possibility.

But it was real, Conner knew as he let the sensual memories flood him, and all he could do now was hope that she'd viewed it the same way he had. Because she was the last person who deserved to get hurt, and—

"Good morning," Lucy said.

Startled, he opened his eyes to find her adjusting the pillow beside him for her to sit up against the headboard. She still smelled terrific, but now she was dressed in a floppy T-shirt he'd never seen before. "You're awake," he blurted.

"I just fed Emma." With a teasing smile, she ran her fingers down the side of his whiskered jaw. "You look like a pirate."

"You look like…" He couldn't find the words. Something wonderful, he knew that much, but his brain still felt foggy. "Uh…"

Lucy waited while he sat up beside her, then seemed to recognize that he wasn't at his best just yet. "'Beautiful' would be fine," she prompted, tugging his pillow into position behind him. "I'd settle for 'great.'"

"You *are* great," Conner blurted, and saw a faint flush of color rising on her cheeks.

"Well, thank you."

"I mean it, Lucy." Here it was barely six in the morning, and she was looking after him with the same attention she'd already devoted to Emma. As though his comfort mattered as much as her daughter's. "You're really something."

"So are you." She shifted positions, turning to look at him directly and holding his gaze as she spoke. "It meant a lot, last night, that you cared about Emma."

"Well, sure." But the way she regarded him so wholeheartedly made him feel a little uneasy. As if she might have forgotten that Conner Tarkington lacked a capability most people took for granted. "Look," he began, and she cut him off.

"I know we have to get back to work today," Lucy interrupted, then shot him a challenging glance. "That's what you were going to say, right?"

He hadn't even thought about work yet, Conner realized. But of course she was right. They had a full day to make up for.

"Because that's fine," she continued, apparently seeing nothing wrong with talking business even before getting dressed. "The foundation is important. And I promise," she added solemnly, with a gesture of crossing her heart, "I'm gonna keep my hands off you the whole time we're in the office."

"It's gonna be a long day," he muttered, and she grinned at him.

"I know. Talk about frustrating."

She wouldn't be talking that way if she viewed last night as a one-time event, would she? He sure wouldn't mind a repeat, either, or even another month of repeats—no man in his right mind would turn down a woman like her—but he had to take some responsibility before anyone got hurt.

He couldn't let her think this meant anything except fun.

"Lucy," he warned, "you know what I told you before, about how there's something missing? I mean, when it comes to love, somehow I never learned the real—"

She lifted her hand to stop him. "Don't worry about it."

"You're sure?" If he had half a brain, he would take her at her word and shut up right now. But his conscience, Conner knew, would keep insisting that Lucy deserved better. "I mean, you're okay with that?"

Without lowering her left hand, she waited until he met her gaze before answering very soberly. "I'll tell you the only thing that's *not* okay, is if you start trying to throw diamonds at me."

She'd already made it clear how she felt about gifts, but combining the sight of her engagement-ring finger with the mention of diamonds made the message even clearer. Lucy Velardi wanted nothing from him except the kind of fun they'd shared last night, which made her exactly the kind of woman he wanted.

"You're really something," Conner said softly, and she grinned at him.

"If I say 'So are you,' we have to start all over again." Then, as he marveled at her ability to remember fragments of conversation at this hour of the morning, she jumped out of bed and grabbed her scattered clothes from the floor, clearly ready to begin the day. "Don't forget, it's your turn to make the coffee."

She had already pledged that today was for the foundation, so there was no reason to be disappointed that she didn't seem to plan on sharing his shower. "Right," he said, but even as he stood up he realized that he couldn't let her leave his room yet. Not without some sense that there was life beyond work. "Look, you want to have dinner tonight?"

It pleased him when she let her gaze linger on his body, even while she answered in a tone as practical as his own movements as he pulled on last night's discarded khakis. "Depends on how late we work. If Emma's still awake…"

"Right," he said again, remembering with a flash of pleasure that the baby was usually asleep by six or seven. "We'll quit early."

Lucy cocked her head, then broke into a smile. "I like your attitude," she announced. "But, Conner, if we *do* have to work late, that's okay. We can order in pizza."

She meant it, he saw, which astonished him. "You deserve better than that," he told her, retrieving his shirt from the floor.

"Better than pizza?" She dropped her handful of clothes into a jumble on the bed and moved toward him. "There's no such thing."

What kind of life had she lived, anyway? Hadn't anybody ever treated this woman to the kind of dinner that would prove she was special? Turning his shirt right side out, Conner halted as she yanked it away and slowly ran her hands up his chest.

"I should've said," she corrected herself, "nothing better than pizza—in bed."

He drew her into a sweeping embrace, marveling at the way she made it so clear what she wanted, and warmed at the knowledge that what she wanted was him. "Lucy, you're amazing."

"No, I'm not," she protested, even as she smiled up at him. "I just know what I like."

Pizza in bed. "You've almost got me hoping we'll have to work late," he said, enjoying the softness of her against him so much that he could almost feel the foundation fading from his awareness.

Maybe Lucy felt it, too, because she resolutely took a step back. "We won't even get started without coffee," she warned, then kissed him with dizzying swiftness and handed him back his shirt. "So let's get to work."

Work occupied them for the rest of the day, in spite of the frequent stirrings that urged him to take her back to bed, take her out dancing, do whatever he could to make sure this magic lasted. But the foundation had to come first, Conner knew, and as long as Lucy was keeping her word about not distracting him in the office, surely he could do the same.

It was tougher than he'd expected, though, especially when he saw her staring into space with a reminiscent smile. But when he stood up, she threw him a guilty glance and immediately returned to her notes, and he forced himself to take the long way to the phone rather than walk directly behind her chair.

"The first day of anything is always the hardest," she told him that night in the kitchen, while they reheated the triple cheese pizza they'd taken to bed with them and never gotten around to eating. "Tomorrow will be better, because we'll know we can spend a whole day in the office together without going crazy."

But that knowledge didn't make the next day any easier, or the next.... Conner found himself reluctant to leave for a late-afternoon meeting with an investment adviser, and Lucy admitted when he came home that she'd slept the whole time he was gone, "because the only thing keeping me awake lately is wanting to be around you." Which prompted him to suggest another day off.

"You've got to get some rest," he told her as they put Emma to bed, "and if you wait until I head for Seattle, you're gonna collapse."

"I'm not working any harder than you are," she reminded him, as if feeding Emma in the middle of the night couldn't possibly count as work. "Besides, we're already getting a day off for Christmas."

Conner flinched. He'd been able to ignore most of the holiday trappings, closing his mind to the decorations in Joel's office and the carols during talk-radio commercials, but if Lucy expected some kind of Christmas spirit from him…

"If it makes you too sad, remembering Bryan," she continued as she pinned the baby's diaper into place, "I can understand that. But I'd rather spend the day with you than anyone."

"It's just…the whole Christmas thing…" Con faltered as he took Emma's blanket from the dresser. "I figured if I skipped it this year, got away from all the reminders—"

"Then you'd survive, right?" Lucy asked gently, fastening her daughter's sleepers.

"Well, yeah." Lights and wreaths and Santas shouldn't make anyone feel like they were suffocating, but he'd discovered last year that the memories of his son's death were far worse during the holiday season than any other time. "When Bryan died, it was like…I don't know, I was surrounded by all these Christmas trappings."

"Not luminarias," she said, prompting him to rack his brain for an image until he remembered the traditional Southwestern candles flickering inside brown paper bags. "Not tamales." She kissed Emma and nestled her gently into the cushioned drawer. "Not going out in the desert." Taking the blanket from Conner, she covered the baby and kissed her good-night, then straightened up and turned back to him. "Why don't we spend Christmas Day hiking Squaw Peak?"

It was a tempting prospect, but she'd said a long time ago that she and Emma were celebrating the holiday with friends. As much as he'd like to share the day with her and the baby, they had a life of their own. He needed to remember that.

"You don't have to give up your plans for me," Conner assured her, and turned out the light before she could see any sign of wistfulness on his face.

Lucy followed him into the hall, leaving the door ajar as she'd done for the past few nights. "I want a picture of me and Emma at the top of Squaw Peak," she announced. "The only way that'll happen is if you get one of those instant cameras and come with us."

Even if she was making that up on the spur of the moment, he couldn't turn down such an appealing offer. "You talked me into it," he said swiftly, and she grinned at him.

"We'll have a good time."

They had a great time hiking the two-mile trail along a mountain that jutted right from the heart of Phoenix, passing a number of other people along the way who were apparently trying out their new gifts of hiking gear. Once again, Con reflected as he clicked off several shots of her and the baby at the end of the trail, Lucy made everything fun. She showed off Emma to half a dozen admiring strangers, shared conversation with everyone they met at the scattered overlooks viewing the city skyline, and when they ran into a cluster of kids during a water break on the way back, she plopped down beside them and asked what they'd gotten from Santa.

Watching her was like watching the spirit of Christmas come to life, he thought, marveling at her ability to share genuinely friendly conversation with everyone she met. And he felt a curious sense of pride that this woman was here with *him*. Out of all the people she and Emma could have chosen to spend the day with, she had picked Conner Tarkington.

Nobody else.

"When school starts," he heard Lucy ask one of the kids, "what kind of things do you like to do after you get out for the day?"

She was asking on his behalf, Con realized with a jolt of awareness. She wanted to show him how easy it was to talk to kids, to ask the kind of questions she'd insisted he should take to the people who mattered.

And the least he could do was to listen to their answers.

It took only ten minutes before the group moved on up the trail, but he found himself taking mental notes the entire time. "You know," he told Lucy as he passed her the water bottle, "I see what you mean. It's different going directly to the kids."

She took a gulp from the bottle and handed it back to him. "You could do that."

He could do that. For the first time since Bryan's death, he could imagine himself having a conversation with someone around the same age as his son. "Maybe, when school starts, I will."

Lucy's joyous smile made him wish he'd had the camera ready, but even without a picture he would remember it for a long time. As long and with as much pleasure as he'd remember her celebratory kiss. "Good for you, Conner," she told him, her eyes shining as she took his hand and started back down the trail. "Good for you."

She and Emma were good for him, Lucy reflected the next day as she let her daughter splash in the kitchen sink while Conner phoned yet another contact. He'd been working doggedly all morning, asking investors to recommend schools where he might talk to children, which was a fundraising angle she hadn't even thought of.

It shouldn't surprise her, though, that he'd made the most of her idea about chatting with actual kids. Personally involved parents would offer even more support for the foundation, and this man was incredibly good at business.

But over the past few days, he'd started letting himself be good at real life as well.

"So I'll be in Seattle on the second, if I could come by and talk to Hannah then," she heard him conclude. "Great, tell her thanks for me." Then another round of goodbyes, another pause and another number keyed into the phone.

His phone demeanor hadn't changed, but the rest of him had. She noticed it again when he came into the living room as she was fluffing Emma's hair with the bath towel, looking almost gleeful as he held out his finger for the baby to grab.

"We need to take some more time off tomorrow afternoon," he told Lucy. "It's all set up."

All she'd heard was him talking to investors, but she hadn't really been paying attention to the calls. Even on the day after Christmas, Conner seemed to have no problem connecting with people he wanted to reach.

"Emma," he explained, gently easing his hand from her grasp, "has never seen *The Nutcracker*."

The Christmas ballet? "Neither have I," Lucy said. She had always dreamed of it, but that tradition was like cheerleading or driving a red convertible—glorious, but not something regular people could afford. Even in Phoenix, where the performances lasted from late November until after Christmas, tickets were still hard to get. "They sell out way in advance."

"It's okay," he assured her. "I talked to some people, and we've got tickets for tomorrow."

But no matter how he'd managed that, he was talking about something far more expensive than a simple day off. "Conner—"

"See," he continued before she could finish her objection, "I'd really like a picture of me and Emma with the dancers. And the only way that's gonna happen is if you come along and take it."

Oh.

Well…

Whether or not he really wanted such a picture, she couldn't very well refuse the same request she'd made of him only a few days ago. "I'd love that," Lucy admitted, and saw the light of relief on his face. "Emma," she told her daughter, "we're going to see the most wonderful ballet in the world."

"I don't know if it's—" Conner warned, and she lifted a finger to his lips.

"For Emma, it will be. For me, too."

She thought the same thing the next day as they settled into what seemed like the very best seats in Phoenix's Symphony Hall. They had juggled the baby's naps and feeding schedule in hopes that Emma would be awake for most of the performance, and so far it looked like the plan would work. Lucy had wished her daughter was old enough for a red velvet dress and shiny black shoes, but for now the baby was as well dressed as any other baby in the audience…and the white sweater-dress she'd borrowed from Shawna was perfect.

Shawna had dropped off the dress last night, after a panicked phone call when Lucy realized she had nothing to wear, and had drawn her into the bathroom for an interrogation about Conner.

"You can try this on while you tell me about him," her friend ordered, closing the door and withdrawing the dress from its drycleaning wrap. "But don't even *think* about telling me there's nothing going on! I saw how he looks at you."

"I'm probably looking at him the same way." She stripped off her T-shirt, realizing only after she dropped it on the sink that the results of Con's attention last night were impossible to miss. "He's wonderful, okay?"

"This is the same guy you couldn't stand living with two

weeks ago, right?'' Shawna teased, generously pretending not to notice her blush. ''Or did I miss something?''

''It's like he's a different person,'' Lucy protested, sliding off her jeans and reaching for the dress. ''This past week, he's finally realized he can relax once in a while. Enjoy life for a change.''

''That's what it looked like the other night,'' her friend agreed, helping her shake the clingy skirt into place. ''No more working every minute, huh?''

''Well, he's still a worker.'' There was no question that The Bryan Foundation mattered to him, even if he seemed more relaxed during his steady twelve-hour sessions in the office. ''And I like that about him—I mean, how he takes things seriously.''

''That doesn't sound like you,'' Shawna protested, and Lucy had to admit she was right. She had never been attracted to serious people before, but there was something different about Conner Tarkington.

He might be serious about things that mattered, but he also knew how to have fun.

And he proved it at *The Nutcracker*. The afternoon was even more delightful than she'd expected, thanks to Conner's remarkable ease at dealing with box-office staff, ushers and program vendors. He belonged in places like this, Lucy had noticed as he guided her through the well-dressed crowd with the assurance that came from lifelong privilege. He might not view it as anything special, but this man's blue-blooded confidence was a pleasure to watch.

It wasn't until the overture began that she realized, with a start of guilt, that in spite of his relaxed demeanor he was going to be faced with the kind of music that had troubled him only last week. Con looked perfectly comfortable right now, but as the performance unfolded she checked his profile for any sign of distress whenever she tore her glance from the stage.

"You doing okay?" she whispered when the music swelled for the entrance of the Mouse King, and he nodded.

"Fine."

"I just thought maybe the music—" she began, and he reached for her hand.

"Lucy, it's all right."

He still seemed all right when the houselights came up after the first act, and she was relieved to notice when they reached the lobby that he looked almost exhilarated. Maybe he was enjoying the performance as much as she was, or maybe, she realized as she saw him watching her, he was simply enjoying her reaction to it.

"Still think it's the most wonderful ballet in the world?" he asked, and she lifted Emma for an imaginary pas de deux.

"It is now. Conner, really, this was so nice of you."

He smiled at her, and the presence of the crowd around them seemed to diminish as she warmed herself in the glow of his eyes.

"I wanted you to have this," he said softly. "Tchaikovsky, whatever…I wanted it for you."

She had never told him her dream of someday dancing on stage, but somehow he must have guessed it anyway. And for her sake, she realized with a quiver of wonder, he was willing to risk listening to the kind of music that had shattered him before.

Lucy felt her throat tightening up, and he must have seen the rush of emotion on her face because he drew her and Emma close to him for a swift, sustaining hug.

"Thank you," she whispered, and he gently squeezed her shoulders as he let her go.

"I'm enjoying it, too. I wouldn't have done this without you."

So she and Emma were definitely good for him, Lucy decided with a flare of happiness that warmed her throughout the second half of the show, and the rhapsodic music seemed to echo her own sense of exultation.

"That was so good!" she told Conner as they made their way out to the plaza after a round of applause that still had her ears ringing. "Did you love it?"

"I loved it."

But his confirmation didn't sound as enthusiastic as her own, and she felt a sudden tremor of guilt as she remembered that she'd completely forgotten the impact of the second half, where the score was more lushly evocative than the first. "And the music... Were you okay?"

He smiled at her, and she saw in his expression a mixture of pride and tenderness. "Yeah," he answered. "I just kept watching you and Emma."

"Oh, Conner..." The realization of what that meant sent a dizzying rush of joy through her, and Lucy raised her free hand to his shoulder, stopping him in place with a heartfelt kiss. "I love you."

"I love you."

The words still haunted him as he drove to the Fast Foto place, which had left a message on the answering machine that his order was ready. It was the excuse he needed to get out of the house, give himself and Lucy both the breathing space they needed. Give them time to relax, time to regain their balance.

To put things in perspective.

"I love you."

She didn't mean it, Conner told himself, deliberately relaxing his unnecessarily tight grip on the steering wheel. It was just the impact of the show, just an emotional reaction to the same kind of music that affected him beyond all reason. Lucy was an exuberant person to begin with, and it was only natural that she'd react with such a statement.

But she didn't mean it. She couldn't. He'd told her twice—three times, if you counted that day at the park— that he'd already failed his only attempt at love, that nobody with his flawed combination of genetics and upbringing could get it right, and she'd assured him that it was no problem.

Which meant her "I love you" was just a surfeit of emotion, a spontaneous exaggeration that shouldn't embarrass either one of them.

It had, though. He could tell from her expression even as he caught his breath that she regretted having spoken. She'd covered any awkwardness with a flow of chatter about the show, about the parts Emma had seemed to enjoy most, and he'd managed to keep up his end of the conversation all the way home…where he was relieved to find messages not only from the photo place, but also from Weller-Tarkington-Craig.

He would phone Philadelphia in the morning, Con resolved, parking outside the row of shops where he'd left the instant-camera pictures of the Squaw Peak hike. After all, he needed to confirm that he'd be returning to the firm within three weeks.

He didn't want to think about that, either.

Fortunately, the hiking photos were an effective distraction. Although Emma had her eyes closed in half of them, and a few others were flawed with overly bright sun or shadows, there was one that made his chest tighten. Lucy was smiling at him with such joyous affection, holding Emma with such comfortable sweetness, that he felt an irrational surge of pride.

As if this woman and child belonged to him.

It was a stupid reaction, Conner knew, but even so he was going to keep this photo. Lucy wouldn't miss one print from the batch, and he'd get her an enlargement in any case. The store clerk told him to come back in half an hour, and he spent the time standing in line to pay for a simple platinum frame that wouldn't distract from the picture of her and Emma.

Lucy was delighted when he gave it to her that evening, although she spent far more time than he had marveling at her daughter's image. "Doesn't she look happy? I love how she's right on the verge of smiling."

"I love you."

She didn't mean it, he reminded himself, watching her tilt the photo against the light from the living room lamp. It was just an expression.

"Yeah," Conner said. "I thought you'd like it."

"This frame, though…" She turned it in her hands, casting him an uneasy glance. "Tell me this isn't anything expensive."

Expensive was a pretty loose term. "Don't worry about it. Anyway, the guy at the photo place said if you don't frame a picture this size, it'll get all beat up."

That must have been convincing, because Lucy nodded as she set the framed photo on the bookshelf and took a step back to admire it. "Well, thank you. I just don't want you spending money on—"

"Uh-oh," Con interrupted. He knew where this was heading, and it wasn't anyplace he wanted to go. "Looks like a fight," he predicted, taking a boxing stance at her side. "Gotta warn you, no tickling."

She stared at him, as if wondering whether she'd heard right. "Huh?"

"Anything else is okay, but tickling is off-limits." He shifted his weight like a boxer, relieved that she was starting to look amused rather than baffled. "You got that?"

"Conner—" she protested, and he grinned at her.

"You mean it's not off-limits?" With a quick lunge, he dived for the soft spot at the side of her waist. "I can reach in like that, and—"

"Conner!" she protested again, but this time it was a shriek of laughter, and within a few moments of wrestling for each other's ticklish spots, they were suddenly back to the level of comfort they'd enjoyed for the past few days. It was as easy as ever to retreat to bed together, to share the night in each other's arms, and in the morning he woke with a sense of relief that Lucy obviously hadn't been serious about loving him.

She wasn't expecting anything he couldn't give.

That assurance made it easier to focus on the tasks of the day, which included calling Philadelphia—no word from Kenny, which meant he'd been needlessly worried—and checking in with his law partners. And, feeling as good as he did right now, Con was pleased to offer his cooperation in visiting a client who'd asked for a consultation at home—a vacation home in Sedona, the resort town a few hours north of Scottsdale.

"I'll head up there this weekend," he promised, already realizing the potential for such a drive. Bringing Lucy and Emma along would turn it into something far more enjoyable than just a business trip, and he'd welcome any opportunity for more time with them. "No problem. Right, then I'll see you on the fifteenth."

The fifteenth was closer than he liked to acknowledge, but it was still almost three weeks away. And if he'd learned anything from Lucy, Conner knew, it was to make the most of the moment at hand.

Which, right now, was a morning in the office.

Together.

Lucy was copying numbers from the checks that had arrived in yesterday's mail, and when he hung up the phone she handed him a deposit slip along with an invoice. "All these investors must have more money than they know what to do with. But that's a good thing, because we just got the bill for the stationery."

It was still an odd sensation, writing checks himself instead of letting a bookkeeper do it, but he'd started the practice to avoid any questions about why The Bryan Foundation paid its clerical help by the week. "Right," he said, taking the checkbook from the drawer and writing Lucy's paycheck along with one for the printer. Then, handing hers across the desk, he looked around for the invoice envelope. "Where's the mail pile?"

When she didn't reply, he turned and saw her gazing at her paycheck with a look of amazement.

"Lucy?"

She blinked, then glanced up at him. "That's it," she said softly, gesturing toward her check. "I made it."

It was the normal, weekly amount, but her expression indicated something much more significant. "What?"

"I've got enough to move out."

He felt as if he'd just been kicked in the stomach. "That's what you've been saving for?" Conner managed to ask. She'd said when they first met that she planned to move out, of course, but that was a long time ago. "All this time?"

Maybe she noticed something strange in his voice, because she looked at him curiously. "Well, sure," she answered, reaching for Emma as the baby set up a sudden clamor. "I can't stay here forever."

"But—" he began, and she interrupted as she lifted her squalling daughter into her arms.

"I know, your parents aren't coming this winter." Holding the baby close against her, she rocked her gently back and forth. "But that still doesn't change anything. I want Emma and me to have our own place."

Of course she wanted that, of course she didn't want to live off the Tarkingtons. But the idea of Lucy moving out made his chest feel tight. "You're not leaving right away, are you?"

She smiled slightly, but he could see on her face a mixture of embarrassment and regret. "It's funny," Lucy told him. "Back when you first showed up, I couldn't wait to move out of here." Emma hiccuped, and she shifted the baby to her shoulder. "After that day playing Frisbee, I wanted to get away from you as fast as I could."

The statement hurt, in spite of knowing very clearly that

he wasn't what Lucy needed…at least not for anything beyond a few weeks of enjoyment. But even so, he found himself tensing every muscle as he asked, "Do you still want to get away?"

Lucy was silent for a moment, and he felt his body preparing for the impact of a blow. Then she met his gaze, looking a little rueful, and said simply, "No."

It was surprising how hard the wave of relief crashed through him. "I don't want you to leave, either," Conner said, knowing even as he spoke that it was a major understatement. He wasn't ready to let her go. Not only because setting up a child-support account in Kenny's name was taking longer than he'd anticipated, but also for a simpler reason. "I'd miss you. And Emma."

"Well, then." She regarded him for a moment longer, her eyes curiously bright, before returning the contented baby to her carrier with a soothing caress. "Back to work. I want to get as many of these letters done as I can before you leave for Seattle."

Seattle. Right. He'd already set that up for next week. But, damn, there was still a lot of work to finish, which meant less time for enjoying his last few weeks of Lucy's company.

In a way, Conner thought with a twinge of regret as he checked off the list of Chicago investors he still had to visit, it would be easier if he could simply invite her and Emma back to Philadelphia with him. But that would be unforgivably selfish. Implying some kind of future, implying he could offer anything beyond fun—well, and responsibility—would be grossly unfair. And Lucy, who said things like "I love you" so easily, didn't deserve that kind of hurt.

Besides, she was already planning for a future without him, planning to move out as soon as the foundation was up and running. And he had to be strong enough, decent enough, to let her go.

Still, there were almost three weeks left.

Three weeks to enjoy every possible moment with Lucy and Emma. To make up for what he couldn't give her by offering whatever else he could.

To make her smile, the way he did that night, by suggesting he order in dinner and surprising her with a candlelight caterer rather than the usual pizza.

To make her eyes light up the next day by presenting Emma with a teddy bear almost as big as the baby herself...although Lucy did warn him again to quit spending money.

She couldn't very well object to the diamond-studded locket he gave her, though, when he explained that Emma's photo deserved a perfect setting. And when he asked her to accompany him to Sedona on Saturday "because I want somebody I can trust to witness this client's signature," he was relieved when she responded with a look of cautious optimism.

"Okay," she agreed. "If you need me at your meeting, that's fine."

I need you.

But he couldn't tell her that, Conner knew, at least not outside of a business context. He didn't need anyone—never had, never would. Whereas Lucy was the kind of person who would give and give and give, pouring out all her affection and passion and joy on someone who could never respond with the kind of long-term love she deserved, and he wasn't going to let that happen.

"All right, then," he said. "Let's leave for Sedona tomorrow morning."

In Sedona, they could finish the client meeting in half an hour and spend the rest of the time on fun. In Sedona, they could add to the storehouse of memories he was already stockpiling for his return to Philadelphia. In Sedona, he would show her the kind of celebration a woman like Lucy deserved.

In Sedona, he could pretend for a single weekend that Conner Tarkington was capable of love.

Chapter Eight

"I'll bet you love Sedona," Conner observed the next afternoon as they turned from the interstate onto the state highway, and Lucy squinted at the horizon in hopes of glimpsing the red rocks ahead. "You've probably been here a lot."

"Actually, just once," she admitted, "back when Mom and I moved here from New Mexico." She had been eleven years old, and furious at the gentleman who'd accepted a job transfer to Arizona without a single thought for all the friends she'd left behind. "I was so mad at the guy she was with, I sulked through the whole trip."

Con glanced at her thoughtfully, then shook his head with a slight smile. "I can't see you sulking. You're more like— You put things right out there."

Things like "I love you," which she'd realized was a mistake the moment she'd said it. For the past three days she'd sensed that Conner was still on guard, that his wholehearted passion for the music at Symphony Hall hadn't convinced him he was capable of any deeper emotion.

Even though his actions sure *looked* like love, he still wasn't calling it that.

"I mean," he continued now, "you're more straightforward than anybody I've ever met."

"Not when I was growing up, though," Lucy said, leaning forward to see if she could spot any dramatic monoliths silhouetted against the sky. "Mom drilled it into me that whoever was paying the bills had all the say."

"That'd be the Boyfriend Of The Month, huh?"

Maybe it was only because the landscape looked so much like the one she'd spent an entire weekend resenting, but the memory of those gentlemen still stung. "Right. So if Jim wanted the phone free every night and I wanted to talk to my friends, too bad. Mom kept saying, 'You don't understand, without Jim we've got nothing. We have to get along.'"

Conner shot her a sudden, startled look of concern. "Lucy," he faltered, "were you— I mean, did anyone ever—"

"No," she interrupted. It was heartwarming, though, seeing how troubled he looked at the very idea. "No, none of them were perverts. They were just bossy." At least most of them, the ones who had insisted on calling the shots. "Where we lived, who we saw, what time we ate. My mom would put up with anything, as long as the money kept coming in."

He tightened his grip on the steering wheel, and for a moment he looked the way she remembered him a month ago, with every emotion firmly walled beyond reach. Then he said, "I see why you're so big on taking care of yourself. Nobody else ever did, huh?"

"No, they *all* did." Everyone had contributed something to the household before moving on...usually in response to her mother's growing dependence. "These guys were always calling the shots, but for as long as they stuck around, everything was fine.'' It was only after they left that her mother would shrink into a heap of misery, and Lucy would have to swallow any signs of anger at yet another abandonment while pretending that of course things would be better next time.

"Damn,'' Con muttered. "That'd be hard on a kid.''

It had been harder to pretend after losing Hal, who used to listen to her childhood adventures, and later Doug the jazz fan—both of whom had left without even saying good-bye—but none of the gentlemen ever lasted for more than a year or two. And in any case, it was all ancient history now.

"Well, so,'' Lucy concluded, "I haven't been to Sedona in a long time. It's probably a lot better place than I remember from that one weekend.''

Her childhood memory didn't include the sandstone-sculpted vacation home where Conner's client lived, and she was pleased that she and Emma had plenty of time for exploring the nearby trails while the meeting dragged on. When she finally witnessed the signing of three documents, Con and the client looked equally pleased at whatever business they'd completed, and her impression was confirmed when they pulled out of the driveway and he raised one fist in a sign of exultation.

"That's the biggest piece of business anyone's brought in all year.''

"Good for you!'' she told him, enjoying his unabashed look of triumph. "Do you get paid extra for it?''

"Well, not me personally, but the firm will, yeah.'' He glanced at his watch and frowned, making her realize how absorbed he must have been—he normally had no problem remembering the two-hour difference between Phoenix and Philadelphia time. "I'll call them tomorrow.''

"Your office is open on New Year's Eve?''

"The partners'll be there, yeah,'' he said, braking at the

entrance to the highway. "Or if not, I'll get them at home. Anyway, what do you say we go see the light show?"

His client had described how one of the Sedona resorts sponsored a festival of holiday lights, with dozens of sparkling exhibits on display every night, but there was still half an hour until sunset. "I don't know," Lucy said, although the idea of lingering for such a spectacle was tempting. "We'd be awfully late getting back."

"Well, we can stay overnight." Conner gestured at the road toward town, which she suspected was lined with resorts meant for wealthy vacationers. "See if we can give you some better memories of Sedona."

This afternoon's walk had already given her a new appreciation of the region's dramatic beauty. But no matter how appealing it might be to spend the night here, there were practical considerations...like the dwindling supplies in her diaper bag.

"I didn't bring anything," she told him. "Emma needs—"

"We can pick up whatever Emma needs. Whatever *we* need, for that matter." Con still hadn't turned the car toward the row of resorts or the grocery stores beyond, but she could see the eagerness in his body. "I'd like to spend another day, do one of those jeep tours." Then he grinned at her, almost melting her heart on the spot. "You know, play like we're on vacation."

It sounded wonderful, but she'd spent the past week vowing not to let herself put the pleasures of sensuality before the commitments of her job. "We're not supposed to be on vacation," Lucy warned. "This was supposed to be a work day."

He regarded her thoughtfully for a moment, and she could see on his face a mixture of admiration and entreaty. "It was," he said finally, "but we've finished our work. And I'm bringing back a lot more business than anyone was expecting. So for now— Lucy, *you're* the one who showed me there's more to life than work.''

When he put it like that, there was no point in arguing. And she didn't really want to argue, which made it all the more satisfying to let him drive into a resort surrounded by breathtaking canyon views. Lucy waited in the car with Emma, who was dozing contentedly, while Conner strode inside and returned with a key but no bellman.

''Kind of nice not having to worry about luggage,'' he said cheerfully as he parked outside a building that looked like a place for visiting royalty. He took Emma from her car seat, unlocked the door and gestured them in. ''Here we go.''

She could live in a suite like this for the rest of her life, Lucy thought, gaping at the splendor before them. Con didn't seem awed by the shelf of books, the leather sofas or the whirlpool spa in the bathroom, but even he stood still when she opened the floor-to-ceiling blinds that revealed a view of the red rock cliffs in the sunset.

''God,'' he murmured. ''My God.''

No matter what else they did tomorrow, she decided, they had to explore whatever had put such reverence in his voice. And the next morning when they asked the concierge for a list of sightseeing recommendations, she was delighted to see the Chapel of the Holy Cross at the very top.

It was a moving start to the day, and from there they moved to the cliffs at Courthouse Crossing, the Red Rock Museum and finally to Tlaquepaque, a dazzling cluster of shops and galleries where they lingered over coffee and compared their favorite mental snapshots of the day. Conner opted for one of her and Emma by the creek before their picnic lunch, and she chose the cliffside trail where the scent of piñon had stayed in her senses ever since.

''They ought to make that into some kind of perfume,'' she observed, and he clapped the baby's hands as if she were applauding.

"Emma votes yes," he announced. "And while we're voting, I bet she'll go for this one, too. Let's stay tonight, and do the whole New Year's Eve countdown thing."

She would have argued harder, Lucy suspected, if she weren't so relaxed from the past half hour of sitting leisurely at the coffee bar, watching people meander through the courtyard and feeling like part of a happy-weekend painting. Tomorrow was technically a day off, they'd bought plenty of diapers at the grocery store last night, and she could wash out her and Emma's clothes in the bathroom sink.

"Okay," she said, and saw Con's start of surprise at such an easy agreement before he immediately presented another idea.

"I'll bet the hotel can get a sitter," he suggested, and she set down her coffee cup.

"No."

Conner looked back and forth from her to the baby. "You want to bring Emma with us," he asked, "to ring in the New Year?"

The idea of Emma blowing horns and waving her fists at midnight was darling, but it would be silly to wake up a contented baby for five minutes of jubilation. "No," Lucy answered, "but we don't need a sitter. We can celebrate right in our room."

"We could, sure." He hesitated, shifting Emma on his lap before returning his gaze to her. "It's just...well, I'd like to watch the countdown with you, see all the confetti and stuff...."

That was sweet. And she liked the implications of beginning the new year together. But a hotel party, with everyone dressed in their holiday glitter...

"I don't know why," Con muttered, "I've just got this idea of how New Year's is supposed to—" Then he broke off, looking abashed. "It's stupid."

"No, it's not," she protested. Especially after the past two years, which she suspected he'd spent in the darkness of solitary anguish. "Everybody gets ideas of how things should be."

"Maybe so." He glanced down at the baby again, then faced her with an expression that seemed almost shy. "Anyway, that's…I guess that's my fantasy for New Year's Eve. It's just—"

"It's a good one," Lucy interrupted, standing up to take Emma from him and settling the baby on her shoulder. Surely, as soon as naptime was over, she could find some reasonable party clothes at the shopping center they'd visited last night. "Let's see if we can get a sitter first, and I need to make sure it's someone Emma likes. Meanwhile, if she's not going to sleep in the car, I ought to get her down for a nap."

Within fifteen minutes she was settling her daughter into the same spacious crib they'd used last night, marveling at Con's ability to arrange another stay at the kind of place most people would spend months saving up for. He dismissed it as casually as if she'd remarked on his ability to open a jar, and left her with Emma while he went to "take care of things for tonight. See you pretty soon."

She dozed off for what felt like only a few minutes before a knock at the door revealed a clerk from the gift shop, carrying a silky red dress that looked as if it had been made for her. "Just call extension 312 if you need anything changed," the girl ordered, and left her with not only the garment bag and boxes, but also a note in Conner's strong handwriting.

I'm enjoying the fantasy already. C.

This was the stuff of fantasy, all right, Lucy decided, holding the dress up in front of her and glorying at the sight in the mirror. She wouldn't change a thing about it, unless it were his signature on the note—"Love" would have been a nice closing—but that was her own fantasy, and meanwhile Conner's was a pleasure to share. Someone at the gift shop must have enjoyed picking out the perfect trimmings for a night of celebration, from the exquisite shoes to the kind of underwear she couldn't wait to show him. The bracelet and earrings worried her a little—those couldn't be real rubies, could they?—but in the spirit of fantasy, she tried them on as well.

No sooner had she finished her dress rehearsal than the phone rang, and Conner announced he'd run into a slight delay. "But there are three sitters coming at six, so you can take your choice or keep them all, and I'll pick you up right after."

He knew how to make things eventful, she reflected, gazing at her reflection with wonder. He knew how to do the whole Prince Charming thing with such dazzling competence that she felt a little awed. But, like he'd said, this was fantasy. This was just one night of enjoyment before heading back to real life.

It wasn't until she opened the last box and found a vial labeled Lucy's Piñon Perfume that she found herself on the verge of tears. This was just too much, too much splendor and grandeur all at once, and she wanted to enjoy every minute of it...

But this was too much.

She took a deep breath and touched her finger to the perfume, dabbed a little on her wrist and the back of her neck, then set the vial down beside the earring box.

This had to stop.

Emma set up a small cry, and Lucy hurried to retrieve her from the crib. Holding her daughter close, she settled down by the window and tried to make herself think.

But all she could think of was her mother holding a vial of perfume with the exact same expression as her own. With that look of giddy enjoyment that came from accepting the kind of gifts she'd been accepting from Conner all week. All those years, all those presents, all those men offering vacations and jewelry and—

And her mother insisting they were tokens of love.

Maybe they were, Lucy told herself, startled at how intensely she wanted to believe that. It was frighteningly easy, all of a sudden, to see how such thinking could sneak up on you. It wasn't so much a case of greed, accepting gift after gift after gift....

It's wanting to believe he loves you.

She jumped up, hurrying Emma away from the mirror so neither of them could see the desperation on her face.

Conner still wasn't saying he loved her. He wasn't even letting her say it to him, and for the first time—all at once, as if a curtain had risen—she wondered whether the gifts were his attempt to make up for that omission.

Because the omission felt darker than she'd let herself acknowledge until now. Felt more ominous. More disturbing.

As if there might be some truth to what he'd been saying all along, when he explained that he couldn't love. Which had to be wrong—after all, even neglected orphans could learn to love as adults—but maybe, after feeling like he'd failed his son and his wife, he was scared to even *try*.

Maybe he'd rather just offer her money...

And here she'd been letting him do it, she realized with a sickening lurch of her heart. Letting him give her ballet tickets, picture frames, diamond lockets and dinners and resort vacations as though that was all she cared about, as though money was as good as love...and she couldn't keep letting him think that, couldn't keep letting him *do* that, it had to stop!

He had to stop. And she had to tell him so.

Tonight.

"Tonight," Conner told her, touching his champagne glass to hers, "you look like fireworks." From the minute he'd seen her waiting for him, so vibrant and glowing that the whole world seemed centered within this woman, he'd felt dazzled at the prospect of welcoming a new year in her company. "All bright, and sparkly, and...and it's like I can't look away, because I don't want to miss anything."

She gazed at him over the rim of her glass, without ever taking a sip. "Thank you." Then she shook her hair off her forehead in a riotous shower of curls, and sent him a challenging smile. "This *is* your fantasy, right?"

That might have been the wrong word, Con realized, because it sounded like all he wanted was some spectacular female sharing his table. "I shouldn't have said that," he corrected himself. "You're more than just a fantasy."

"Well, good." Lucy glanced down at the bracelet sparkling on her wrist, then met his gaze with a troubled expression. "I was getting worried, there."

Just because he'd given her something to enjoy? "No, come on," he protested. "I wanted you to have something nice, that's all."

She set down her champagne glass, still untouched, and from the sudden tension in her bare shoulders he realized that she was preparing for something significant. "Conner," she said, "listen to me. I don't *want* ruby earrings."

She wasn't even wearing them, he realized with a start. It wasn't like she needed anything extra, looking as good as she did, but—

"I don't want you throwing money at me," Lucy continued, then drew a shaky breath and looked at him straight. "I just want...you."

He felt a rush of elation, immediately followed by a tremor of warning—she wasn't talking long-term, was she? She couldn't be thinking beyond the next few weeks, could she?

No, Con decided, she was smarter than that. Knowing him the way she did, she sure wouldn't go looking for heartbreak. She was just being her usual, straightforward self, assuring him that money wasn't why she wanted him.

"Same here," he answered, and saw the light of relief in her eyes. Damn, she must have been worried about him pitching a fit, insisting that her smile was worth any price. Which was actually pretty close to the truth, even if she didn't want to hear it. "I like making you happy."

"Well, good. So quit buying me things." She reached across the corner of the table, touching his shoulder as if her order needed all the emphasis she could manage. "I mean it. You don't owe me anything."

But she was wrong there, Conner knew. A few pieces of jewelry were trivial compared to what she'd done for him. "I owe you everything," he corrected her, feeling a sudden tightness in his throat. "Lucy, you got me through this whole holiday season."

"I wasn't doing it as a favor!"

"No, I know. I know." She was doing it because she cared about him, same as he cared about her, so why did she sound so upset? "And I'm not trying to make this some kind of a trade deal. It's just, I see you and Emma, and I want to…"

He faltered, knowing he was close to shaky ground. Wanting to take care of her and Emma wasn't what she needed to hear, even though it was the rock-bottom truth. Wanting to make her happy might be more acceptable, and that was true as well…but already Lucy was finishing the sentence for him.

"You want to help us," she said, "but that's not your job." Then she fixed him with a stern gaze, as if daring him to answer otherwise. "Is it?"

Maybe not technically, but he'd be damned if he was going to give up caring for her. "Lucy…"

"Look," she interrupted, evidently sensing his uneasiness, "I'm asking you to promise me something. No more gifts."

That would be a tough promise to keep, he knew. It wasn't like photos and jewelry and celebrations were the only way to make her happy, of course. But it wasn't like he had anything else to give.

"How about," he asked lightly, "just on your birthday?"

"No," she said, and her troubled expression didn't change. "Conner, I mean it. No more gifts. I can't do it."

She was serious about this, Con realized, and there was no way out except agreement. So he took her hand, clasped it in his and rested it over his heart.

"No more gifts," he pledged, knowing even as he spoke that there had to be something else he could give her. This woman deserved so much more than a promise to forget her birthday, and yet aside from another two weeks of entertainment, what the hell did he have to offer?

If only he could love her...

But he'd been down that road already, and he wasn't going to put Lucy through the same despair he'd already inflicted on Margie. For a few months, sure, he could go through all the motions, but when it came to the long term, that sure didn't add up to love.

He'd thought it would, when he married the ideal woman for a rising young attorney. He'd thought anyone could figure out how to love a family, even if they'd never experienced it firsthand, simply by remembering birthdays and providing the right gifts, offering regular compliments and remaining scrupulously faithful.

But he'd realized two years ago that such habits weren't nearly enough, and that Margie had seen through him all along. She had refrained from complaining until after he let Bryan die, but she'd been right on target when she told him after the funeral that he was simply incapable of loving anyone.

"You promise?" Lucy asked, and he gripped her hand tighter.

This woman deserved the best he could give her, and what that meant was to get out of her life before these first few weeks of exhilaration faded. To let her forget about him the minute he returned to Philadelphia.

And if the thought of leaving her made his soul ache, well, that was just too damn bad.

Conner reached with his free hand for his champagne glass and downed the contents in three quick gulps before concluding his pledge.

"I give you my word," he said, and released her hand. "But, Lucy, just so we're clear…if you ever need me for anything, I'll be there."

She watched him silently for a moment, looking a little troubled by his conclusion, then straightened her posture and gave him a bright smile. "Well, that's nice. Thank you. I might need you to carry me back to the room if they're going to keep filling our glasses."

She hadn't taken two sips all evening, but he responded in the same lighthearted tone that carrying her would be his pleasure, and he proved it to her shortly after midnight even though Lucy insisted she could walk just fine. She could, he knew, but he liked how she felt in his arms—so warm, so light and exuberant against him, as if he could follow wherever she floated.

And, damn! he was going to miss her.

It was his first thought the next morning, and he suspected that the old superstition about repeating the same thought all year long might be valid this time around. Conner spent most of the drive back to Scottsdale fantasizing about miracles—about discovering he'd actually loved Margie and Bryan all along and simply never noticed it, about Lucy declaring she and Emma wanted financial security more than lifelong love—and felt a shameful sense of relief when she assured him that napping all the way home would be fine with her.

"Emma and I will stay out of your way," she yawned, and left him to his own thoughts. She did the same thing at home, devoting herself to the laundry without even questioning why he attacked the work piled up in the office so fiercely. Of course she would blame it on the two-day vacation, he realized when she poked her head in the office to say good-night; of course she would assume that he was making up for lost time by starting the new year with renewed determination.

Which was true, in a way. Work had always been his refuge, and even though he still couldn't risk more than twelve hours it was convenient to have so much work on his desk. Convenient that he'd have it with him tomorrow in Seattle, where otherwise he might find himself missing Lucy too intensely. Convenient, Con reflected ruefully as he packed his travel bag in the dark to avoid waking her at midnight, that this three-day trip would give him time to figure out how to make things right.

Because he had to make sure she was taken care of before heading back to Philadelphia.

He'd generated two new lists for handwritten notes, which should keep her in paychecks for another month, and left them for her to find after she returned from dropping him at the airport tomorrow morning. But that still wasn't enough. Somehow he had to come up with more than a child-support account, which Lucy could very well refuse, without breaking his promise of no more gifts.

It wasn't until he heard a whimper from Emma, who fell silent again a moment later, that he realized the baby might be his best bet. After all, taking care of his niece was completely different than taking care of a woman he couldn't keep in his life.

A woman who wanted the best possible life for her daughter.

Which made it fortunate, Conner realized with a flash of triumph as he retrieved his trust-fund number from the office, that he'd never promised anything about gifts for Emma…

Emma seemed fussy the next morning, maybe sensing the tension in the car as they arrived at the Phoenix airport. "Too much travel," Lucy observed, waiting while he took his carry-on bag and computer from the trunk of the car. "Either that, or she's wishing you didn't have to fly."

"It's all right." For once he would welcome the turmoil of being trapped in a metal shell miles above the earth, because at least it would take his mind off Lucy. Off the need to play fair, the need to look out for her over the long term.

The need to leave her free for someone who could love.

That's the best you can do for her.

He knew that. Conner shouldered his bag and slammed the trunk shut.

You've got to do it.

He knew that, too. And he had to give Lucy his keys to drive home with, but that still didn't make it any easier to turn and face her.

To mumble something about taking care, checking for messages, seeing her Thursday, whatever else people said at airport drop-offs. To know that this morning was only a preview of the final goodbye.

"I'll miss you," Conner blurted, and she threw herself into his embrace with all the fervor he'd longed for last night while clenching his fists against the mattress to keep from waking her up.

"I'll miss you, too," she murmured, cupping her hands against his face for a farewell kiss and surprising him with the sheen of tears in her eyes.

God, was this as hard for her as it was for him? He pulled her back against him, holding her as close as he could even while his mind railed at his screaming senses that he had to let her go. They couldn't spend the whole day here at the airport curb. They couldn't spend the rest of their lives together.

"We'll get through this," Con said hoarsely, and managed to let her go.

But it took every fiber of strength he possessed to walk

through the glass doors of the terminal, still feeling her body in every cell of his own, and not turn around.

He couldn't turn around. He couldn't go back. No matter how much it hurt to leave her now, it was better this way.

It was better this way.

It was better this way.

"All better," Lucy told her daughter, adjusting the blanket in her car seat and wishing she could move Emma up front. Having company beside her would make the drive home go faster, although she'd probably hurt just as much at home as she was hurting here by the airport curb.

Because he hadn't looked back. Not once. She'd stood by the car waiting for him to turn around, waiting for him to wave goodbye, waiting even after he disappeared into the distance and left her with the stark realization that Conner was already gone.

That his absence had begun a long time ago.

"I just didn't realize," she murmured to the baby, who didn't seem to be paying much attention. "Everything was all right until I said I loved him...."

But what was she supposed to do, keep it a secret? Pretend she hadn't noticed he was giving her money instead of love?

"We'll get through this."

Right. Of course they would. Maybe he just needed a few days apart to get used to the idea that he could love her and Emma just fine. To realize their relationship didn't necessarily have to end when he returned to Philadelphia. To recognize the difference between offering gifts and offering his heart.

She had done the right thing, Lucy assured herself as she drove home and put Emma down for a nap. She'd explained as clearly as she could that presents weren't what she wanted, and now it was up to him to acknowledge that he was capable of more.

At least she hoped so.

But the discovery of more work in the office startled her. Conner must have been up all night, setting out new assignments for her, and the implication was confusing. It would take at least another month to finish this many letters, but wasn't he leaving sooner than that?

"He said he was only here until January fifteenth," she told Shawna on the phone that evening. "But he's left me work that'll last way beyond that."

"So you think," her friend asked, "maybe he's planning to stay longer?"

"I don't know." She rested the phone against her shoulder and rinsed the coffee mugs they'd left in the sink. "His company wanted him to go see this client in Sedona, and they're doing a whole bunch of business together. But you'd think he would've said something."

"And the way he looks at you *isn't* saying something? Lucy, he's crazy about you!"

She wished she could believe that. But he certainly hadn't mentioned any plans for a future together, although the thought had sneaked into her fantasies several times over the past week. "I guess I'll find out," Lucy said as she opened the dishwasher. "I told him in Sedona, I didn't want any more gifts—I just want him."

"Put it right out there, huh?"

"Well, what else could I do? If he doesn't love me, he doesn't." She jammed the mugs into the top rack and slammed it shut. "Anyway, men leave."

There was a silence. Then her friend said gently, "Not when they love you."

Well, maybe not. And while saying goodbye at the airport this morning, he'd sure *looked* as if he loved her. "Maybe being apart will make him realize it," Lucy murmured. Maybe he was already missing her as much as she missed him....

But he didn't call that night, and when she fed Emma at

two in the morning and saw no messages on the answering machine, she felt a twinge of dismay. He might just be busy, of course, but how much time would it take to phone and say hi?

This was bizarre, staring at the answering machine and wishing for a flashing green light. How many times had she sat here in the dark, dreaming of her unborn child, or half-asleep while Emma drowsed through a midnight feeding, and wishing fervently for a moment of contact? Never once, and she'd been alone in the house from March through November. But until now, she had never felt such a void.

Until now, she had never realized how acutely silence could hurt.

The silence didn't keep her from finishing eleven letters the next morning, before she realized that even a mariachi CD would be better than waiting for Conner to call. So it was against the music of "La Cucaracha" that she heard the doorbell ring, signed for an overnight-delivery letter, and saw with a flicker of surprise that it was addressed to her.

Not in his handwriting, though. Something official looking, the size of a business packet, but with the elegance of a wedding invitation on thick, creamy paper. She ripped it open and drew out a letter announcing that Conner Tarkington's niece could choose from any of the following schools for her college scholarship—

What?

Maybe it was a marketing scam, Lucy decided. Nobody was asking for donations, but maybe it was some kind of practical joke.

Her hands were cold, though, and drawing a full breath seemed to take an enormous effort.

Conner was sending her money.

Exactly the way Kenny had done.

She folded the letter back into thirds, then grabbed the top edge and yanked with both hands.

But the paper was too thick to tear, and she desperately

crumpled it between her fists. How could he *do* that? What made him think a scholarship for Emma was any better than ruby earrings? It was different, she had to give him credit for that, but it was still throwing money at her, and right after he'd promised "no more gifts."

Unless he'd sent this last week. She unfolded the crumpled page with shaky hands and scanned it again, but the dates were wretchedly clear. Conner must have decided on the way to Seattle yesterday that he should phone some trust administrator and…and pay her off.

Because that's what this was. A way of detaching himself without actually saying the relationship was over. Not as directly as Kenny had said it, but still he had to know how she'd react. He had to know she couldn't take this, couldn't let him spend that kind of money—much less for his list of "the following schools." That was exactly the kind of control she'd seen from her mother's gentlemen, and that wasn't something she could accept. He might think she'd change her mind if it benefited Emma, but—

Emma deserves to go to college.

Lucy faltered, clenching the letter in her fists, then set it down on the desk and picked up her daughter from the baby carrier. Still laboring for a full breath, she held Emma close against her and tried to take comfort in the baby's soft warmth.

Emma deserved the best of everything.

"Don't you?" she whispered to the baby, who cooed in response. "You do, sweetie. Mommy wants you to have the best life you can."

Such a life might not have included many frills, but nobody *needed* satin quilts and bronze baby shoes and new portraits every month. Nobody needed pony rides, either, or steak dinners and designer fashions and a car on their sixteenth birthday. But Emma would have everything that mattered, and that vow hadn't changed since Lucy made it last spring.

So, yes, Emma deserved to go to college.

But not like this. Not with some gentleman decreeing which schools were acceptable. She couldn't raise her daughter with the same "have to get along" attitude that she'd endured from her own mother, couldn't put Emma through the kind of life that sacrificed every scrap of pride to ensure that the bills were paid.

Because if her daughter was going to have a decent life, there were things that mattered far more than college. And one of them was self-respect.

Which meant refusing to accept any other gifts from a man who offered money instead of love.

"This has to stop," she murmured to Emma, swallowing against a sudden tightness in her throat. "I'm not letting anyone boss you around." Or worse yet, walk out as soon as the child grew attached to him. "I promise, I won't *ever* let that happen to you."

Emma offered no response as she returned to the office, but Lucy already knew from the ache in her heart what she had to do. She couldn't stay here, letting herself slide back into the tempting comfort of depending on a Tarkington's generosity. She had to make her hands stop trembling long enough to stack these notes in a neat pile, pack everything she owned into a couple of shopping bags, and find someplace else to live.

Now.

Before Conner could fly back from Seattle. Before he could coax her into staying, which she already knew he could do far too easily. A night in his arms, a promise that things would be different this time, and she'd be right back in the same pattern she'd grown up watching.

And so would Emma.

"We don't need Conner," she assured her daughter in a shaky voice. "He isn't a scumbag—he probably tried really hard to love us—but he said all along he couldn't do it, and Mommy just wasn't listening."

Emma wriggled in her embrace, and Lucy kissed her forehead through suddenly tear-clouded vision.

"I'm not making any more mistakes like that," she told the baby, shifting her to one shoulder and letting the tears spill over in a rush. "I was stupid once before, and I was almost stupid again this time." This time she'd pretended that unspoken love would make everything all right, and wound up accepting far more than she should. "But I promise you, Emma...that's never going to happen again."

Chapter Nine

This would happen again, Conner promised himself as the last two kids and their parents left SeattleSweets with his thanks for a good hour of opinions on after-school care. He was going to keep this up, keep meeting kids and talking to them and functioning—even with the eight-year-old boys—like a normal, reasonable adult.

No more hiding from grief. No more avoiding memories of Bryan. He was going to talk with as many children as he could, face whatever turmoil might come up, ache if he had to, and then move on.

Like he was moving right now, he acknowledged as he took off through Pike Place Market on the way to his next meeting.

And it was all thanks to Lucy.

She'd given him the courage to face these kids, given him so much more than she seemed to realize. Which made it all the harder to know he couldn't ask her for anything more, couldn't even give her the kind of thanks she deserved....

Better stop thinking about Lucy.

A scholarship for Emma wasn't nearly enough, but there had to be something else he could do.

Inviting her to Philadelphia wouldn't be fair, not when he couldn't offer her the kind of love that worked. Although, Conner remembered with a jolt of hope, she hadn't actually *said* she wanted his love.

She'd just said she wanted him.

So might she want him the same way in Philadelphia?

Stop thinking about Lucy!

But the question nagged at him for the rest of the afternoon, through two more investor meetings, then all the way back to his hotel...where he forced himself not to dive straight for the phone and ask about her day, tell her about the kids, do whatever it took to maintain the connection between them. This whole trip was supposed to help them drift apart, help him do the right thing, and calling Scottsdale every time he thought of her was contrary to the whole spirit of easing off gradually.

The least he could do for Lucy was give her the gift of withdrawal.

But even so, his second night without her was tougher than the first. He found himself envisioning the neighborhood surrounding his Philadelphia townhouse, trying to remember whether he'd ever seen a dance studio nearby, wondering if she might enjoy the coffee vendor he passed every morning on the way to work. He was getting way ahead of himself, Conner knew, but the fantasy of Lucy and Emma staying with him was impossible to set aside.

Which meant, he resolved the next day while waiting for a cab to the airport, that he could at least *ask* how she'd feel about it.

Just ask. No pressure. If she didn't like the idea, he wasn't going to push her—that would be almost like asking for love, which was pointless. Stupid. A complete waste of time.

But just asking if she'd like to visit Philadelphia…there was nothing wrong with that.

Still, he wasn't going to ask her on the phone. In person was better, and he'd be home in another six hours. Always assuming, Con reminded himself when his flight took off and he opened his laptop, that this pilot knew what he was doing and got them back to Phoenix in one piece.

"Sir, can I get you anything?" the flight attendant asked, and he realized he was gripping the armrests of his seat more tightly than usual. It took him a moment to respond, to maintain that everything was fine, and he remembered with relief that he hadn't yet reached his twelve hours of work. Surely a summary of the Seattle commitments would keep him focused on business.

Or maybe on the distance to the emergency exit, as usual, but either way he wouldn't be obsessing about Lucy.

About how soon he would see her. About how much he'd missed her. About why, a few hours later, she still hadn't answered the phone.

Of course she had no idea what time his flight would arrive, and he should have called her for an airport pickup earlier instead of waiting until somewhere over Utah. But maybe it was just as well she'd gone out with Emma someplace, because hearing her voice might make it harder to wait before asking her to Philadelphia.

And he had to ask her just right.

Even though a cross-country trip was probably the kind of thing a woman like Lucy could do at a moment's notice, he couldn't just blurt it out. No, he had to keep things relaxed. Easy, not demanding. Not expecting, not really even hoping.

Because that never worked.

"We'll be landing in a few minutes, sir," the flight attendant told him, and Conner glanced at his watch without loosening his grip on the armrest. Lucy would surely be home by now, but he'd have to wait until they landed to try phoning again. And by that time, he could take a cab home a lot faster than waiting for her to drive in from Scottsdale.

Taking a cab, it'd only be another hour before he was walking in the door and…

Stop thinking about Lucy.

But to see her smile, to hear her laugh, to hold her close again.… This could work, Con told himself, closing his eyes to let the vision of her take shape. She'd said only a few days ago, at their New Year's Eve dinner, that she wanted him. And she hadn't said anything about wanting love.

"Ladies and gentlemen, welcome to Phoenix. The local temperature is seventy-one degrees, and we thank you for flying with us today."

The landing was smoother than usual, maybe because he couldn't seem to get his mind off Lucy. Although, considering that within fifty-five minutes he'd have her in his arms again, maybe there was no point in trying to think about anything else.

It took him more than an hour to get home, though, with late-afternoon traffic clogging the streets, and he felt his impatience simmering higher than usual by the time the cab driver dropped him at the front door. No sign of Lucy when he stepped inside, which meant she was in the laundry room, one of the bedrooms or just coming in from the garage.

"Lucy?" he called, starting for the laundry room because that was closest, then realized that the baby swing in the corner was gone. She must have decided to rearrange things, done some kind of massive cleaning, because somehow the whole house felt different…although he couldn't tell exactly what had changed.

None of her clothes in the laundry room, none of Emma's blankets. It was funny how much emptier the small room felt without her nearby, although she was probably coming back any minute from the grocery store or wherever she'd gone.

He deposited his laptop on the dining-room table and took his travel bag to the bedroom, where the bed was made more smoothly than he remembered ever seeing it. Lucy had really gone out of her way to spruce things up, with everything neatly in place…except on the dresser, where his car keys sat in the very center of the polished mahogany surface.

She wasn't at the grocery store, then. Not when he'd told her to take the car whenever and wherever she wanted. Which meant she and Emma must have walked over to the park across the street, and he could be there in two minutes.

Conner pocketed his car keys and started down the hall, wishing he'd thought to bring Emma a balloon for enjoying at the park. In fact—

He stopped short at the guest-room door, staring at the sudden absence of baby blankets, of the cushioned drawer beside the bed, of all the trappings that meant a baby lived here.

What the hell?

The room was strangely tidy, as if no one had occupied it in a long time. And there, on the dresser where he'd changed Emma's diapers for the past month, lay an envelope…and Lucy's ruby earrings.

He felt a tremor of panic racing through his veins, even as he tried to make sense of the image before him. Same as he'd done when he saw Bryan in the street, felt himself hurtling from disbelief to despair to stark, raw grief—and back to the certainty that this couldn't be happening, this was all just some bizarre mistake.

Lucy couldn't have moved out.

But he had trouble picking up the envelope—his hands didn't seem to be working right—and when he saw his name on the front he felt a cold weight spreading from his heart through his body.

The wrinkled letter inside was from the trust company he'd used to fund Emma's scholarship, but the top margin contained a note in Lucy's handwriting. Writing he'd seen on dozens of message slips over the past five weeks, writing as fluid and vibrant as Lucy herself. Writing which seemed to wobble on the page, impossible to take in, until he drew a deep breath and squinted at the message.

''The office notes are organized for whoever the temp agency sends to replace me, because I just can't take this. Thanks, anyway.''

And that was all.

But it didn't make sense. She couldn't be moving out just because he'd arranged an education for Emma.

Could she?

No, that was ludicrous. That was impossible. That was like Bryan dying. Things like that just didn't happen right out of nowhere, without any warning.

''I don't want you throwing money at me.''

But he wasn't throwing money at her! He was looking out for her daughter, which was a completely different thing. This wasn't like buying her gifts, this wasn't like ruby earrings.

Earrings which she'd left sitting on the dresser.

And there, Conner saw with a sudden twist of despair, there was the locket he'd given her. There was the bracelet from New Year's Eve. The framed picture of her and Emma on top of Squaw Peak...what was she thinking, leaving all these gifts in a neat little pile?

What the hell was she *doing?* Giving back everything he'd meant for her and Emma, leaving without a word of farewell—well, unless you counted that note on the scholarship letter—but that didn't make sense. None of this made sense, it had to be some kind of mistake.

Lucy couldn't just walk out. Not like this.

He crushed the letter in his fists and hurled it onto the

bed. This wasn't happening. This wasn't possible. He had to straighten this out.

He had to find Lucy.

Shawna might know something, and although he'd never seen her phone number he still had Lorraine's. The elderly sitter was delighted to hear from him, asked about Emma, and sounded shocked when he explained that only Shawna could tell him where Lucy and her baby had gone. "You tell my granddaughter," Lorraine instructed, "that if she knows where to find Lucy, she'd better spit it right out."

But Shawna flatly refused. "Lucy doesn't need you throwing money at her," her friend insisted. "If she wants to call you, she knows where the phone is, but don't hold your breath."

She knows where the phone is? If she was living someplace without a phone, she must have taken Emma to some fleabag apartment…and, damn it, that didn't make sense! "Just tell me where to find her," Conner repeated in his best intimidate-the-witness voice, but it didn't work on Shawna. Which meant his only other option was the temporary agency—she must have called someone about a replacement for her job—but he wasn't likely to get much help from a temp agency after business hours.

Still, he tried every possibility in the phone book before admitting defeat and driving over to Shawna and Jeff's apartment…only to find it deserted, which must mean they were working a night shift.

He tried phoning again at two in the morning and got no answer, and again at five before realizing there was no use pursuing Lucy's friends when the temp agencies would open in another few hours. And if it took him all day, Con resolved as he returned to the phone book a few minutes before seven, he was going to get things straightened out…because he had to make things right.

He had to make her understand.

Damn it, he had to find Lucy!

* * *

"We have to find you a bigger sweater," Lucy told Emma, bundling her daughter into the baby sweater that had fit just fine until now. Emma was growing faster each day, it seemed like, and this sweater was only another example. "But for now we'll just use the old one and put Mommy's sweater on top of it, because we're going outside to the pay phone."

Van and Mary Ellen, who ran the diner where she'd worked until last month, had told her to call back early this morning and see if her replacement had returned from Christmas vacation in Denver. If not, they'd be glad to have her start work immediately.

"You can stay in the kitchen with me like we used to," she promised the baby, "if Rose doesn't come back. But if this job doesn't work out, we have a whole week to find something else. So we're going to be fine."

Emma seemed satisfied with that, and Lucy carried her out to the pay phone at the corner of the mobile home park where they'd moved in yesterday. It had been a relief to know she could afford the deposit with enough left for cleaning supplies, and an even greater relief that such a small unit didn't need much cleaning, because after leaving the Tarkingtons' place in such perfect shape that no one could claim she owed them *any*thing, she was tired of scrubbing tile.

Still, if the diner would hire her back to scrub carrots or dishes or whatever needed it, she'd jump at the chance. And when Mary Ellen asked if she could come back to work this afternoon, she was delighted to agree. That would give her a few more hours to organize their new home, to find the best place for Emma's swing, to hang the freshly washed towels in the bathroom to dry.

To convince herself that leaving Conner's gifts behind—even the photos, which she missed even more acutely today—was her only possible choice.

"Because," she told her daughter as they returned to the tiny trailer, "if we kept letting him give us things, we'd never take care of ourselves again. We'd sit around hoping he still loved us, and that's not how we want to live. Is it?"

Emma wriggled in her arms, which Lucy decided to take as an expression of agreement. "We don't need him taking care of us," she assured the baby as she fished the key from the pocket of her jeans and twisted it in the lock. The maneuver took all her strength, but maybe dripping oil on the hinges would help. "We can open doors just fine."

She repeated that to herself three times over the next hour as she carried Emma back and forth from the laundry room, returning for the soap she'd left behind, and finally retrieving the towels she'd used to scrub the floors last night. Everything else she could wash in the kitchen sink, but she wasn't going to put Emma near a towel which had touched those pitted linoleum floors.

There was no point in paying to use the laundry-room dryer, though, when she could just as well hang the towels in her own bathroom. She hadn't really appreciated the convenience of a free washer and dryer at Conner's house, Lucy reflected as she dropped the wet load in the chipped white washbasin and shook out the first damp towel.

But independence mattered far more than convenience.

She draped the towel over the flimsy shower rod and picked up the next, then heard a knock at the door. Tracie already? The two-doors-down neighbor had introduced herself yesterday and promised to stop by for iced tea sometime, but nine-thirty in the morning was a little early for iced tea...especially with no teabags in the house. So, in case Tracie needed proof that this wasn't a good time for visiting, she took the wet towel with her.

But when she opened the door and saw Conner outside, she very nearly dropped it. The sight of him was so unexpected—and so disturbingly welcome—that she felt a rush of sensation all through her skin before she could remember that this man didn't belong in her life.

He didn't seem to realize that, though, because he stepped inside as soon as she opened the door. Looking exactly the way she'd seen him in her dreams last night, with that endearing mixture of well-hidden shyness and innately compelling confidence. "Lucy," he demanded, "what are you *doing?*"

It was none of his business, but even so her heart had already picked up speed at simply having him so close. Which was a bad sign, she knew. She had to remember the importance of taking care of herself. "Hanging up towels," she answered, gesturing with the one in her hands.

"No, I mean—" He stared at her in disbelief, then yanked the towel from her grasp and dropped it on the kitchen table. "I got home and you were gone!"

How could *he* be upset when he was the one who'd broken that no-gifts promise? Lucy folded her arms across her chest, hoping such a show of defiance would make her feel as strong as she looked. "Didn't you get my note?"

"Yes," he said bitterly, "after the temp agencies closed for the day. So I started calling first thing this morning, and found someone who said you'd talked about her old neighborhood." His gaze moved across the entire unfinished room in one horrified moment, then returned to her with an incredulous expression. "You just packed up and moved *here?*"

"I was planning to move all along, remember?" she reminded him. He had no right to sound so accusing, to look as if she'd lost her mind. She knew perfectly well what she was doing. "And it's time Emma and I got a place of our own."

"But—" Conner broke off, hesitated a moment, then shoved his hands in his pockets and looked at her straight. "Back in Sedona," he said grimly, "you said you wanted me."

She still did, which made it hard to stand her ground. Lucy backed up a few steps, trying to regain her balance, but even though he made no move toward her, she could almost feel the heat radiating from him as he burst out, "You said you loved me!"

She had, she still did, and all the while he'd kept insisting that he *couldn't* love her.

But she hadn't really believed it until that final payoff arrived.

"I made a mistake," she replied, picking up Emma from the baby carrier, which rested outside the bathroom door in the narrow hallway. "That's why we had to get out."

"Get out and come *here?*" Glancing at the battered walls and the stained sofa, he turned to her with a look of barely suppressed fury as he gestured toward the baby. "Lucy, you can't raise her in a place like this! We've got a perfectly good house sitting vacant."

Not exactly vacant, and that was as big a reason as independence to stay away from the Tarkingtons' house. Maybe even bigger.

"I'm not moving back in with you," she protested, and he cut her off with a quick lift of his hand.

"Fine. No one's asking you to. I'll be in Chicago next week, and I can move the— Hell, I'll move out today if you want."

He meant it, Lucy realized with an aching tremor of regret. He would actually move into some hotel to make sure she and Emma were taken care of, but he wouldn't dream of fighting to keep them in his life.

"Whatever it takes," Conner concluded, shoving his hands in his pockets again as if realizing how easy it would be to touch her, and what a mistake that would be. "But I can't let you stay here."

As if he had any say in where she lived! As if she was still his responsibility.

"Where I live," she reminded him through gritted teeth, "is not your decision."

He acknowledged that with a sharp breath, and she could see him make a deliberate effort to relax his posture. Then he braced himself against the doorframe and met her gaze, sending another unwanted flutter of warmth through her. If only the man didn't look so good.

"I'm worried about you," he said, making her heart lurch in spite of her better judgment. If only— "And Emma."

She felt a sudden flicker of panic at how easy it would be to give in, to let him keep providing the kind of gifts she'd found herself all too ready to accept. At how easy it was to imagine enjoying another few years together. Looking forward to his lovemaking, living comfortably on his terms, letting him dictate where she and Emma spent their days...

"No, I can't," she blurted, and saw his startled reaction to the intensity in her voice. Still watching her with a newly curious gaze, he looked as if he'd just noticed the same weakness she felt, and when he shifted his stance from the door frame, she instinctively took a step back and lifted both hands. "Conner, please just get out of my life. This is hard enough as it is."

He didn't move, which should have been a greater relief than it was, but she could see the crackle of anger in his eyes. "It *should* be hard, damn it! You can't just walk out and tell me to quit taking care of you and Emma."

But that was exactly what she'd been telling him all along, and his last gift was proof that he'd never really understood her. That he never really would.

"Yes, I can," she retorted, turning back to smooth the crumpled towel on the kitchen table as a shield of activity. "You're not my boss anymore."

"Fine, I'm not." The grittiness in his voice reminded her all too clearly of how he sounded in bed, and when she made the mistake of glancing his way she could feel the familiar heat still resonating between them. "But—"

"You're not my boss," Lucy interrupted, "and you're not my…my…" She couldn't quite finish the sentence—after all, he'd never been her boyfriend, exactly—but Conner seemed to have no problem concluding it for her.

"Your lover," he said bleakly, as if only now realizing that he'd never quite been that, either. Except in a technical sense.

Which wasn't enough.

No matter how good they'd been together, it wasn't enough.

"You said all along," she acknowledged without quite meeting his gaze, "you couldn't love anyone. I just didn't want to believe it." If only she'd believed it, if only she'd taken him seriously, it would have saved her a lot of grief. "I—I wish I'd listened."

From the barely suppressed pain on his face, she could tell he wished the same thing. "Lucy, I'm sorry," he muttered. "I didn't want you to get hurt."

An apology didn't make much difference, now that the damage was already done. But a man like him would live by such niceties, she knew, which made his latest gift suddenly easier to understand.

"That's why you sent Emma the scholarship money, isn't it," she observed, picking up the flattened towel. It wasn't just taking responsibility for his brother's baby, but trying to make up for the hurt. And yet, either way, it wasn't something she could accept. "Because that's all you'll ever let yourself give."

His jaw tightened, but he didn't attempt to deny it. Instead, he reached for the towel in front of her and held the top half for her to meet with the bottom half. "Even so," he said, "I want to take care of you."

Of course he did, given his sense of family duty. But responsibility wasn't love, and it never would be.

"I know you do," Lucy told him, taking the half-folded towel and finishing the job herself as a signal that there was nothing left to discuss. "But that's not what I want. You can't *give* me what I want," she concluded, moving to open the door for him, "and there's no point even talking about it."

From the darkness in his eyes, she could tell he recognized the truth of that. Still, it took a long moment of waiting, of watching his gaze move from her to Emma and back again, before she saw him square his shoulders in acceptance. As he headed past her to the door, she realized with an ache of regret that her last glimpse of Conner Tarkington would always carry with it the echo of his parting words.

"Damn it, Lucy. I wish I could love you the way you deserve."

Slamming the door behind him was a mistake, Conner knew. It was stupid, it was childish, it was the kind of thing Kenny might have done. It wasn't like Lucy was going to change her mind about him if he went around slamming doors.

Missing her and Emma was even more stupid. He couldn't love them, anyway, so what was the point in wishing they'd come back? After all, it wasn't like he *needed* Lucy to feel whole. It wasn't like he'd spent the past three days missing her exuberant laughter and the warmth of Emma's tiny hand in his. He was better off without them cluttering up his attention, taking time away from his work, because he flat-out couldn't offer Lucy what she wanted.

Even so, he found himself tensing at every stoplight on the drive home, trying to think of how he could have handled the past half hour better. He'd argued the wrong line, gotten her defenses up to the point where she might refuse any assistance whatsoever. And yet how could he let her and Emma stay in that rattrap?

Maybe slamming doors wasn't the answer, Con admitted as he opened his own front door, but—

"Hey," said Kenny.

The greeting was so familiar that it took him a moment to realize his brother hadn't been here all along. Conner had quit expecting him after Christmas and New Year's came and went with no word of his arrival, but nonetheless some long-buried part of himself recognized his earliest companion with an instant flash of acceptance. "When did you get here?"

"Twenty minutes ago." Kenny had evidently made himself at home, because already he'd laid out a putting strip on the living room floor. "I saw your stuff in my bedroom, so I took the other one," he said virtuously, taking aim at the ball and executing a flawless putt. "Want to go play nine holes?"

Nine instead of eighteen, Conner knew, was a concession to his longtime insistence that nobody could afford an entire morning away from the office. "No, I can't. I've got a lot of work backed up."

"C'mon, I'll spot you three strokes." Kenny picked up the ball and tossed it up for a one-handed catch. "Besides, I need some practice. See, I might be getting in a lot more play if everything works out. I've got a great plan for—"

"Hold it," Conner interrupted. There were more important things to discuss than the latest scheme for attracting a tour sponsor. But apparently his brother viewed Lucy as less important than dreams of glory, because he persisted.

"No, this is gonna be what I need. Full sponsorship—"

"I don't want to hear about it!" Con told him. "What I want to know is, did Mom get in touch with you about Emma?"

With a sigh, Kenny abandoned the game of catch. "I had to promise to come visit before she'd even talk about new clubs. So, you satisfied?"

He should have figured their mother would recognize the

fastest way of getting Kenny to show some interest in father-hood, even though such a show wouldn't fool anyone who knew him. "She really wants you to be a dad, huh?"

"Looks like." His brother lined up the ball again, then glanced around the room as if only now noticing there was something missing. "I thought she said Lucy was staying here."

Until yesterday, he had thought the same thing. Even this morning, before he tracked her down in that shabby trailer park, he'd felt certain there was still hope of her returning. But that hope had been replaced by some kind of a void that ached whenever he moved. "No," Conner said tightly. "She left."

"Couldn't stand living with a lawyer, I bet." Kenny shot him a cocky grin, not even waiting for a response before returning his attention to the putt. "You can put me in touch with her, right?"

Yeah, he could, but...

"She doesn't need you messing with her," Con warned. She needed someone who could love her for a lifetime, someone who could give her the kind of wholehearted car-ing she deserved. Someone who could get her and Emma all the—

Oh.

"Unless," he added deliberately, "you're planning to come up with some child support." No matter how she felt about gifts from gentlemen, Lucy couldn't very well refuse to let her child's father pay for a decent standard of living. The only question was whether someone who lived like Kenny could come up with a reasonable amount of money, month after month.

Looking almost smug, Kenny adjusted his grip on the putter. "Well, Mom said she'd help me out...she's really excited about having a granddaughter." Which made sense, although their mother would be in for a surprise if she expected Lucy to accept any gifts for her baby. "So, yeah, this kid—Emma, right?—is gonna do all right for herself."

That ought to be enough, Conner knew. All he wanted was for Lucy and Emma to be taken care of, regardless of who paid for it, so he ought to be satisfied.

Hell, he *was* satisfied.

"Okay," he muttered. "Long as you've got the account set up."

Kenny nodded, took a practice swing, then followed through with another perfect putt. "Maybe I'll take her to a tournament sometime," he said, flashing a victorious grin as if acknowledging the applause of spectators. "Lucy likes 'em." Then, sobering slightly, he shot his brother a questioning glance. "You met her, right? How does she look?"

That was more concern than he'd expected from Kenny, and for a moment he hesitated.

"I mean," the golfer continued, picking up his ball, "did she get fat, having a kid and everything? You've seen it. Not with Margie," he added in a placating tone, evidently seeing Con's scowl. "She was fine, but you know how, well, some women get all messed up. But Lucy used to look really good."

Just concentrate on what matters, Conner ordered himself fiercely, tightening his fists in his pockets. It didn't matter that Lucy deserved far better than this from her baby's father. It didn't matter that Kenny sounded perfectly willing to pop back into her life as long as she looked good. After all, she'd already dismissed him as a scumbag. No, all that mattered was getting her and Emma into a reasonable place of their own.

"The child-support account's already set up, right?" he demanded, and his brother returned his glare.

"Mom said she's fixing it with the bank...not that it's any of your business." He pocketed the golf ball, then straightened up with a defiant expression. "What's the matter, you don't trust me to take care of my kid?"

That was an easy one. "No."

"Look who's talking," Kenny retorted, and Con felt his lungs tighten. He *had* failed his son in the worst possible way. But before he could respond, his brother raised both hands in a gesture of apology. "Hey, I didn't mean— Forget it, okay? Anyway, the account's all set up. Emily's gonna be fine."

"Emma," he managed to say over the roar in his head. There was no point in feeling any sense of anger, of desperation—he didn't *have* feelings, damn it! "Her name is Emma."

"Emma, right." With his usual good cheer already back in place, Kenny slapped him on the back. "So, come on…let's go play nine holes, and you can give me Lucy's phone number."

"She doesn't have a phone," Con grunted. "You'll have to go see her."

"Well, after the ninth hole I'll stop by there. And meet my kid—I bet she's cute, huh?" As if suddenly remembering his plans for the baby, he retrieved a beribboned teddy bear from his golf bag and displayed it with a self-satisfied flourish. "You figure, Lucy and me…she's gotta be cute."

So Kenny was going to show up at the trailer, hand over a teddy bear, and come back bragging about his daughter?

Yeah, probably.

"You don't mind driving, right?" his brother continued blithely, following him toward the office where the stack of mail on his desk loomed as the only possible retreat. "I took a cab from the airport, because I figured you'd have a car already." Then, when Conner reached for the letter opener, Kenny shifted plans with easy swiftness. "Hey, let's make it tonight instead. Head over there together. You can bring whoever you want—you've gotta be seeing someone by now, right?—and we'll go have dinner someplace."

A double date with his brother and Lucy? The image refused to crystallize in his mind, which was just as well, because she'd never agree to such a disaster in the first place. Besides, with all his talk about lining up a date and whose car to take, Kenny hadn't even thought of the first problem with inviting her out for a night on the town. "She's got a baby, remember?"

"You've never heard of baby-sitters?" With an indulgent smile, his brother dropped into a vacant chair and put his feet up on the edge of the desk. "Con, you've been working too hard. You need to get out more." Then, as if to assuage any remaining doubt, he offered a breezy reassurance. "Lucy's a lot of fun. You'll like her."

He already liked her.

Already wanted her.

But he didn't truly love her, and he sure didn't *need* her. He didn't need feelings, either—and he wasn't feeling anything, anyway, so that took care of that. Conner picked up the letter opener and slashed the first envelope, concentrating on movement. On logic. On control.

He couldn't very well deny Kenny access to the mother of his child, and he sure couldn't stand in the way of Lucy getting some long-overdue financial support, but this whole situation was more than he wanted to deal with. And the only solution, he knew, was to focus on work. "I've got to meet the foundation attorney in Chicago," he said, and set down the letter opener.

"What, today?"

He glanced at the letter—another offer of funding from a private trust in Montreal—and gritted his teeth against the memory of Lucy whooping with delight over such news.

"Today, next week…we've got a lot of material to go over." Anytime would work, even though they'd planned it for next week. "Might as well get it out of the way."

Kenny accepted that with his customary ease. "Well, hey, I'll be glad to drive you to the airport," he offered, swinging his feet off the edge of the desk. "No sense leaving your car there, right?"

Maybe not, but he wasn't letting Kenny take over one more piece of his life. "Get your own car," Conner snapped. "I'm driving myself."

"Fine, whatever," his brother muttered in the same injured tone he used whenever someone refused another loan. "Have a good trip." He started out of the office, then turned at the doorway and flashed the familiar grin that meant he'd remembered another request...a request he fully expected to see granted. "Just make sure and leave me directions to Lucy's place."

Chapter Ten

"We don't need Conner," Lucy told Emma, holding the bright plastic teaspoons over the baby carrier and guessing how much yarn it would take to reach from here to the ceiling. "We don't need any gentlemen at *all*. Mommy's got a job, and we're going to fix up this place so it's all nice and pretty, and you'll never even remember that we used to live with that—"

Lucy broke off. She couldn't really call Con a scumbag, even now. But how could he go around saying things like, "I wish I could love you the way you deserve" and expect her to believe it? If he really wanted her, he'd be willing to let her risk her heart!

After all, she'd endured other losses. She could take another risk. But not for someone who didn't even want to try.

She scrambled to her feet and reached for the roll of yarn, still wishing she could forget the sound of his voice and the taste of his skin and the exquisite comfort of those few days where he'd let himself love her—even though he'd never used the word.

"See, sweetie, the spoons will hang right here," she told her daughter, measuring off a length of yarn. "And pretty soon you'll be able to make them move just by reaching up there. Because *you're* not afraid to try new things...."

Unlike some people, who didn't want to believe their heart could work just fine if only they would let it. He obviously didn't want her enough to believe that Conner Tarkington could love, and no amount of wishing was going to change his mind.

"And Mommy's *never* going to sit around wishing for some man to love her, the way your grandma used to," Lucy continued as the baby nodded off. "Because I can take care of us just fine, so—"

A knock at the door interrupted her, and she let Emma guard the teaspoons while she went to answer it—still trying to squelch the same embarrassing rush of hope she'd felt each time Tracie had stopped by—maybe Conner had changed his mind.

It wasn't Tracie this time, though, she saw with a shock of recognition.

It was Kenny Tarkington.

"Lucy," he greeted her with the same carefree smile she remembered loving a long time ago. "You look great."

So did he, technically, although the differences between him and Conner were far greater than she'd noticed the first time she met his brother. But Kenny still dressed in the newest designer golf wear, still had the same familiar cleft in his chin, still carried himself with the same blue-blooded confidence she'd always admired. He just didn't make her blood sing.

Regardless, though, the man was Emma's father. "Come in," she invited, wondering what had brought him here the very day after she'd said goodbye to his brother. Could Conner have summoned him to start taking care of her and Emma? "When did you—"

"Con told me how to get here," he said easily, and she felt her heart constrict. Such a scrupulous transfer of responsibility was just what she could expect from the man she'd told to get out of her life. And he had done exactly what she asked…which shouldn't leave her feeling so hollow.

Kenny didn't seem to notice any uneasiness on her part, because he was eyeing her prepregnancy jeans with frank appreciation. "You look really, really good," he observed.

But her mouth felt dry, her breath felt tight, and it was all she could do to refrain from asking about his brother.

"Thanks," she mumbled, turning to lead him down the hall. "Emma was just drifting off, but she might not be asleep yet. You want to see her?"

"Sure, okay," he said, although he sounded a little uneasy at the prospect. "Is she…" Then, when Lucy lifted the dozing baby from her carrier with a flash of pride in how adorable Emma looked for this introduction, he took a step back. "I mean," he faltered, "she's not gonna spit on my shirt or anything, is she?"

He deserved worse than spit, if that was his first response to the miracle in her arms. "Shirts wash," Lucy snapped, then remembered that Emma needed to think well of her father. This meeting should be a pleasant one, so she made a deliberate effort to relax and smile as she handed him the baby. "She'll be three months old next Thursday."

"Yeah?" Kenny glanced at the pink-blanketed bundle, evidently not even caring that the baby was still asleep. "So, anyway… She's really cute and everything," he offered, shifting from one foot to the other as if calculating how quickly he could hand her back, then returned her to Lucy with an expression of relief. "Look, I gotta tell you…my mom is really excited about having a granddaughter."

A mere flicker of enthusiasm would probably seem "really excited" to someone like Kenny, she thought, already hoping Emma would never ask whether her father had ever seen her. There was no way to make this meeting sound good, and there wouldn't likely be many others. Still, maybe a grandmother would be more affectionate.

"I think," Lucy offered, steeling herself to say his name with an air of casual nonchalance, "Conner has some pictures of Emma if you'd like to send her one." Gently returning her daughter to the carrier and closing the bedroom door, she led Kenny back to the living room where she wouldn't have to watch his indifferent gaze skip past the baby.

He took a seat on the orange plaid sofa, already shaking his head in response to the offer of a picture for his mom. "No, see, she's more interested in the real thing. That's why I came out here, is—well, of course I wanted to see you."

It was almost like a dance routine, she realized, watching Kenny turn on the charm. The rakish smile, the way he angled his body toward her…were those the same well-practiced gestures she'd fallen for last winter?

"You really do look good," he continued, evidently taking her curious regard as a confirmation of interest. "But, anyway, the other day my mom and I were talking about some tour stuff, and she came up with a great idea." He leaned forward, bridging the distance between the sofa and her straight-backed chair. "If you and I get married, she can see more of Emma."

"Married?" Surely this wasn't a proposal, but he didn't sound quite like he was joking. "Why would I want to do that?"

"We were going to get married, remember?" he interrupted, sounding so defensive that she realized he must be serious about the idea. For some reason, he must have convinced himself that marriage would be a good thing, although his uneasiness spoke otherwise. "I just wasn't ready."

And now he was? A man who'd held Emma for all of ten seconds before handing her back with a sigh of relief?

"You're not ready now, either," she told him, tucking the leftover yarn into the pocket of her jeans and wishing she could dispose of Kenny so easily. Maybe his mother wanted to see more of the baby, but what a ludicrous way to go about it! "Send your mom a picture instead."

"That's not enough." The intensity in his voice startled her, but when she saw the mixture of pleading and desperation on his face she realized that Kenny must have more at stake than a desire for fatherhood. "She wants a granddaughter. You know, all she had was boys, and now here's a chance to do girl stuff."

But wanting a girl in the family was no reason for a marriage. "She can come out here and bake cookies if she wants," Lucy offered. Would that qualify as "girl stuff" for someone as high-society as Kenny's mother? "Or embroider napkins, or talk about clothes, or whatever, but she'll probably want to wait until Emma's a little older."

He didn't even seem to hear her, he was so focused on his sales pitch. "And if we get married," Kenny persisted, then broke off abruptly and let out his breath in a rueful sigh. "Look, okay, maybe we weren't the greatest couple in the world." He flashed her the same apologetic grin that she'd come to dread during their month together, and only when she folded her arms across her chest did he try another tactic. "I mean, we've both moved on, right?"

"Right." She had moved on to his brother, but that wasn't something she planned to mention. After all, Conner had made it very clear—by sending Emma's father to take over the responsibility he'd claimed for the past six weeks—that he was definitely out of her life. "And there's no going back."

"Well, no, see, we wouldn't have to. I mean, we wouldn't have to pretend like we're in love or anything," Kenny continued, evidently warming to his new approach. "But if you think about it, this is really a win-win situation all around. We *all* get something out of it. My mom gets a granddaughter, I get the fees paid, you get some great vacations, clothes, a car with a chauffeur, you name it.''

As if that would make things any better. As if that would make it easier to stop wanting Conner....

"We could still have our own lives," he concluded in a burst of energy, settling back on the sofa and gesturing with both hands open. "You know, I'd be on the tour and you could do whatever you wanted. It's just, that way my mom wouldn't have to file for custody or anything like that."

She couldn't have heard him right. "Custody?" Lucy repeated faintly, and he shrugged.

"Oh, you know, give her granddaughter every advantage—it'd just be a lot simpler to get married, like we were gonna do in the first place." He stretched uncomfortably, as if to release the kinks from his neck, then met her gaze with an abashed expression. "My fault we didn't, okay? I admit it."

She had never in her life felt as if the slightest breath might send her spinning to the floor, but right now she couldn't seem to do anything but stare at him. Still hearing the word "custody," still trying to imagine whether it could actually happen. Could his mother want a grandchild that much?

"Look," he said defensively, "my mom can do a lot for Emma." Which any social worker would probably agree with, if it came down to a custody hearing.... "And Warren, her husband, he's a great guy. You couldn't ask for better grandparents."

Warren, she remembered through a shivering wave of nausea, was a judge. Whereas the only judge in *her* life had been at juvenile court when she was arrested for shoplifting. Was that something a social worker would learn about? Lucy twisted her fingers together, struggling for a full breath as Kenny continued.

"And if you want the whole church wedding thing, that's fine, I don't have any problem with that. Or Las Vegas, whatever, it's your call."

Would a wedding make it harder or easier for his mother to file for custody? She had no idea, no idea whether it would make any difference to a judge deciding between a wealthy grandmother and a struggling single mom. No idea what to answer, who to ask, where to look for help.

"What if," she faltered, "I don't want to get married?"

"Aw, Lucy." He looked pained at the very idea, and his next words confirmed that she was right to be afraid. "Come on. Don't make things hard."

She could feel her hands trembling, but it seemed important not to let Kenny notice any sense of panic. Not to give away what little control she still had. "Let me think about it, okay?" she managed to suggest in what sounded like a normal tone of voice, and he glanced at his watch.

"Yeah, hey, I've got a tee time at noon." As if the discussion was concluded to his satisfaction, he stood up and gave her an appealing smile. "You want to come along, get a drink at the clubhouse?"

And talk about what his mother planned to do with Emma? About how they wouldn't have to pretend they were in love, as long as Kenny married the mother of this coveted grandchild? Or did he genuinely believe she'd enjoy an afternoon of margaritas when her life was on the verge of collapse?

"I have to work," she said numbly, and Kenny shook his head in dismay as he turned toward the door.

"You sound like my brother, you know that? Mr. Workaholic."

Conner. A lawyer. She needed a lawyer, and surely he wouldn't have suggested his mother seek custody. No, all she had to do now was ask him for advice.

But she'd told him to get out of her life.

"The guy could be playing golf," Kenny concluded,

"and instead he takes off for Chicago." Which sent her half-formed hope of rescue spiraling into the dust. "Anyway, I'll call you tomorrow—no, wait, you don't have a phone yet." He picked up a grocery coupon from the kitchen table, scrawled a number on it and handed it to her. "I'll be all over the place, but that's my car phone. You call me, okay?"

She couldn't call Conner, Lucy realized. But surely some other lawyer could make sense of this, find some way to keep Emma safe.

"Right," she murmured, glancing down the hall toward the bedroom where her daughter slept. "Tomorrow."

Kenny hesitated at the door, evidently noticing the wariness in her posture. "I know I threw a lot at you all at once," he said apologetically. "But us getting married is a good idea. Oh, and I forgot something." Hurrying out to the gleaming black sports car in her driveway, he grabbed a teddy bear from the front seat and handed it to her with a flourish. "Here, this is for Emma. Anyway, give me a call."

Calling Conner in Chicago wouldn't do any good, Lucy admitted after a long conversation with the diner's last customer of the day. Calling Conner would be no different from calling any other attorney, and after hearing about Marian's experience in small claims court, she knew better than to expect help from the legal system.

"I wish it were different," the elderly lady concluded. "But people who don't know the law are no match for people who do. Of course you might want to try the legal aid society, but it sounds like this other family has all the money on their side."

Which was absolutely true, she reflected as she turned the Open sign to Closed and began wiping down the counter. Van and Mary Ellen had taken the afternoon off for their daughter's birthday party, leaving her in charge of closing, but it was mindless work. A good thing, because she'd spent the past several hours operating on automatic, putting one foot in front of the other with no real awareness of anything except the horrifying questions hurtling through her brain.

Would it make any difference that the Tarkingtons had more money than she'd ever seen in her life? Would it matter that Kenny's stepfather was a judge? Would that give him an advantage if it came to reading juvenile shoplifting records from ten years ago?

She didn't know, and she was afraid to ask.

"If you ever need me for anything, I'll be there."

But she couldn't depend on Conner now, Lucy acknowledged as she wrung out her cloth and started on the other half of the counter. Not when her problem was with the Tarkingtons in the first place. He might be the greatest lawyer in the world, but she couldn't expect him to put aside his bone-deep family loyalty at a time like this.

Besides, what could he do? What could *any* lawyer do? Go tell a judge that Emma belonged with her birth mother, get a bunch of social workers involved to the point where she couldn't simply take off for Mexico, and leave them hoping for the best?

She reached the end of the counter and glanced at the baby carrier, which fit perfectly against the tiled backsplash. Emma was awake now, gazing contentedly at the plastic teaspoons hanging from the carrier handle, and Lucy felt her heart twist again at the sight of her daughter's dreamy expression. No matter what happened, Emma came first. Nothing—not pride, not self-respect, not even independence—mattered as much as this baby.

And Conner had always understood that. But somehow he'd either let his mother believe that Emma would be a wonderful addition to the household, or else he had no idea that Kenny had arrived with a marriage proposal.

Yet before he left for Chicago, he'd told Kenny where to find them.

"You can't raise her in a place like this!"

No, oh, no. She gripped the damp cloth in both hands and braced herself against the counter across from the sink. He couldn't have been so determined to move her and Emma out of the trailer that he'd suggest his brother come back and marry her. No matter how strongly he felt about responsibility, surely he wouldn't have recommended that his mother seek custody of a granddaughter she'd never met.

Lucy flung her cloth at the sink, saw it hit the floor, and choked back a cry of despair.

How could the Tarkingtons *do* this to her? How dare they threaten her baby? How could they possibly think they had any right to a child Kenny'd never wanted in the first place?

But she knew how, and she knew there was no point in resenting the way the world worked. Conner's family was no different from anyone else with money and, for that matter, neither was he. She'd seen it over and over, men showing up with lovely promises, wonderful gifts, saying just what you wanted to hear, and leaving the minute you believed them.

Gulping against the tightness in her throat, she picked up Emma, holding the baby close as she tried to stop herself from crying. Crying wouldn't help matters any, because she still had to come up with a plan. And she might as well do it here at the diner, because Shawna got off work at four and she could use the phone in the kitchen to ask for advice. So after finishing the cleanup and her daughter's four o'clock feeding, she settled down on the blue bar stool and called her oldest friend.

"Kenny's back," she announced, "and he wants to get married."

"The scumbag?" Shawna sounded more incredulous than alarmed, but of course she didn't know the whole story yet. "I thought he was in Asia."

Lucy shifted Emma in her arms, not quite willing to return her to the carrier even with its comfortable nest of blankets. "He says his mother wants a grandchild." And over the past few hours, the reasoning behind that desire had begun to make more sense. "I think she's afraid that otherwise, I might marry somebody else who'd wind up adopting Emma, and she wants to keep her granddaughter in the family."

During the following silence, she could almost hear her friend contemplating the same questions that had troubled her all day. And Shawna's response echoed her own first thought.

"What's this Mrs. Tarkington like? Is she nice?"

"I don't think so." From what little she'd heard—she'd answered the phone once when Kenny's mother called last spring—the woman didn't possess much of a loving heart. "Conner said their family's never been that close. And she didn't sound anything like *your* grandma, you know, nice and comfortable and friendly. She sounded…I don't know, polite. But that's all it was."

"So there's even more of a reason," her friend observed, "not to marry this lady's son. I can't believe you're actually thinking about it!"

Neither could she, except… "Kenny said she's gonna file for custody of Emma," Lucy blurted, closing her eyes as if to keep everything out of her awareness except the baby. But the trick didn't work. In spite of the comforting warmth in her arms, there were still dangers swirling in every direction. "She might have a chance, too, since her husband is a judge and they're rich. And on paper, I wouldn't look so good. Because, remember, back in high school?"

Shawna's swift reassurance felt disturbingly shallow. "I don't think they can look back that far. Lucy, you were sixteen! And you've been Miss Perfect Angel ever since."

A Miss Perfect Angel who'd never held any job for more than a year, who'd taken far too long to earn her diploma, who was raising her illegitimate daughter in the cheapest possible quarters. "I'm just not sure if a judge would see it that way."

Her friend evidently recognized the possibility as well, because she took on a more practical tone. "Worst case, you work out a deal. Emma can spend a weekend with Grandma every now and then, and the rest of the time they leave you alone."

That might work, although she hated the idea of Emma hearing well-bred remarks about her mother's unfortunate background, Emma torn between two wretchedly different ways of life, with people who claimed to love her on either side of the gap. "But sending her off to Philadelphia by herself..."

"So you go with her. They're not gonna throw you out of the house."

Lucy drew a shaky breath. "Not if I'm married to Kenny."

There was a silence as the statement lingered in the darkness of the diner kitchen. Then Shawna protested, "You shouldn't have to marry a scumbag. Unless..." Her voice softened, as if she'd suddenly spotted a note of hope. "You're not in love with him, are you?"

If only she could pretend that she loved him, if only she'd never loved his brother, the idea of marriage might work. But she couldn't imagine forgetting about Conner, even if she could persuade herself to marry Kenny.

"I haven't loved him in a long time," she admitted, nestling Emma closer to her. "But, actually, that part wouldn't be a problem. He said right up front, we'd both live our own lives."

"So," her friend observed wryly, "he can sleep with whoever he wants."

That was probably his reasoning, and she wasn't about to argue with it. "I don't care who he sleeps with, as long as it's not me. Because Conner's brother—" Lucy broke off, appalled at the very idea. "I couldn't do that."

Shawna hesitated. "Don't take this wrong," she said slowly. "I know you said it's all over and you never want to see him again. But if this whole thing is about the Tarkingtons wanting custody of their granddaughter, it might be a lot easier if you just married Conner."

She felt her heart falter, felt a heaviness in her veins. "That'd be even worse. He doesn't want me."

"Oh, come on, I've seen how he looks at you! Being married to him wouldn't be any hardship."

Yes, it would. Because in a loveless marriage with Conner, she would be constantly wishing for more.

"If I'm going to marry a man who doesn't love me, I'd rather it was someone I don't care about. Like Kenny." She squinted at the shelf of paper towels across the room, trying to remember which ideas had sounded feasible over the past few hours. "But there's got to be something else I haven't thought of."

"Brainstorming, right?" Shawna asked, and immediately fired off a suggestion. "Give them some other baby. Some nice orphan who'd love growing up with a rich family."

If she knew any such orphans, that would be the perfect answer. But no amount of wild brainstorming would replace the three basic options she'd spent all day resisting.

"I could hope," Lucy began, "that if we wind up in court, there'd be a judge who thinks mobile homes are better than mansions." That might be risky, yes, but it was still a possibility. "Or I could take Emma to Mexico and hope they never find us." Except her daughter shouldn't have to grow up as a fugitive. "Or... I don't know. There has to be something I can do!"

Her voice broke on that vow, and Shawna offered the same conclusion that was already haunting her. "Not too many good choices, are there?"

Lucy gulped against the threatening tears, knowing she couldn't afford to break down with her daughter at risk. "I just have to do what's best for Emma," she said, burying her face against the sweet warmth of the baby. "Even if it's marrying Kenny."

"Maybe it wouldn't be so bad," her friend offered. "Maybe he'd spend all his time playing golf, and you could go back to dance class."

Maybe so. She drew a long, shaky breath, trying to imagine living with Kenny Tarkington until her daughter grew up. As long as she kept her mind on Emma—and off Conner—maybe she could stand it.

"And at least that way," Shawna continued, "there'd be no chance of losing Emma. I don't think they could take her, anyway, but I can see why you'd rather not risk it. If she were *my* baby, I'd do whatever it took to keep her."

Which was exactly the reason, Lucy resolved as she pulled Emma closer to her, why she was going to marry Kenny.

But before she agreed to anything, she needed to make sure her daughter would be safe.

So when she called him the next day during her lunch break, she delivered her ultimatum before he could even ask for a decision. "I've thought about us getting married," she told him, hunching her shoulders against the chill in the diner kitchen, "but first, you need to promise me something. If I marry you, nobody gets custody of Emma except me."

Kenny hesitated a moment. Then he responded, "As long as Mom can see her whenever she wants, I don't see any problem with that."

"You need to write it down," Lucy warned. "Make a legal contract and everything. Because I'm not just taking your word."

"All right, fine," he said impatiently, "we'll do a prenup. So we're getting married, right?" Already he was sounding more carefree, more like his usual good-time self. "How about next week in Las Vegas? That work for you?"

This wasn't going to be anything like the wedding she'd dreamed of, a joyous celebration of life with a man who would never abandon her, but she had to remember that what mattered was keeping Emma safe. "All right."

"Great. My buddy Stu flies charters out of Scottsdale Airpark, he can take us up there…we'll have a good time." Even with the clamor of the kitchen around her, she could almost hear the party taking shape in his mind. "Bring some friends if you want. My brother'll be back—"

"No!" The thought of Conner at her wedding, the thought of seeing him at all, was more than she could face. She would have to meet him at family gatherings over the next twenty years, but she couldn't start yet. "I don't want him there."

"Conner?" Kenny sounded baffled. "He's a nice guy, just a workaholic—well, you saw, right? Mom said you were doing some work for him."

"Kenny," she managed to protest, hoping her voice didn't sound as shaky as she felt. Because she had to convince him—the very idea of another meeting was too much to bear, and she could no longer expect any help from a man she'd ordered out of her life. "Please. I don't want to see Con."

"He was a lousy boss, huh?" She could hear the amusement in his indulgent response, and it set off a tremor of relief…even through the cold heaviness that had weighed on her heart all day. "Well, don't worry about it. We can get married on our own."

He was on his own, Conner saw when he arrived home and found no sign of Kenny. Not that he'd expected his brother to sit around waiting for him, but still he regretted it. Ever since leaving Chicago this afternoon—hell, ever since leaving Phoenix two days ago—he'd been wondering about Lucy.

Had she accepted Kenny's offer of child support? Were she and Emma okay? He could ask her himself, but she'd made it very clear that she didn't want him as part of her life.

Which shouldn't surprise him, Conner knew. It shouldn't hurt. It wasn't like he'd expected her to love him or anything.

It wasn't like he *needed* her.

He needed information, though, and he was relieved to see a note from Kenny waiting for him in the middle of the floor. But when he grabbed it, he discovered with a mixture of irritation and relief that the note had nothing to do with Lucy. Instead, his brother had written, "I got tickets to the game tonight—Philadelphia's playing Phoenix—so check at Will Call if you make it back on time."

A basketball game? Well, he could ask about Lucy just as well there as he could at home. So he made the half-hour drive to the arena, found a parking place and collected his ticket from the Will Call window, realizing that Kenny must have run into a well-connected golf buddy to get seats like these. With five minutes to spare before the tip-off, he spotted his brother in the third row at center court, chatting with a blonde and a redhead in form-fitting ASU shirts.

"Hey, you made it!" Kenny greeted him, sending the college girls off with an easy caress for each one. "I figured when you said you'd be home tonight, you could use a break."

He had a good three hours of work to catch up on before reaching his daily quota, but finding out about Lucy was more important. "Yeah," Conner said, settling into his seat and glancing at the players just heading onto the court. "So, how'd it go?"

"Their center might not play tonight, but— No, look, there he is. This is gonna be a great game."

It probably would be, if he could just keep his mind on the ball. "Right," Con agreed, looking around for a vendor. His brother had a beer in front of him, but he wanted more than that. "What I meant was, how'd it go with Lucy?"

Kenny glanced up from the court and gave him a triumphant smile. "We're getting married."

He couldn't have heard right. The crowd must have been cheering or something, even though there wasn't much happening on the court, but he couldn't have heard right. "You're getting married?" he repeated, wondering with a sudden jolt if that could be why she'd ordered him out of her life. No, she hadn't even known Kenny was coming. "You and Lucy?"

His brother nodded complacently. "I guess after all this time apart," he observed, crossing his legs and leaning back in his seat, "she realized I'm pretty irresistible." Then he spread his hands in a gesture that mocked humility. "Hey, what can I say? You know how women are."

But Lucy, he thought with a thud in his heart, wasn't like those college girls who saw nothing beyond the carefree surface. She wasn't the kind of woman to fall for a self-centered golf pro.

Who was Emma's father.

And she'd loved him once....

"When did this happen?" Con asked before realizing it didn't actually matter, but Kenny answered him anyway.

"I went and saw her the other day," he said, still looking pleased with himself as he returned his gaze to the pregame warmup. "Met the kid, too, she's really cute. She'll be saying, 'Hi, Daddy' in no time."

She probably would, he realized numbly. Lucy would make sure Emma saw the best of her father, would dress her up for family outings, would smile at Kenny while he guided her first steps.

"We're not doing the whole church wedding thing," his brother continued. "Mom can't complain—she already got one of those from you."

Which was true. He and Margie had exchanged vows before the rector at St. Martin's-in-the-Field...the same church where, nine years later, they had returned for Bryan's funeral.

"So we're gonna do it the easy way instead," Kenny continued. "We'll head up to Vegas next week. I'd ask you to come along, but Lucy said she doesn't want to see you. What'd you do, anyway, short her paycheck or something?"

"What?" He still felt off balance, as if this couldn't actually be happening, but the idea of it happening so soon disturbed him even more. Even if Kenny was simply co-operating with their mother's wish for a grandchild, how could Lucy abandon her desire for independence so quickly?

"My guess is, she got fed up waiting for a raise—you sure weren't paying her much. I mean, did you *see* where she's living?" His brother reached for the beer in the cup holder before him, then waved at a distant vendor before turning back to Con. "Don't worry, you won't be missing anything. The wedding's not that big a deal."

But it still didn't seem possible. "Lucy said," Conner asked slowly, "she wants to marry you?"

"What, you're surprised?" Kenny sounded more amused than offended, then suddenly a glimmer of understanding crossed his face. "Oh, you're thinking about that other time. Yeah, I guess she wasn't too happy with me then…but, see, I already explained to her how I just wasn't ready last year. She's fine with it now."

No, she couldn't be. She had said flat-out, that night in the laundry room, that she hadn't loved Emma's father in a long time—but somehow he must have persuaded her to give him another chance. Maybe by apologizing for last year? Or maybe she had persuaded herself, wanting Emma to know and love her father.

"So we're flying up to Vegas next week," Kenny said, lifting one finger as the vendor approached their row and offered Conner a beer he didn't want. "Look, if you'd like to come with us, it'll be a fun trip. Lucy can't hold a grudge if I want my brother at the wedding."

That wasn't his biggest worry, not right now. Right now all he could think about was why she'd agreed to such a wedding in the first place. "I'm just not sure," he said, gesturing the vendor away, "that she knows what she's doing."

"Lucy?" Kenny gave him a baffled look as the players retreated to their benches for the opening announcements. "Hey, maybe she didn't go to the same schools *your* wife did, but she's a lot smarter than you think. Lucy knows what she's doing."

Maybe she did....

"I can take care of myself and my daughter."

God, maybe she did.

"You can't give me what I want."

"So, how about some congratulations, huh?" Kenny prompted him, then met Conner's gaze with a sudden look of contrition. "Hey, is this— I'm sorry, man. I thought you were over Margie and...all that."

He was. He was. But his brother seemed to see something in his expression that demanded a show of concern, because he was lifting both hands to gesture a halt.

"Look, Con, I'm serious. The wedding's not that big a deal. If it's gonna mess up your head, you don't need to be there."

Whether or not it messed up his head wasn't the point. What mattered was Lucy getting what she needed. But why the hell would she need to marry Kenny?

Unless she wanted Emma to grow up with a father.

Unless an apology for not being ready was enough to satisfy her that Emma's father had changed.

"She really said she wanted to marry you?" he repeated just as the game-opening buzzer shrilled, and Kenny glared at him in exasperation.

"You wanna call her, ask her yourself? Yeah, I messed up last year—I'm not saying I didn't—but I told you, she's over it!"

All right, then, he thought numbly as the players raced onto the court. Maybe an explanation was all she'd needed, and his brother had evidently given her that.

So she'd made her choice, and she'd chosen Kenny.

Her child's father. Her first love.

He had to live with it.

But living with a lead weight in his chest was harder than he remembered, Conner realized as the basketball game dragged on. All around him people were cheering, swearing at the referee, shouting over hotly contested points, but somehow he couldn't take in enough air to yell along with them. The vendors continued offering their drinks, but he couldn't quite bring himself to swallow a soda or beer. And when the game finally ended, freeing him to return to the work piled up on his desk, he still couldn't seem to feel any sensation in his body as he drove home and looked at the office clock.

Ten-fifteen. Technically he couldn't work beyond one-fifteen without breaking his self-imposed limit, but at least he could get something done before then.

Something to get his mind off Lucy.

Something to keep him going.

It took until midnight before he hit his stride, but by one o'clock he was feeling the familiar exhaustion, the welcome blankness that meant his escape had worked. Conner started another summary, glancing back and forth from the keyboard to the clock on his desk until it reached one-fifteen.

He stood up, stretching his arms behind his back...and then, with a savage shove, he pushed the clock off his desk.

Work was all he needed. If he could just work long enough, hard enough, get this summary done, start the next proposal, he could forget about everything else. Forget the hollow ache in his chest, forget the sharp pain whenever he tried to breathe too deeply, forget about Lucy showing Kenny how Emma loved balloons.

Work was all that mattered.

Work was everything that mattered, he reminded himself as the night wore on. The whole idea of a twelve-hour quota was stupid, pointless, because who *cared* how long he stayed at his desk? Nobody at all. It was too late to make any difference to Bryan, and it wasn't like he needed to worry about anyone else.

Except Lucy.

Conner braced his elbows on the desk and rested his forehead against his hands as the sky outside his window lightened from black to gray.

Burying himself in work wasn't going to help Lucy.

And whether or not she needed his help, whether or not she wanted him in her life, he had to make sure she and Emma were okay.

He stood up again, repeated the stretch of his shoulders, then reached to turn off his computer.

Maybe Lucy knew what she was doing, he reminded himself as he watched the screen image fade from view. Maybe she saw something in his brother that no one else had ever seen. Maybe she really could take care of herself.

But, either way, he needed to be there for her.

And if that meant setting Kenny straight during his daily round of golf, then it was just about time to start.

Chapter Eleven

He had to start with the right approach, Conner told himself as he watched Kenny tee off at the first hole. Laying down the law might have worked when his brother was ten years old, but he needed something more effective now. Which was why he'd agreed to a full eighteen holes, because that would offer a better opportunity for delivering the message he'd rehearsed all the way over here.

Somewhere on the course, he needed to make it clear that Lucy and Emma deserved a wholehearted kind of love. The kind that didn't involve flirting with college girls at a basketball game. The kind that put them first, year after year after year.

The kind he'd never experienced himself, which was why he recognized the danger of marrying without it. And why he had to warn Kenny that Lucy deserved far more than just a casual commitment.

But first they had to play a few holes, get into the rhythm of the game, and by the second hole he had to admit that, even though this morning he was having a harder time with his shots, he'd missed the challenge of golf lately. Over the past few years he'd moved more and more meetings from the country club to the office, which might explain why he missed two easy putts in a row.

"You're not doing so good," Kenny observed as they headed for the third hole. "You used to play your best game first thing in the morning."

"I'm out of practice," he admitted, pocketing the score-card and returning his putter to the bag. Ten years ago he'd been more than a match for his brother, but no practice and no sleep were a bad combination.

"It'll come back," Kenny assured him, squinting at the teebox ahead and giving him a reassuring clap on the back. "Nothing to worry about. Besides, you were working pretty late last night."

He had returned the clock to its place on the desk a few minutes after seven, just in time to make a pot of coffee before inviting himself along to the golf course. But he'd done without sleep before.

"I can handle it," he told his brother, and Kenny reached for the driver. Taking sight of the flag in the distance, he executed a perfect swing which, Con realized with a tug of pride when he finished his tee shot, was a few yards short of his own drive.

"Nice one," his brother observed as they headed down the fairway, and waited until they'd finished their approach shots before raising a question on the way to the green. "So, anyway, you want to come to Vegas next week? I figure on going up there early, see a few shows, all that."

"With Emma along?"

Kenny looked blank for a moment, then seemed to rec-ognize the name. "Oh, the baby. No, well, Lucy can get a sitter or something."

There would never be a better opportunity for his warning about putting family first, Conner decided. But it took him the rest of the trek to come up with the most effective opening, which he finally found as they parked the cart. "Have you thought about what it'll be like," he asked, "living with a baby?"

Kenny shrugged, evidently not viewing the issue as a major concern. "Well, it's not like I'll be spending that much time with her. There's always sitters—hell, there's always Mom. She's the one who wants a granddaughter."

Con reached for his putter, wondering how Lucy could even consider marrying someone who thought so little of her baby. "I don't think Lucy'll want to leave Emma with Mom *or* a sitter that often."

"Well, she doesn't have to." Kenny took his own putter from the bag and they started for the green, where both their balls lay a short distance from the cup. "Unless she wants to come on the tour with me."

As if she'd consider accompanying a high-flying golfer to a different city every week. "You're staying on the tour?" Conner demanded, and his brother gave him a baffled glance.

"That's what this is about, remember? Mom said she'd sponsor me."

With a sudden jolt of clarity, he realized what must have brought his brother out here—their mother's hope of buying a granddaughter for the cost of a tour sponsorship—and a flash of anger shot through him. How could she think Lucy would ever trade her child for a wedding ring? How could Kenny care so little for what mattered to his wife?

"You could've mentioned that," he muttered, knowing even as he spoke that his brother had already tried to describe the latest plan for acquiring a sponsor, and he'd refused to listen. But to use Lucy as a bargaining chip? "My God. I can't believe you'd marry her just to give Mom a granddaughter!"

"Hey, Mom's helped me out a lot," Kenny snapped,

shooting him a defiant glance as he reached to mark his ball. "At least *one* of us makes her feel needed."

He'd thought that same thing a few weeks ago, but it still horrified him to see his brother's belief that any desire was available simply for the asking. "That's what you call it, making her feel needed?" He took a steadying breath before sinking his putt, then turned to face his brother a few feet away. "I call it using people."

"Easy for you to say," Kenny muttered. "You don't *need* any money, the way you live, but some of us have a life!"

With the edgy irritation rising higher, Con retrieved his ball and took a stance by the cup. "Some of us," he said grimly, "don't use women to get a life. Some of us believe in taking responsibility for ourselves."

"News bulletin, buddy." His brother lined up the shot and flexed his shoulders, making a visible effort to restore some sense of tranquility. "That's why I'm getting married."

"You're only getting married," he retorted, "because Mom wants a grandkid. Am I right?"

Kenny returned his attention to the putt. "Well, I'll get something out of it, too," he said, raising his eyebrows in a suggestive smirk as he hit the ball toward the cup. "You've seen Lucy. She still looks pretty damn good."

Conner moved to block his shot, feeling a rush of fury building within him. "Hold it. She's not just some—"

"Yeah, she is," Kenny said, staring at him as if he couldn't believe such an outburst. "What do you care, anyway?"

"I—"

"You want a turn at her?"

The dam burst, and with every cell in his body erupting in rage Conner shot his fist into his brother's face. "I love her!" he yelled as Kenny fell backward onto the grass, looking as stunned as he felt.

"What the—"

"I love her," he repeated, feeling the words shooting through his blood with a power he'd never felt before, but which felt desperately, fiercely right. "Look," he told his brother, who was still watching him in disbelief, "you're not getting your hands on Lucy. Because I love her, Kenny. My God, I love her!"

Without even waiting for a response, he took off running for the clubhouse. He had to find Lucy, he had to tell her what should have been obvious a long time ago. How could he not have seen it? Con wondered, ducking past a startled foursome and racing toward his car. How could he have missed all the signs?

The way her laughter danced in his memory.

The way he thought about her even while working.

The way he longed to make her happy.

The way he imagined her wherever he went, worried about her getting hurt, dreamed about her in his arms, wanted her for the rest of his life.

This was love, all right, and why had he thought he couldn't do it? Just because he'd never seen it before, never felt it before, he'd told himself the Tarkingtons were incapable of love—and maybe that was true of his parents, but it sure wasn't true of himself.

Because he loved her. All of her. Her fire. Her compassion. Her stubbornness. Her grace. Her strength, her flaws, her determination, everything about her was precious, was perfect, was what he'd been waiting for all his life. That kind of wholehearted love had never happened during his marriage, but Lucy mattered more deeply, more intensely than anyone he had ever known.

And he needed to tell her right away.

The only problem, he realized as he spotted his car across the parking lot and took off at top speed, was finding her. Knowing Lucy, she probably had another job lined up already, and camping out on her rickety doorstep until she came home didn't strike him as the best way to celebrate the awakening of his heart. But a neighbor offered directions to a nearby diner, which must be the same one she'd worked at last month, so he raced down Scottsdale Road, hoping he'd catch her before the place got too busy.

Somehow, a whole restaurant full of customers didn't feel like the ideal setting for his first heartfelt declaration of love.

But he'd waited long enough, Conner knew as he shot through a yellow light. Too long, because if he'd just recognized the truth sooner they could have been together by now—planning for a future wherever she wanted, sharing a home with Emma, building a family that he would cherish for the rest of his life. So this time, he wasn't letting anything stand in his way.

This time, he was going to love her the way she deserved.

This time, he was going to love with all his heart.

Conner looked like he'd just emerged from a storm, Lucy saw as he burst through the front door of the diner, his eyes wild and his body almost vibrating with some kind of energy she'd never seen before. If anyone else had come in looking like that, she would have called Van from the kitchen—but this man couldn't possibly be wired on drugs.

And even though she didn't want him in her life, she couldn't very well throw him out in front of half a dozen customers.

So instead, she approached him with a full coffee cup and waited until he took a seat at the counter before setting it down in front of him. Then, as she edged back—the intensity radiating from him was a little unnerving—he grabbed her hands, and she caught her breath.

"Conner, what's going on?"

"Look," he blurted, "I should've figured this out way before Kenny started talking about marrying you."

So he'd heard the news. And either he'd come to wish her happiness, or to warn her that Kenny wasn't an ideal husband…as if she might not already know that. But before she could pull away—she didn't need the warmth of his touch reminding her how much she still wanted this man—he delivered a surprise she had never expected.

"I love you, Lucy. You *and* Emma. And I want both of you with me for good."

Less than a week after announcing he could never love her the way she deserved? And yet it was alarming how desperately she wanted to believe him. "But—"

"Kenny's only in this for himself," he said, glancing at the nearby customers before returning his intense gaze to hers. "You can't marry him."

Was that what this declaration of love was all about? Taking over his brother's responsibility? Lucy jerked her hands away. "If it means keeping Emma," she said fiercely, "I *can* marry him, and I will."

"What?"

His shocked expression relieved her more than she cared to admit, because she didn't *need* the comfort of knowing Conner was still a fundamentally decent person. "You haven't heard," she asked, backing up a step to view him from a slightly safer distance, "your mother was planning to sue for custody?"

"Did Kenny tell you that?" He must have seen the affirmation on her face, because his eyes darkened with what looked like barely suppressed fury. "Son of a— Mom might've said something about wanting Emma in the family, but I can't believe she'd try—"

"He said she wouldn't have to file for custody if I married him!"

She could almost see the moment when Con's fierce anger was masked by a look of professional expertise, but that didn't diminish the heated energy radiating from his body. "Lucy, forget about that. She wouldn't have a chance. Emma's yours."

As a Tarkington *and* a lawyer, he should know, and the

rush of relief that swept through her was so intense she felt herself sway against the counter. Emma was safe. Emma was hers, no matter what, and if it had been any other lawyer delivering such good news, she would have thrown her arms around him and shouted for joy.

But this man had started the whole transfer of responsibility in the first place, and she couldn't help the flicker of resentment inside her even as she focused on the most important part of his message. "Are you saying Emma stays with me," she asked carefully, "no matter what?"

"No matter what," he answered, then turned to glare at a customer down the counter who was loudly clearing his throat with his coffee cup held high.

Before Lucy could respond, Mary Ellen emerged from the kitchen and hurried to offer a refill, which meant Lucy was now on her break. And that was just as well, because her hands were shaking too badly to lift a coffeepot. Which didn't make sense, not when Emma was going to be fine, but the flood of relief was so impossibly strong that she still didn't feel quite steady on her feet.

Con rose from his seat, reaching for her hands again, and this time she met him halfway, because even though his family was to blame for all this turmoil in the first place, she needed the comfort of his touch right now.

"You don't have to marry Kenny *or* me to keep custody of your daughter," he said softly. "I promise you that. But, Lucy, I love you."

It was frightening how badly she wanted to believe him. But…

"I want us to be married," he continued, making her wonder for a dizzy moment if she'd stumbled into some fantasy world where every wish came true at once. First her daughter's safety, then Conner saying he loved her, and now—

"And I want to be Emma's dad," he concluded. "This

time, I won't mess it up. I want to look out for her, too, give you both whatever I can."

Which jerked her with a sudden, alarming wrench from the fantasy back into the world she knew. Lucy pulled away, forcing herself to stand straighter, and took a quick breath before asking, "Are you trying to take care of us again? Is that it?"

Conner moved the coffee cup out of the way and leaned forward on the counter, meeting her gaze directly. "Look," he said, "all this business about how you can take care of yourself—that's fine, I know you can. But you don't *have* to, Lucy. Because I really want you in my life."

In a way she wished she could simply believe him, accept his declaration as the truth. If only she could throw aside any worries about dependence and bury herself in the warmth of this man, with his familiar body and his equally soothing reassurance, for the next fifty years. But she'd been through enough grief already.

"I want to take care of you and Emma both," he concluded, meeting her gaze with such sincerity in his eyes that she almost cried out—please, let this be true! "I love you."

He must believe it himself, Lucy realized with a pang of yearning, because he couldn't sound so earnest otherwise. But all along he had focused more on responsibility than on love. She knew perfectly well, after those years of watching her mother, that even the most heartfelt declaration didn't necessarily mean anything. "That's sweet," she said carefully. "Thank you."

Conner hesitated, as if waiting for something more, then she saw a look of dismay cross his face. "You don't believe me, do you." He glanced away, evidently struggling for the right response, then back at her. "I didn't realize it soon enough, either," he admitted. "But all of a sudden, it was like—"

"I *do* believe," Lucy interrupted, "you feel responsible for us. But, Conner, that's not the same thing as love."

With an impatient shake of his head, he stood up and stared down at her. "Look, I know I said I couldn't love you, but that was wrong," he announced, meeting her gaze until she felt herself growing warm from the light in his eyes. "Because, Lucy, I really do love you."

It would be so easy to give in, to take him at his word. "I wish I could believe you," she managed to answer, trying to remember the pain of abandonment before she could melt into his arms. "But how do I know you won't change your mind again?"

She saw his muscles tighten as if to absorb a blow, then he squared his shoulders. "I'd tell you to trust me," he answered, "but that might take a while. What'll it take for me to prove it?"

Oh, if only she *could* trust him! But with all his gifts, with all his attempts to make things easier for her, this man had never understood the difference between responsibility and love.

And yet people could change, couldn't they? Maybe not often, but maybe things would be different this time. So maybe she shouldn't deny herself, or Conner, the chance for him to prove it.

"Maybe I could believe it," she said on a shaky breath, "if you can promise you'll quit trying to take care of me and Emma."

Conner stared at her, frustration evident on his face. "I can't promise that," he protested, and she felt her heart sink. "Lucy, I love you! Of course I want to take care of you."

Of course he did. And he would never see anything wrong with using her to satisfy his own need for responsibility, the same way all those men had used her mother.

She gulped back the knot of tears in her throat, hoping she could end this without crying. "I know you want to," she blurted, "but that's not what I want. Your whole *life* is about taking care of people, controlling things, and I can't let you do that to me."

"But," he began, and she raised her hand to stop him. She had to get back to work, start another pot of coffee, check on Emma in the kitchen, but most of all, she had to get him out of here.

"Just go somewhere else, all right?" Nothing should hurt this much, but she couldn't seem to stop wanting him even while she knew she could never have him. So she came around the counter, took his hand, and guided him toward the door. "I'm glad you came—I'm glad I don't have to marry Kenny—but I can't deal with any more Tarkingtons."

"Lucy," he protested, and at the sight of his stricken expression she felt the first rush of tears spilling over.

"Please," she cried, opening the door and taking a step back, "just leave me alone!"

He started to reach for her again, then she saw him halt. Take a breath. And turn away. But just as she let the first sob escape, he turned back from the door with one last glance that mingled frustration and compassion.

"You got it," he told her, and left.

She didn't get it, Conner told himself, heading out of the diner with half the customers still watching him suspiciously…as if he'd tried to offer a threat, rather than his heart. She honestly didn't believe he loved her, and damned if he could figure out why.

But there was no sense making her cry, making her look like she'd just lost her best friend. Not when he wanted to *be* that best friend. If she didn't want him right now, okay, but he wasn't giving up. He'd try again later. Maybe not today, not while she was so upset, but—

I've got to make this right.

The only question was how to do it. With anyone else, he'd send an order of flowers now and come back tomorrow, but flowers weren't right, because flowers were a gift. So what was he supposed to do? Wait until next week? Hang out around her trailer like some kind of stalker?

There had to be something he could do, he vowed as he drove up Scottsdale Road. He hadn't thrown off a lifetime of telling himself he couldn't love, of refusing to risk his heart, only to turn around and withdraw the minute things got tough. What he needed, Con decided as he arrived at home and saw Kenny's car already there, was something to convince her he loved her.

Her and Emma, both—it wasn't like he could ever forget the baby who'd smiled at him out of nowhere. He loved Emma, too, damn it, and Lucy just didn't get it!

It was almost like she didn't *want* to get it, but why would she hesitate? Why wouldn't she believe his declaration of love with the same openhearted enthusiasm, the same sweet confidence she'd shown ever since they met?

He walked inside and stopped short.

There was a woman in his living room.

And she was tickling Kenny.

"Hey, Conner." His brother looked up with an abashed grin, but made no move to disentangle himself from the redhead. "I was just telling Heather, it looks like I won't have to be in Las Vegas next week."

There was the answer, Con realized, right on the sofa in front of him. Lucy must have heard plenty of "I love you" declarations from Kenny, and look how that had turned out.

"You won't," he snapped, and started down the hall. Even though Heather didn't seem too concerned about privacy, this was nothing he needed to stick around for. But Kenny stopped him with a question.

"How'd it go? Is she going to marry you?"

"Maybe not." The words stuck in his throat, but he turned back to explain the problem to the scumbag who'd caused it. "She's got this crazy idea," he told Kenny with a pointed glare, "that she can't trust anyone named Tarkington."

"Oh, hell." His brother evidently picked up on the accusation, because he stood up and sent the redhead toward the door with a quick caress. "Look, Heather, I'll see you later, okay?" Then, when she departed with a coy wave, he returned his attention to Conner. "You told Lucy you love her, right?"

Over and over. Like he'd never told anyone before, although he must have said something like that to Margie back at Cornell. "Yeah, but she doesn't have much faith in men, after that stunt you pulled last year. She doesn't want to believe it."

With a frown of concern, Kenny headed for the kitchen. "Well," he said, taking a beer from the refrigerator and gesturing an offer to Con, who shook his head, "you've got to convince her, that's all." He scanned the counter for a bottle opener, then seemed to realize some more advice was called for. "Roses are good. Women like roses."

Roses were just another gift, though, and she'd already made it clear that she didn't want the kind of gift you could wrap. But half an hour ago he'd offered her his heart, and she had burst into tears. Conner felt a sudden stab of desperation. What the hell could he possibly give her?

"Or a diamond," Kenny continued, evidently warming to the topic, "the size of a golf ball."

Whatever he gave her, it sure wouldn't involve jewelry. Nor money. Nor an education for her daughter…but, damn it, there had to be something he could do for the woman he loved! "Lucy doesn't want diamonds."

"Women always want diamonds," his brother insisted, locating the bottle opener in the drawer where Lucy had kept Emma's teaspoons and neatly popping the lid off his beer. "Look, I'll see if I can get you a deal on some kind of ring—I'm serious, I want to help. You'd be good for Emma."

That caught him off guard. He hadn't given much thought to how Kenny would feel about someone else parenting his baby. "You think?"

Kenny shrugged an acknowledgment. "I figure," he said

before taking his first swig, "you'd make a hell of a lot better dad than I would."

Which wasn't saying much, Conner knew. "I didn't do so good with Bryan," he muttered. Even though he wouldn't make the same mistake twice, it was only fair to let Emma's father know the truth. "He thought I didn't care about him."

That didn't seem to worry his brother. "Yeah, well, what do kids know?" He set down his beer, then braced his hands against the breakfast bar and looked at Con directly. "Maybe you never said so, but you loved the hell out of that kid. Otherwise, why'd you fall apart when he died?"

It took him a moment to find his breath, and even then he couldn't quite find an answer. "I—"

"Look," Kenny interrupted, straightening up again as if to dismiss the question, "if pretending you never loved him is what got you through the whole thing, that's fine. But you'd still be good for Emma."

With a sudden flash of certainty, he remembered how he'd felt when he held Emma for the first time. When the baby had dozed against his heart. But his brother had already moved on.

"So," he concluded, "if I'm going to get my tour sponsorship—Mom won't care who marries Lucy as long as it's legal—you've just got to convince her you love her."

That was what mattered most, Conner reminded himself. Everything else, Bryan, Emma, even the sponsorship issue would have to wait until he could make Lucy see that he'd never change his mind about loving her. That they could stay happily married for the rest of their lives.

But he still had no idea where to start. Especially since she didn't want to believe him, after her experience with his family.

"I hope," he said hoarsely, "I can talk her into it."

"Man, so do I." Kenny sounded surprisingly intense, which touched him until his brother continued, "Because one of us *has* to marry her. Mom's really serious about this granddaughter thing.''

This granddaughter thing?

"Too damn bad!" Con exploded. "If Mom thinks she's getting Emma—"

"Well, isn't she?" Kenny reminded him, looking a little startled. "I mean, that was the whole reason for getting married in the first place."

The idea still infuriated him, but there was no point denying he wanted to marry Lucy. Still, he'd have to make it clear that Emma was off limits. Nobody had any claim on the baby except for Lucy herself.

Not even him.

"It's up to her," he said fiercely, "whether she wants to get married or not."

His brother shrugged. "It'd just be easier, that's all," he explained, dropping the bottle opener back in the drawer. "Warren said filing for custody would be a long shot."

So Warren was in on this, too? He had actually offered advice on filing for custody of another woman's child?

Apparently so. But—

"There's no way anyone's filing for custody," Conner announced, squaring his shoulders as he ran through a mental list of threats. If all he could do for the woman he loved was to guard her daughter, then that's what he'd do right now. "I'm not letting that happen."

"Fine," Kenny agreed, leaning against the breakfast bar and taking another swig of his beer. "But first, you've got to marry her."

"No, first I've got to straighten them out." Even if it meant flying to Philadelphia and warning his mother off, he'd make damn sure Lucy never heard from some lawyer threatening to take Emma away. "This family's put her through enough already—and it stops right now."

Chapter Twelve

Right now used to be her favorite time of the day, Lucy reflected, kissing Emma's tummy and laying her down to sleep. Watching her daughter drowse off for the night, knowing she was safe and warm and happy, had been one of the first pleasures of motherhood, and sharing the bedtime ritual with Conner had made the twilight hour even more special.

The way he'd helped with the fuzzy sleepers and soft blanket. The way he'd met her eyes as she gently closed the bedroom door. The way he'd taken her hand and—

She wasn't going to think of that now.

Because the only way to start enjoying Emma's bedtime with all her heart, the way she used to, was to put Conner Tarkington out of her mind.

To stop fantasizing about how things might have turned out.

To quit remembering how much she wanted him. Still.

She turned off the light and sat down on the edge of her

bed, struggling against the memories of those other bedtimes. For some reason they were stronger tonight, as if his claim of love had reopened the barrier she'd managed to erect long enough to get herself and Emma away.

To get them back on the road to independence, self-respect, all the essentials she'd given up far too easily and would never abandon again.

Oh, but if only she could believe he loved her...

"Lucy?"

That sounded like a voice outside her front door, but not until the call roused her did she realize that there'd been a knock, maybe two or three, while she sat here yearning for Conner. And it was unnerving to discover she could get so lost in fantasy that she didn't even hear someone knocking at her door.

Lucy hurried to peer out the darkened kitchen window and recognized the same car Kenny'd been driving the other day, which meant she didn't need to worry about some stranger dropping by. Still, after Con's reassurance that no marriage was necessary, she couldn't imagine why he would show up now.

"Look, it's fine about not getting married, but I don't have all night," she heard Kenny call. "If you're in there, would you please open up?"

It was the "please" which reassured her—well, that and knowing he didn't have all night. She turned on the light, opened the door and saw him standing outside, looking ready for some serious partying.

"I'm not coming out with you," Lucy told him, and he reacted with a start of surprise.

"Hey, no, I didn't mean for— There's something I need to tell you, that's all."

All right, then. As long as he was heading out to find some playmate for the evening, it seemed safe to assume that he'd accepted her phone-message cancellation of their wedding. After all, he could tell his mother he'd *tried* to win her a granddaughter, shrug off the failure with his usual good cheer, and go on to the next tournament without breaking a sweat—so it wasn't likely he'd come to suggest she change her mind.

But if he'd come to tell her something about Conner....

"Come in," she invited, clenching her fingers against the hope that Conner had sent...what? She didn't even know, couldn't even think of what he might say, but still she watched Kenny saunter through the doorway with her heart feeling poised on a very steep edge.

But when she offered him a seat across from her on the orange sofa and he stayed standing, his hands jammed in his pockets, she realized that he must be feeling awkward about something.

Which, for Kenny Tarkington, was probably a first.

"Look," he said, staring at the floor as if he couldn't quite meet her gaze, "I'm sorry I didn't stick around when you got pregnant, okay?"

What? Of all the things he might have said, an apology was the last she would have expected. Unless, once again, Conner had tried to enforce what he thought was right. Which would be just like him, taking responsibility for everything he could.

"Did Conner tell you to come apologize?" Lucy demanded, rising to face him. "Because I have had it up to *here* with—"

"He doesn't know where I am," Kenny interrupted, and apparently that denial gave him the courage to sit down and adjust the crease of his tan silk slacks before meeting her gaze with a sober expression. "But I talked to him half an hour ago, and he's still hurting."

What, just because she'd seen through his attempt this morning to resume taking care of her? "Did he say that?"

Of course he wouldn't say that, she realized as soon as she asked it. Conner would never tell anyone he was hurting. But something must have penetrated Kenny's usual blithe indifference, because he answered slowly, "I just don't think you're being very fair to him, that's all."

"That's none of your business," she snapped, turning away long enough to close the bedroom door. If Emma's father was going to sit out here talking about unfairness, this might very well turn into a shouting match.

But when she returned to her seat across from Kenny, he still seemed uncharacteristically serious. "Well," he said, "actually, yeah, it is my business. Because *I'm* the one you're mad at, right?"

Lucy drew a deep breath. She wasn't going to yell. This man wasn't worth yelling at. "Kenny," she managed to answer in a voice so calm it impressed her, "this may come as a surprise to you, but not everything is about you."

"You're mad at me," he continued as if she hadn't even spoken, "but you're taking it out on Conner. And he doesn't deserve that."

"I'm not taking anything out on him!"

Kenny hesitated, glancing down at his hands, then seemed to come to a decision, because he turned to her and snapped, "The hell you're not. He shows up to tell you he loves you, and you tell him you don't believe him?"

But that was her only practical choice. "I don't," Lucy explained. Not because she was taking anything out on Conner, but because— "I can't."

"Because you can't trust the Tarkingtons, right? Ever since I didn't come back from Atlanta."

It had started long before that, but Kenny's defection was all the more proof that depending on *any* man was a bad idea. Expecting a gentleman to take care of you was downright stupid, no matter how much money he might throw in your direction, and expecting him to love you for a lifetime was an even bigger mistake.

"So," Kenny concluded in a more reasonable tone of voice, "you think all men are like that."

Maybe not all men, no, but she didn't need any more

heartache in her life right now. Which meant she needed to remember what happened when you let a gentleman call the shots.

"Yeah," she answered, pulling the sofa cushion from behind her and smoothing it across her lap, "pretty much all men *are* like that."

"Not Conner."

Conner, who kept insisting he wanted to take care of her and Emma.

Who wished he could love her the way she deserved. Who had tried to compensate for his distance by buying her gifts.

Although he hadn't tried that at the diner today.

Nor had he lied when she asked for a promise he couldn't give.

Instead he had promised that Emma would be safe, no matter what. Same as he'd promised, back in Sedona, that he'd be there if she ever needed him—and he *had* been there today, even though she'd already told him to get out of her life.

But he hadn't. He had been there for her all along, bringing Emma to pick her up from the catering job, guiding them both to the top of Squaw Peak, sharing his plans for the foundation, taking turns with the coffee every morning…

"And he's hurting now," Kenny continued, which twisted her heart. Conner didn't deserve that, not after everything they'd shared. "He said I destroyed your faith in men."

"It wasn't just you," Lucy muttered. Over the years, she'd seen dozens of men walk out on empty promises, mostly to her mother, who had never learned *not* to believe them. "I've seen it happen again and again."

"Not with Con."

No, she realized with a jolt of recognition, Conner wasn't responsible for her mother's mistakes.

Or her own.

He wasn't the one who'd forgotten the importance of never depending on gentlemen, who'd pretended to believe things would be different with a good-time golfer, who'd joyfully accepted another flurry of gifts without any mention of commitment.

And yet here she'd been acting like all the disappointment, all the humiliation, all the betrayals she had ever endured were his fault.

Lucy dug her fists into the cushion until she felt the ache of pressure against her thighs, but it didn't take away the hollow sensation in her heart. Kenny was right. She'd been taking out a lifetime of resentment on someone who didn't deserve it, and it hurt to think that she could have inflicted the same kind of pain on Conner that she'd seen dished out by other men.

Or maybe even worse.

"Anyway, so that's why I came to apologize," Kenny concluded, standing up and adjusting the cuffs of his shirt. "I'm sorry, okay?"

"Okay, fine." It didn't matter whether he meant it or not, what mattered was making things right with Con. If anyone should be apologizing right now, it was herself. And even though it meant asking Kenny for a favor, she wanted to do it in person. "Can you wait a minute while I get Emma, and drop us off on your way out? I need to tell Conner I was wrong."

"I just talked to him, remember, when he called to check for messages? He's on his way to Philadelphia."

Already? She felt a sickening thud in her stomach. After five weeks of saying he was here until January fifteenth, he'd taken off now? Right after she refused to believe he loved her?

Oh, she had to explain her mistake, but how was she going to do that? Asking for a ride was bad enough, but asking for a plane ticket to Philadelphia—

"I don't know how long he's gonna stay," Kenny offered, "but I can tell him to call you."

She couldn't ask for a last-minute plane ticket. That was right up there with diamonds, mink coats, the kind of thing she would never, *ever* accept.

Because there were limits to what her pride would allow...and a trip to Philadelphia was way beyond those limits.

"Tell him," Lucy said raggedly, "to call me at the diner. Here, I'll give you the number."

Kenny stuck the paper in his pocket, carefully smoothed the line of his slacks, then headed for the door before turning back at the threshold. "So, anyway," he said cheerfully, as if the hardest job of the day was safely behind him, "I'll see you around. Uh, tell Emma 'hi' for me."

With a jaunty wave, he stepped outside, leaving her to lock the door behind him and bury her fists in the sofa cushion, wishing she could erase the past seven hours and start over again.

Conner was hurting, and it was her fault. This morning he had finally broken through his habit of solitude, opened his heart for the very first time, and what had she done? Bad enough she hadn't believed him when he said he loved her, just because she was afraid to risk the pain of abandonment. Worse yet that she'd told him to get out of her life, that she didn't need him or want him or even trust him to know his own mind.

And now, on top of all that, how long would he have to wait before she could make up for it?

Well, Lucy reminded herself as she moved to the kitchen and began the after-bath cleanup, she would probably hear from him at the diner tomorrow, but still, a phone call wasn't the same as apologizing in person. If only she had the money, she would pack up Emma right now and take a cab to the airport, get the first plane to Philadelphia and show up at his house.

If only.

No, it was no good thinking that way. She could've asked Kenny for the money, sure, but nobody could accept that kind of favor and still preserve any shred of pride. And waking Emma from a sound sleep only to fly across the country was a crazy idea. She couldn't do that.

But if only, if only she could make things better for Conner.

I want to do that.

The certainty startled her, it felt so incredibly clear and so desperately urgent. Yet it rang with the force of truth, with the same passion she felt for protecting her baby, for making sure Emma had whatever she needed.

Because you do whatever you can for the people you love.

And that, she realized as a rush of tears welled into her throat, must be how Conner felt about her. That was why he kept insisting he wanted to take care of her and Emma. You couldn't love someone and not want to make things better for them.

No matter what it cost you.

Lucy squared her shoulders and headed for the bedroom to find her purse, where she'd saved the grocery coupon with Kenny's car-phone number. If she had to break the vow she'd kept for a lifetime, if she had to ask for plane-ticket money the same as her mother asking for favors, she was going to do it. She was going to throw her last shreds of pride to the wind, if only she could reach Conner before he retreated into that solitary shell.

If only she could tell him she loved him.

If only she wasn't too late.

It was later than he'd anticipated by the time his mother and Warren returned home from some art gallery opening, and Conner wished he'd called on the way here. He hadn't trusted himself to stay calm over the phone, and a face-to-face confrontation would be more effective with no warning, but that lack of notice meant killing almost four hours in the cedar-paneled library while refusing the butler's repeated offers of refreshment.

Still, the wait allowed his anger to coalesce into a fine edge of determination, which he knew could only help his case. And by the time he heard Hughes open the front door shortly before midnight, he was ready for whatever battle needed fighting.

Neither his mother nor the judge looked prepared for a battle, Conner saw as he entered the living room, where Warren turned from the butler with a cordial welcome.

"Conner, good to see you."

"You're back sooner than we expected," his mother greeted him, but behind her friendly smile he could see a hint of concern. She was the one with something at stake here, and she was the one he needed to confront.

"I wish we'd known you were coming," Warren said genially, "we could've skipped the opening." Then, while handing his topcoat to Hughes, he shook his head to counter any protest from his wife. "I know, it was for a good cause. Anyway, if you two will excuse me...."

With a kiss for Grace and a handshake for Conner, he headed down the east hall, and she gestured an invitation back into the library.

"Warren was up all night," she said apologetically, adjusting the sash of her black opening-night dress, "writing for some case this morning. Have you been waiting long?"

All right, they might as well get right down to business. Before Hughes could offer any more refreshments, Conner closed the library door behind them and turned to face his mother.

"Kenny said you were talking about getting custody of his daughter."

She didn't show any sign of contrition as she seated herself on the leather sofa in the center of the room and waited for him to join her. "I'm hoping," she said, turning the diamond bracelet on her wrist with the same habitual gesture he remembered, "he'll do that himself. Settling down and being a father would be good for him."

Maybe so, but it was a pointless wish. "He's not going to do that, Mom. You know it and I know it." And when her expression didn't change—she knew it, all right—Conner delivered his ultimatum. "I'm here to make sure nobody even tries for custody of that baby."

That got a reaction. She abandoned her fidgeting with the bracelet, straightened her posture and met his gaze with a look of disbelief. "Why not?" she protested. "What kind of life will she have otherwise? Her mother doesn't sound like—"

"Her mother," he interrupted, "is great." That wasn't nearly enough of a description, but this wasn't the time or place to explain his own feelings for Lucy. "And she doesn't need anybody threatening to take her daughter away."

"Conner, nobody's threatening her!" His mother sounded genuinely shocked. "I feel sorry for her, trying to raise a child on her own, and if Kenny isn't ready to settle down yet, she'll need some help."

Fine, maybe that sounded reasonable here in Philadelphia. But anyone who knew Lucy, anyone who'd spent more than half an hour with her, would see the problem with such help.

"She won't take it," Con said. "Not from any of us. And I told her she'll never have to." He saw a protest forming, and raised his hand to cut it off. "So I need to make sure you're clear on this. Nobody's taking her baby."

His mother stared at him, as if trying to make sense of a baffling code. "What's this about?" she asked.

It couldn't be that hard to understand, and he wasn't going to let her play dumb. Conner stood up and glared at her from his full height. "You're not trying for custody," he said flatly. "I mean it."

But that expression of bewilderment was still there. "I don't think I've ever *seen* you so—"

"I'm looking out for Lucy, that's all!" he interrupted, and her quizzical gaze softened into recognition.

"Conner," she asked, "are you in love with her?"

All right, maybe his mother knew him better than he thought. "For all the good it does," Con muttered, shoving his hands in his pockets. "I've got to go back there and figure out how to prove it."

"Oh, my."

She sounded more sympathetic than he'd expected, but he couldn't afford to let himself wish for his mother's understanding after all these years of doing without it. No, he needed to stay focused on his mission.

"I have to make sure," he said, sitting down again so he could meet her gaze more directly, "that Lucy's got nothing to worry about from you and Warren. So you need to give me your word you're not taking Emma."

There was a moment of silence. Then she asked in a careful tone of voice, "You really think this young woman can do more for her daughter than we can?"

"Yeah. I do." Anyone who'd seen Lucy with Emma would recognize the same thing. "She loves that baby, Mom. You should see 'em together, it's like—" Conner broke off, trying to think of the words for such joyous, wholehearted love. "I've never seen anything like it."

His mother sat very still, but he was aware of a sudden tension in her posture. "You certainly never got that," she murmured, "from me or your father."

Oh, hell. He hadn't meant to get her started on the failures of the past. After all, she'd apologized long ago for those years under the haze of prescription drugs. But just as he drew a breath to argue that it wasn't worth mentioning, she lifted her chin and continued resolutely, "I know you didn't. We were never there for you…and you don't know how much I regret that."

If it was anything like the regret he'd felt about Bryan, he had a pretty good idea. But that was all in the past, so he hurried to offer the first reassurance he could think of.

"I turned out okay."

She nodded, squaring her shoulders in a gesture that reminded him of Lucy. "You turned out very capable," she said. "Very good at taking care of everyone around you."

"Well, yeah," Con agreed. "That's what I do."

His mother gave him a rueful smile as she resumed her twisting of the bracelet. "But you don't let anyone take care of *you*."

No, but what would be the point? He'd learned a long time ago that he couldn't expect anyone to take care of him.

"It's always," she continued, "what you can do for them." Which, again, was pretty much on target. Hadn't he told Lucy only this morning that he wanted to take care of her and Emma? "You'll give whatever you can to the people you love, but you won't let it work both ways."

"I— Well, no." He had never let it work both ways, had never let himself need anyone.

Except Lucy.

For the second time, the realization struck him with startling force. He loved her, he wanted her, yes—but he needed her, too.

More than he'd ever let himself need anyone, he needed her. Her joy, her vitality, her way of looking at life. He needed her.

But she didn't need him.

Apparently his mother saw no sign of the tumult within him—or maybe she did—because she rose and gestured to her writing desk as if to indicate that the conversation was finished.

"I will write Emma's mother a note," she announced, "and tell her Warren and I have no intention of seeking custody. And you can give her that."

"Yeah," Conner managed to answer. "I will."

She turned to her desk, leaving him to wonder whether he'd just been treated to a maternal lecture or whether he was forcing every thought into the context of Lucy. But the thought nagged at him as he left his mother unfolding a monogrammed notecard and wandered into the front room, where Hughes had turned out all but the foyer lights.

Had he ever told Lucy he needed her?

Probably not, Con admitted as he picked up the hundred-year calendar on the bookshelf and twisted it to January. He couldn't imagine baring his soul like that, virtually asking for a cool dismissal. He hadn't even thought of it until his mother came up with that business about love working both ways.

But if he wanted to take care of Lucy, he needed to let her do the same for him.

The way she'd tried to do all along.

He turned the dials on the calendar back through the past few weeks, watching the dates click across every time she had offered him coffee, offered him a shoulder to lean on, offered her nurturing comfort and her joyful exuberance and her steady insistence that he could talk to children, he could be trusted with Emma, he could love with all his heart.

And he did. God, he did.

But he hadn't let Lucy love *him* the same way, not as long as he kept insisting that all he wanted was to take care of her and Emma. He needed to make things right, needed to explain that she meant far more than a one-way responsibility, but he couldn't phone her until she arrived at work tomorrow morning, and that was too damn long to wait.

No, Conner decided, he had to catch the next flight out, regardless of when it left. The chauffeur would be faster than waiting for a cab, and Jenkins never retired until well after midnight, so all he had to do was head out to the garage. Glancing at his watch, which showed he'd been pacing around with the calendar a lot longer than he realized, Con hurried back to the library to tell his mother goodbye.

Goodbye and thanks, because whether or not she intended to offer such thoughtful guidance, she'd done a pretty good job of mothering tonight.

He found the library empty, but on the desk was Lucy's note. And when he glanced down the hall and saw the light in the master bedroom just going dark, he stuck the note in his pocket, scribbled a thank-you to his mom and headed back to the foyer. Then, bracing himself for a rush of cold air, he opened the front door.

And there, coming up the walk with Emma in her arms, was Lucy.

Asking for Conner would be the only hard part, Lucy told herself as she started up the walk, repeating the assurance she'd chanted ever since the cab driver entered this neighborhood. It was one more in a series of "the only hard part" promises she'd used to keep herself going for the past several hours, ever since Kenny had agreed to book her a plane ticket online and handed her what looked like an alarming amount of money.

But she'd gotten herself and Emma to the Phoenix airport, onto the plane, all the way to Philadelphia, and now to Chestnut Hill by concentrating on nothing but the next hard part. She couldn't let herself think about what would happen if Conner had already given up on loving her.

No, all she could think about was climbing those gray stone steps, snuggling Emma as warmly as she could, and asking whoever answered the door if she could please talk to—

Conner? She blinked at the figure of a man against the light in the doorway, suspecting it was only wishful thinking that made him look so much like the man she wanted, but then she saw him fling it open and come racing down the steps.

"Lucy!" he blurted, throwing his arm around her shoul-

ders and guiding her swiftly toward the house. "I was just—
Come in, you're freezing out here."

She had worn every sweater she owned, and wrapped
Emma in too many layers to count, but the chill of the night
air was almost as bad as the chill of fear that had followed
her all the way here. "Thanks," she managed to answer,
untangling the blankets from her daughter while keeping her
eyes on Conner. He didn't look annoyed at the sight of her,
but of course he'd probably offer this same instinctive hospitality to anyone who showed up on his doorstep at midnight.

"Let's get you in the kitchen, it's warmer there," he directed her, reaching for the baby and ushering them both
through a dimly lit room that looked like something out of
a high-society movie. "What are— I was just coming to tell
you—"

"I had to find you," she interrupted before he could finish
the sentence. If he'd been planning to tell her goodbye in
person, she should at least get through her apology first.
"Conner, I'm sorry I didn't believe you." No, wait, she had
to explain it better than that. "I mean, I love you." If only
she could see his face…. "And I'm hoping," she said shak-
ily as they entered the kitchen and he flicked on the light,
"you still love me, because—"

Then he turned to face her, and she saw in his eyes the
light of incredulous relief, of wholehearted joy. "Lucy," he
said hoarsely, reaching to draw her closer with Emma still
nestled against him, "I will always love you. Always."

She felt a wave of exhilaration shimmer through her, a
dizzying crest of the same relief she'd seen in him. Conner
hadn't changed his mind about loving her, and this time she
could believe him, believe that he loved her for real. For
good.

For always.

"Oh, good," she whispered, and he tightened his embrace so she could feel the pulse of his heartbeat against her cheek. "Oh, I'm so glad!"

Emma chose that moment to gurgle what had to be an agreement, and Lucy saw Con's answering smile. "I'm glad you brought her," he said, pulling a chair away from the butcher-block table against the yellow wall. "Here, sit down. Does she need anything?"

After a late-night feeding and diaper change before leaving the airport, the baby would likely sleep for another six hours, but right now, everything either of them needed was right here in the room. Warmth, light, a place to relax and enjoy the certainty that this man still loved them.

"All the way here, I was afraid of being too late," Lucy told him with a sigh of relief, sitting down and holding out her arms for Emma before remembering she still hadn't finished her apology. "Conner, I *know* you're not going to change your mind about loving us, and I'm sorry I didn't trust you. None of that was your fault."

"No, look," he protested, nestling the baby in her arms and taking the chair at right angles to her, "I'm the one who's sorry." He waited until she adjusted Emma against her shoulder, then met her gaze across the table with a sober expression. "All this time I was trying to make you my responsibility, instead of my love."

And all this time she'd been resisting it, not realizing the difference between responsibility borne of duty and the kind that came from love. "But I can be both, right?"

He reacted with a start of surprise. "Both?"

"I mean," she continued, hoping they each appreciated the same sweet balance between giving and receiving, "I see why you want to take care of me, and that's okay. Because I want to take care of you, too."

Conner caught his breath, then reached for her hands. "I need you to do that," he said, and for a moment he looked almost shy. "I need you, Lucy. More than I ever wanted to admit."

She had never expected such an admission, either, from a man who'd spent his whole life taking care of everyone around him. But knowing what it must have cost him to acknowledge that, she felt all the more certain.

This was a love that would last them both a lifetime.

"We need each other," she told him, and saw the light of relief in his eyes. "Both of us." But that didn't go far enough. "All three of us," she amended, and moved Emma to sit propped up in her lap. Even though the baby would doze off again in a moment, at least she could be part of the circle right now. "You and me and Emma."

"Listen, about Emma—I realized tonight, I *can* be a good father," he promised, meeting Lucy's gaze with a look of sober confidence. "On the way out here, I was thinking about something Kenny said. For a long time I didn't want to remember it, but Bryan was the first person I ever loved."

She felt a flood of emotion in her throat, hearing him acknowledge his son for the very first time. "Of course you loved him," she said gently. "He was part of you." He had awakened this man's heart, which made Bryan all the more special. "And he always will be."

"Yeah, you're right. I can think about him now." On his face she could see a mixture of shyness and certainty. "But loving you and Emma...." Conner looked at the baby again, then back at her with a curious intensity in his gaze. "This time, I'll remember to say so. I'm gonna make sure you know it."

She already did, but even so the promise was sweet. "We already know it," she assured him. "But we like hearing it. Both of us."

"All three of us," he agreed, breaking into a smile. "Even if one of us is falling asleep." Then he stood up, pushed his chair back and knelt down in front of her, taking the baby's curling hands in his. "Emma," he said, "I want to marry your mom. And I want to be your dad."

She felt another rush of joy, imagining how someday

Emma would hear this whole story of how Daddy proposed to Mommy *and* her. And she had to gulp back the lump in her throat before she could respond without bursting into tears. "That," she answered for her daughter and herself, "would make us very happy."

He let go of Emma and leaned forward to pull Lucy into an exuberant hug. "I *want* to make you happy," he said. "I want to take—" Then he broke off, sounding abashed. "Ah, hell."

But he could have finished the sentence, no problem. "Conner," she protested as he drew back, "I don't mind you taking care of me as long as I can take care of you, too. And you're gonna let me do that, right?"

He met her gaze, looking almost sober for a moment, then she saw a quick grin flash across his face. The same look of challenge, of adventure, she'd seen only a few times before and could hardly wait to coax forth again.

"Right," Con answered, shoving his hands in his pockets as the smile warmed his eyes. "I'm looking forward to it."

So was she. "Good, because you need more fun in your life." And it would be a pleasure to help him find the balance between work and play that they'd enjoyed all through Christmas. "As soon as we're married—"

"I want to marry you," he interrupted, "right now."

Getting married at one in the morning might be a little tricky, but she liked the way he was thinking. And the wedding fantasy she had toyed with until he sent that scholarship letter flashed with a sudden renewal of hope. "What about at the chapel in Sedona?"

His answering smile confirmed that he remembered their morning there as brightly as she did. "Good. I don't know if they can take us first thing tomorrow, but the sooner the better."

And what a treat to know that she could leave all the arrangements to him. That his gift for getting things done would benefit more than just the foundation…and that each of them could provide their own gifts to this marriage.

"I just have to call Shawna and Jeff," Lucy said. "And see if your mom and Warren and Kenny can make it."

He shot her a startled glance. "You want them at our wedding? After everything they—"

"Conner, they're your family!" She couldn't deprive Emma of grandparents who would love her, and although she doubted Kenny would ever take much interest in the baby, at least he had come through tonight. Which would be a good story to share with Con once they finished their plans. "Families belong at weddings. Just not on the honeymoon."

The way his eyes gleamed at the very word sent a thrill of heat up her spine. Oh, even with Emma along, this was going to be the kind of honeymoon that would keep her tingling with anticipation—and, later, with memories. "You've got something in mind?" he asked, and the raw awareness in his voice raised a matching tug inside her body.

"Well," she said a little breathlessly, "you don't have to be back at work until next week, right?" And when he nodded, she hurried to lay out the plan that had taken shape on her way across the country, when she'd kept herself from giving into despair by dreaming of the ideal outcome. "I thought maybe, instead of packing up everything at home and flying back to Philadelphia, we could drive."

She could see the moment he recalled the fantasy they'd shared last month at the lake, because his smile looked suddenly younger. More carefree. "The red convertible."

"Yes!" Lucy crowed. "Do you like it?"

"I like it," he answered immediately. "I love it." Then he swept her into a gleeful hug, with Emma supported between them, and kissed her with such passion, such celebration that she felt herself gasping and laughing at the same time. "I love *you*."

They couldn't start kissing the way she wanted to right here in the middle of his parents' kitchen, Lucy knew. But it took all her strength to pull away from his embrace, and she needed some kind of reward for that. "Say it again?"

Conner took Emma from her, evidently recognizing the convenience of a baby as a barrier, and sat down across from her. "I love you," he repeated, and the truth of it leapt between them with shimmering force.

She swallowed. This was probably the best time to ask for what she wanted most. "Enough to start talking about gifts?"

He gazed at her quizzically, but didn't raise any objection. "I know you said not to buy you anything," Con acknowledged, "but I really want to give you a ring."

That was fine, that was no problem. She would love to wear a symbol of this man's love. "With your name inside it, okay?" she requested, and he nodded. "But that's not all I want."

"Red convertible?" he guessed. "It's yours." Then, evidently seeing the uneasiness on her face, he stopped in the middle of the promise. "Or," he suggested gently, "something for Emma?"

"For our daughter, that's right." She almost hated to ask while he was feeling on top of the world, but there was still something missing from the happily-ever-after picture she'd dreamed of. And maybe it was too much to ask right now, but—

"I think," she said in a rush, "next Christmas, Emma should get a new brother or sister."

"Aw, Lucy." With the baby in his arms, he rose again and pulled her to him for a soaring, promising kiss. "I think," he murmured, "that'd be a wonderful Christmas present. For all of us."

And it was.

* * * * *

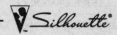

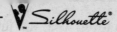

If you enjoyed what you just read,
then we've got an offer you can't resist!

Take 2 bestselling love stories FREE!

Plus get a FREE surprise gift!